TOLD IN SILENCE

Violet seems to lead an ordinary existence — single, working in a shop and living with her parents in rural Kent. But her life has already been touched by tragedy. At twenty-one, Violet, a young widow, lives with Harvey and Laura Blackwood, her late husband Jonathan's parents. Rocked by grief, Violet shuts herself away from the world, but cannot escape reality. Then Max Croft, an old friend of Jonathan's, enters her life. However, she knows that there are secrets behind her husband's death which threaten to shake her faith in everything she knows about their past life together . . .

Books by Rebecca Connell
Published by The House of Ulverscroft:

THE ART OF LOSING

REBECCA CONNELL

TOLD IN SILENCE

Complete and Unabridged

ULVERSCROFT
Leicester

First published in Great Britain in 2010 by
Fourth Estate
An imprint of HarperCollins*Publishers*
London

First Large Print Edition
published 2011
by arrangement with
HarperCollins*Publishers*
London

British Library CIP Data

Connell, Rebecca.
  Told in silence.
  1. Widows- -Fiction. 2. Family secrets- -Fiction.
  3. Large type books.
  I. Title
  823.9'2–dc22

  ISBN 978–1–4448–0814–8

Published by
F. A. Thorpe (Publishing)
Anstey, Leicestershire

Set by Words & Graphics Ltd.
Anstey, Leicestershire
Printed and bound in Great Britain by
T. J. International Ltd., Padstow, Cornwall

For Joy

'The cruellest lies are often told in silence'
— Robert Louis Stevenson

PART ONE

Violet

July

2008

At the airport I felt the first stirrings of a change. I watched my shadow gleaming ahead in the bright reflective floor as I walked towards the café's reddish cocoon. Curved walls rising and curling inwards to meet me; warm globular lights scattering sparkles across the tables. It struck me that I had never seen these things before. I had grown so accustomed over the past few months to reseeing the same surroundings that the realisation that there could still be first times, for anything, gave me a brief sting of surprise.

The plane was late landing. I felt impatient as I scanned the arrival boards from my café seat, and this sensation too was unfamiliar. I imagined Harvey, shifting slightly in his window seat, every so often glancing at the heavy gold watch that he always wore, but otherwise betraying no flicker of discontent. Lately I had mastered his level of restraint without even trying. Now, though, I could feel my fingers wilfully flexing with annoyance, my heart beating a sharp erratic tattoo against my ribs. Anxious not to be late, I had driven too fast up the motorway, numb with fright after so long away from the wheel. It had taken half an hour of patrolling the cool white airport shopping arcade for the panic to subside. I had left the café until last, deliberately stringing out the minutes as I watched the plane's arrival tick back and back, balancing what little entertainment I could find against the delay.

I ordered a coffee and drank it in tiny sips, the acrid taste prickling on my tongue. It was another twenty minutes before the news that the plane had touched down blinked out at me from the screen. Although I knew it would be a while longer before Harvey emerged with his luggage, I gulped the last of the coffee down hastily. I would walk over to the arrivals gate and wait there. The decision, small though it was, flooded me with pride; I was too used these days to having my decisions made for me. I found myself smiling. I had dreaded this mission for weeks, but now that it was drawing to its conclusion, I wondered what I had been worrying about. I took a swift look around the café: an elderly couple huddled over a teapot, a bored beautiful young woman flicking through a magazine, a teenage boy plugged into headphones and oblivious to his parents. *I'm one of you*, I thought. And it was true — from the outside, no one would be able to tell the difference between us. I stood up.

As if by magic, a waitress materialised at my side. All false nails and false smile. 'Are you off?' she cooed.

I nodded uncertainly — what business was it of hers? I started to move away, but she followed, her tanned forehead creasing a little now with what looked like annoyance. I turned back, my eyebrows raised politely.

'That'll be one ninety-five, then, please,' she said. Simple though they were, it took a strangely long time for my brain to filter and decipher the words. Reflexively, my hand went to my pocket, but I knew it was pointless. I had come out without a handbag, without any money, without a credit card, without anything at all except the car keys. Two hours earlier, it had been as much as I could manage to force myself through the door. I felt my cheeks flush and panic grind into gear; a sharp needling noise in the back of my head, a sudden ache in my stomach. Uselessly, I patted the pocket again. The waitress had taken a step back now, arms folded. Out of the corner of my eye I could see the elderly couple, watching, waiting. Their faces were suddenly full of suspicion.

'I'm sorry,' I said. My voice sounded far

off. The curved red walls of the café began to swoop and slide around me. 'I . . . I don't — '

'Don't worry about it,' the waitress said. I had expected her to be angry, but her voice was soaked in pity. I glanced up sharply, and saw it reflected in her eyes, as clear as glass.

I spun on my heel and walked away, as quickly as my legs would carry me. I could feel those eyes boring into my back, making their judgement. For a second I wanted to turn back, to explain to her that although I might well pass for a wayward teenager in her eyes, I was a respectable married woman, that I had simply been going through a difficult time, and that sometimes the everyday practicalities of how to move through the world had a tendency to slip away from me. But she wouldn't have understood — few people did — and of course I wasn't married; not really, not any more. I pressed my fist, cold and hard as a diamond, against my chest, and breathed in. That much I could manage, but it didn't shut out the little voice hissing at me in the back of my head. *What sort of person goes into a café and orders a coffee, without remembering that they have to pay for it? An idiot. A madwoman.* I gritted my teeth against the voice, but I knew by now that attempting to quell it was pointless.

Unconsciously, I had kept to my original plan; my feet had taken me to the arrivals gate. Dozens of passengers snapped into focus in front of me, flooding through the double doors. It was too early for the plane to be Harvey's, but nevertheless I found myself scanning the faces intently. As the crowd cleared I saw a man hovering on the opposite side of the barriers: middle-aged, balding, dressed in dilapidated tweed as if he had come from a shooting party in the country. He was holding a sign with the words 'AU PAIR' printed in large black letters across it. Underneath, in shakier lettering, 'Natalia Verekova' — much smaller, as if the woman would be more liable to recognise her job title than her own name. He was acting out a pantomime of exaggerated distress: craning his neck forward and waggling his head from side to side as he scanned the crowd, looking at his watch, brandishing the sign desperately aloft. This woman had obviously let him down. Natalia Verekova. It was a Russian name, I thought. Suddenly a memory flashed into my mind; a finger rubbing back and forth along my cheekbone, slowly and rhythmically, familiarising itself with the angular line. *Your bones are Russian*, he had said. I had no Russian blood, as far as I knew, but I had liked the idea that my face hinted at a more exotic lineage than the one I possessed — it had made me feel tightly packed with mystery.

All at once I imagined myself walking across the cool polished floor towards the man in tweed, holding my hand out to greet him and introducing myself as the woman he was looking for, apologising for the delay. I could see him nodding and smiling, looking at me and accepting me without suspicion. I would travel back with him to some country pile and meet his children, and there I would be ... catapulted into another life. For a second, the random force of the thought and the strength of the longing that came with it made me dizzy.

With a jolt I realised that I was staring at the man in tweed, and that he had noticed, his eyes on me, was coming forward fast through the crowd. Another morass of people was spilling out of the double doors and he had to raise his voice to be heard above the chattering throng as he reached me. 'Natalia?' he said, yellowing teeth showing in an eager, uneven smile. 'Natalia?'

I shook my head and backed away, and in the same instant I saw Harvey, his smooth silver head swaying back and forth like a snake's as he searched for me in the crowd. The man in tweed was reaching out an uncertain hand, frowning now. I broke away from him and half ran across the hall, ducking into the one place where neither he nor Harvey could follow me. In the ladies' cloakroom I stood in front of the long row of mirrors, stretching vertiginously down the corridor into bright white space. I ran some cold water on to my hands, and they felt burning hot, shaking violently as if I had a fever. I had a crazy urge to laugh, and I forced the sound back unsteadily into my throat.

My reflection stared back at me; black hair in a soft cloud around the face, dark indigo eyes, a mouth that fell naturally into lines that looked sulky, even when they did not feel so. It seemed that this woman was someone other than myself — someone who could pass for a glamorous au pair in a plush country home. It was only a fantasy, of course, one that had passed as quickly as it had come, but the bright flare of excitement that it had given me remained. There in front of the gleaming mirrors, I felt something shift in the back of my mind and come into focus. For months I had felt so dull and tarnished that I had stopped trying to recall how I had been before. The memory came to me now unbidden, and it made me lift my chin and shake my hair back from my face.

Out on the concourse Harvey was standing stock still, his head raised to the clock. He was looking at it, motionless, watching the second hand glide round and round. Some thirty feet behind him, the man in tweed hovered, mercifully with his back to me, worriedly shifting from foot to foot. I hurried over to Harvey and touched his coat sleeve lightly. He swung round to face me, and I thought I caught a spark of irritation in his cool blue eyes.

'Hello, Dad,' I said quickly, and his face softened.

'It's good to see you, Violet,' he said, holding out his hand for me to shake; always the same formality. 'You managed the journey all right, then?'

'It was fine, but we'd better get going,' I said. 'Laura will have lunch ready by one, and you know what the traffic can be like.'

He nodded slowly, but I could see I had displeased him; it was the 'Laura', of course. I pretended not to see, picking up one of his bags and hauling it over my shoulder. Out of the corner of my eye, I thought I saw the man in tweed approaching, and started to walk fast, down towards the car park, my footsteps pounding in my head, trusting that Harvey was following. My heart was hammering stupidly.

He caught up with me by the car, watching as my fingers fumbled shakily with the keys. 'Who was that man?' he asked. 'The one who was talking to you when I arrived.'

So he had seen me after all. 'No one,' I said. 'At first he thought he knew me, but he didn't.'

Harvey looked suspicious, wearily so, as if it were almost too much effort to see through such an obvious lie. 'You must be careful, Violet,' he said. 'You could get yourself into trouble.'

Grindingly, I reversed the car. He was way off the mark with the kind of trouble he was referring to, but I had learnt by now that Harvey could see a sordid sexual motive in almost any contact I had with any man, no matter how old, unattractive or obnoxious. In some ways, he had taken over the role of jealous husband — not that it needed taking over, as Jonathan had never been that way inclined. I had been the jealous one. All the same, I nodded as I swung the car out on to the motorway. All the way back, I felt his eyes on me. After two weeks without him, I had forgotten the relentlessness with which he could watch me, even in such a confined space — without embarrassment, without deviation. At first, it felt strange. Soon enough, as I drove, I felt the inevitable familiarity of it seeping coldly through me, numbing me from head to toe.

* * *

Pulling into the driveway, I caught a glimpse of Laura through the cream curtains, her outline flickering there for an instant before they snapped shut. I knew she would have been waiting there for some time, as if by keeping vigil she could somehow ward off disaster: a violent ball of flames blowing the plane to smithereens, a snarled, ugly pile-up on the motorway. It was understandable, I supposed, but that morning it felt like another new irritant. Laura had no business to take such a responsibility on herself, or to presume that she had any divine power to influence anyone else's fate.

As she cautiously pushed the front door ajar and came forward to meet us, barefoot, the thought seemed even more ridiculous. There was something insubstantial about Laura — a kind of transparency that made it too easy to look past her, through her. Hair the shade of straw, the negative of my own. Pale colourless eyes and papery skin that looked as if you could effortlessly scratch it off with your fingernails. She was a slight woman, barely five foot two, and when she craned her neck up to look at Harvey, I saw the pale blue tendons strain and push against their thin covering.

'Welcome back, darling,' she said. Her tone was calm, but her eyes were wet with anxiety. Harvey touched his hand briefly to the small of her back and kissed her hairline. It was a smooth ritual that I had seen a thousand times. 'How was your flight?'

'Dull,' he said. 'There was a woman next to me who insisted on telling me her life history, even though I patently had no interest in anything she had to say.'

Laura shook her head, as if barely able to believe the temerity of the woman, before she turned to me. 'And you, Violet?' she asked tentatively. 'You managed the drive all right? Everything was fine?'

'Yes, Mum,' I said. I saw Harvey shoot me a glance of satisfied relief. 'Everything was fine.' I could have told her about my panic on the way to the airport: the spasms that had racked my cold hands as they gripped the wheel, seemingly independent of me; the way my head had reeled at the sudden sharp smell of diesel on the motorway as I wound down the window to get some air; the sense of desolation I had felt as I got out of the car and realised I had no idea how to walk to the correct terminal. She would have been sympathetic — too much so. It was easier to keep quiet.

'You left your handbag,' she said, her hands fluttering nervously in the direction of the coat-stand. 'I was worried that you wouldn't have any money to pay for the parking.'

'Dad dealt with that,' I said quickly. When I had driven to the barriers, the overdue realisation that I would have to pay for the privilege of parking my car had felt like a complete surprise — and yet it was something I had done many times before, a ritual that most people would perform as smoothly as breathing. Well, it didn't matter, I told myself as I busied myself with untying my boots. Anyone could make a mistake. Despite my thoughts, my fingers were stiff and clumsy with the laces and, for just a second, before everything snapped back into focus, I felt as if I were being confronted with some incomprehensible, soaringly complex mathematical puzzle that I would never be able to solve, that made no sense at all.

I followed Laura into the kitchen, which was thick with the smell of roasting meat. As she lifted the lid off the largest saucepan, clouds of potato-scented steam billowed forth, clinging to our hair and clothes. Laura was a good plain cook, but she was an obsessive checker, barely able to go a minute

14

or two without testing the status of everything she was cooking, with the result that she slowed down the progress of every meal she made. It was already almost half past one and nothing seemed to be ready, despite her pleas before I left to be back on the hour. I watched her turn to the pan of broccoli. Anxiously she fumbled with the oven gloves, tipping the lid to the side, releasing the heat, and my hand itched to reach out and slam the burning lid back on, no matter how much it hurt. But of course I didn't. I did nothing at all. My limbs felt heavy and hopeless.

'Did Dad say anything about the trip?' she asked presently, addressing the vegetables rather than me. The concentration with which she avoided looking at me betrayed the casualness of her tone.

'No,' I said truthfully. Since he had retired from the law firm to which he had given over forty years of ruthlessly efficient service, Harvey occasionally took a fortnight alone away from home, usually to somewhere hot and mildly exotic: Spain, Greece, Bulgaria. The trips were usually taken without much in the way of prior warning, or indeed of explanation. On a practical level, it was almost impossible to imagine what Harvey actually did on these jaunts away. The idea of him sunbathing on the beach was ludicrous;

even in my mind's eye, I could not strip him of his suit and tie, and the image of him sitting primly on a sunlounger, fully dressed, briefcase in hand, was one that alternately amused and confused me. Of course, it was none of my business. It was difficult to begrudge him a bit of solitude, particularly as it was bought with the money he had earned, even if in his absence the house did feel even emptier and bleaker than usual. All the same, I knew that Laura wondered and worried. She didn't like him out of her sight, or more precisely, I suspected, she didn't like herself to be out of his.

'He seems rested, anyway,' she said, nodding with an air of finality. I knew that she would never ask Harvey directly about his trip; incredibly, my one-word answer seemed to have got the curiosity out of her system. All the same, I thought I saw a fleeting sadness cross her face as she turned back to the stove.

'He does,' I agreed, although in reality I wasn't sure. If an alcoholic stopped drinking, he was just an alcoholic without a drink, and if you allowed some of the tension to relax from a coiled spring held between your hands, then what you were left holding was still, after all, just a coiled spring.

'I think this is ready,' Laura announced cautiously now. Her hands fluttered around the pots and pans as if she were trying to calm an angry mob. 'Will you help me dish up, or would you rather go and sit with Dad?'

It didn't matter. Surely even she could see that. I knew what she was trying to do: give me decisions, give me back some responsibility. It was a pity that she thought I was capable of so little. *But look what happened when she trusted you to drive to the airport,* the voice at the back of my head hissed. *You panicked, you forgot your money, you could barely even lift your hands off the wheel. This is about your level.* I bit my lip. I helped Laura dish up, and she was disproportionately grateful.

Harvey was sitting at the head of the dining table, his back ramrod straight, the newspaper he had brought from the plane held up before him. He was frowning and intently scanning its pages, seemingly totally absorbed. It was only in the second in which he folded it and smoothly returned it to the floor that I saw that it was in Spanish, a language he didn't even speak.

'This looks excellent,' he said to Laura, bestowing one of his tight smiles on her. His eyes travelled over the dishes of pulpy vegetables, hard little bullets of potato, anaemic meat carved and carefully arranged on a platter. It was impossible to tell whether or not the compliment was sincere. With a flash of clarity, I suddenly saw the meal as it would appear to someone outside our enclave; joyless and functional, a means to an end. Harvey had once been something of a gourmet, if not a gourmand. That was lost now, like so much else, and bizarrely, the thought made my chest constrict for a second. I sat down, keeping my eyes on my plate.

Laura sat down last, clearing her throat. Her hands drifted together, clasping loosely as she bowed her head. 'Lord,' she said quietly, 'for the food we are about to receive, may You make us truly thankful. Bless the land from whence it came and all those who receive it.' She paused, took a breath. Staring at my plate, I felt all the muscles in my neck tighten. *Don't say it,* I thought. The vague, blurred discomfort I always felt at these moments had inexplicably sharpened today into a fury that I found I could barely contain. The pale blue swirls around the rim of my plate started to go bright and fuzzy before my eyes. For a moment I thought that Laura would break the habit of the past nine months, raise her head and go on with her meal. But of course she didn't. 'And, Lord, please bless Jonathan,' she quavered, her voice bending with that predictable crack.

'Commend him to Thy spirit and let him watch over us.'

She wiped each eye in turn with the tip of her finger, laid her hands flat down on the tabletop for a moment, and then rose to serve the vegetables. As I had waited for the inevitable words, I had genuinely thought that when I heard them, I would jump from my seat, slash my arm viciously across the table and send the dishes smashing to the floor. Instead I nodded when Laura asked whether I wanted broccoli, sat quietly and chewed my way numbly through the meal. Inside, I turned this new rage over and over in my mind, examining it, exploring it. At its core was something very simple. I didn't want Jonathan's name trotted out over the dinner table as if it were public property. He had been mine as much as theirs. Maybe more. I wanted some choice in when he was spoken of. I wanted some ownership, some right to him.

★   ★   ★

Our past is so real to me that I can't see it as something dead and gone; it's always there waiting. I can picture myself there in the office with him as clear as day. Whenever he comes near me I feel my skin prickling all over. Air rushes into my lungs and makes me gasp, my heart thudding against my ribs like a crazed demon trying to rip its way out through my skin. Surreal bright spots pop, tiny fireworks at the corners of my vision. I know that this is lust, but it feels more like danger, and it frightens me. I'm barely eighteen, and this is too big for me. I can't rein it in.

My desk is barely fifteen feet from his. I file papers, forward emails, take messages, all the things a secretary is supposed to do, but my real job is watching him, nine hours a day. Most of the time it seems he barely notices that I'm there at all. Even when he speaks to me his eyes are elsewhere. I watch him flicking through files, frowning down in concentration at the bright white sheaths of paper. When the sun shines through the window behind his desk, the light that bounces off these papers sparkles across his face and I ache at the way it illuminates his bones. His dark golden hair is always perfectly smooth; he wears dark expensive suits that look as if they were lovingly fitted to every line of his body; his lips are full and almost feminine. He's so nearly a dull, passionless pretty-boy, and yet there is something in the set of his shoulders and the hard slash of his jaw that tells me otherwise.

He looks . . . I think, the unfamiliar words coming readily to my mind as I stare at him across the room, *he looks as if he can handle himself.*

I know now that this is what people mean when they talk about fate. When I decided to take a summer job before starting university, I barely considered my choice of workplace. It was nothing but a means to an end, a way of earning money. I circled a temp agency's ad at random. I didn't even care whether or not I got the job, but now that I'm here, I know that it is where I was always meant to be. Every morning I make him a cup of coffee, black with two sugars, and I press my lips against the side of the burning cup for just an instant before I take it in to him. When I'm back at my desk watching him curl his fingers around the place where my lips have been, it's all I can do not to cry out. This frustration keeps me awake at nights — hot and restless and impatient, wanting him, needing him. When I do sleep I sometimes dream of him, but in these dreams he's just as elusive as he is in life, always a crucial few inches away from me. His name is Jonathan Blackwood. He is thirty years old and an associate lawyer at the firm; his father, Harvey, is a partner. He wears no wedding ring. This is the sum total of what I know about him. No — I know one more thing. I know that he was made to love me.

One Wednesday I see the time display on my computer click on to six o'clock, and I don't move. It's late September, and the last of the light is fading outside. Autumn has come early this year and I can see the leaves falling darkly from the trees that flank his window. In two days I will pack up my things for the last time and walk out of his life to begin my own, at university, in Manchester. For these last few days, I don't want to leave his office until he does. He is bent over the desk, writing notes on a pad of paper, lost to everything else. His lips move slightly, unfathomably, as he writes. I lean back in my chair and surrender myself to the pleasure of watching unobserved. I don't know how much time passes; only that the room gradually shrinks and glows until it seems that we're caught in the only pocket of light in the whole universe and the darkness outside has graded through to pitch black. This should feel strange, but it doesn't. It feels as if I have come home.

Suddenly, he raises his head and I feel the force of his gaze on me. 'Violet,' he says. 'Why are you still here?'

I straighten up in my seat. 'What time is it?' I ask.

'Nine o'clock.' He speaks with faint surprise. 'I don't know where the time's gone tonight.' He pauses, and I know I am supposed to fill the silence, but I am mute and frozen to my seat. 'Why are you still here?' he asks again.

'I thought,' I begin, and clear my throat to ease the tightness, 'I thought you might want me to stay, in case you needed anything.'

He stands up abruptly, snatching his briefcase and stuffing the pad of paper into it. 'God, I am sorry,' he says briskly. 'I had no idea — you should have said something. I meant to leave hours ago myself. Let's get these lights off and lock up. I expect everyone else has already left.'

Hearing him say it makes it real. We're alone here. I watch him click his desk lamp off, and want to scream for him to stop. I stand too, but I don't move away from my desk. At the door he glances over at me, looks away, then back again. His brow creases in confusion, or indecision. After a few moments he comes across the room to stand in front of me. Close up, I can see the faint golden hairs pushing through around his mouth and chin, and a flash of how they would feel against my fingers comes to me so clearly that I can't help making a small sound, deep in the back of my throat. He puts his hands palms down on the desk, leaning in slightly towards me.

'Is there something wrong?' he asks.

I can smell the dark spicy scent of his aftershave, and his fingers are just inches from mine, and suddenly a wildness overtakes me and I think, why the hell not, why shouldn't I get what I want this time? I don't reach out and touch him. I don't tell him that I think I love him. I know, instinctively and deep in my gut, that the most brazen thing of all is not to say a word or move a muscle, and that's exactly what I do. The realisation seems to come to him slowly, drip by drip, easing its way through his body and changing the expression on his face so subtly that I can't pinpoint the moment it switches. All I know is that first he's looking at me with detached concern, the way that any employer might see his secretary, and next he's just a man staring at a woman.

'I didn't . . . ' he says slowly. He doesn't finish the sentence, because he's realising that of course he did know, he's always known. I stare steadily back at him, and then I back away, inch by inch until my back is flat against the wall. I feel the silky fabric of my stockings catch against the cold plaster. He moves towards me in slow motion, never taking his eyes off mine. When he is as close as he can be without touching me, he puts one hand, flat and deliberate, against the wall above my shoulder — centimetres from my face, a knife just grazing my ear. I'm trembling, waiting, feeling the heat rising off him. He slides the other hand down the opposite side of the wall until it is level with my waist, then curves it swiftly inwards, slipping against the small of my back. I feel his touch on me like an electric shock. He pulls me towards him, roughly against his body, and suddenly I'm closing my eyes and giving myself up to it, kissing hard and fast. When he pulls back for a second, his face is dazed and surprised.

Later, much later, he whispers, 'I don't want to hurt you,' and I say, 'You won't.' At eighteen, I am filled with confidence and certainty, and I have no suspicion that I am wrong. When I'm lying in bed beside him, finally still and listening to him breathing, I pinch the back of my hand so hard that tears spring to my eyes. I don't wake up. This is a dream from which I won't surface for another two years, but when I do it will be with such violence — eyes streaming, limbs aching, throat straining for breath — that it will almost kill me.

★　★　★

The morning after Harvey's return from Spain, I walked into town for my shift at the shop. Every Friday and Sunday for the past four months, I had done the same thing. Laura had been the one who had seen the job advertised in the shop window, had noted down its details on a scrap of notepaper and pushed it under my bedroom door without a word. I hadn't thought it worth my while to argue. Even I could see that I couldn't sit in the house for the rest of my life. It was a kind of rehabilitation, I supposed — an undemanding job designed to reintegrate me into society — and like all rehabilitations, it felt at once painfully repetitive and ridiculously daunting.

Finding my way to the shop was usually like sleepwalking, my feet blindly steering me on a course they knew by heart. That morning I made myself stop and look as I walked, forcing the blurred, remote shapes around me into reality. Trees, lamp-posts, buildings, people. It was a hot day, and I could feel the sweat trickling down the back of my neck and catching in my collar. Everything I saw seemed to have a kind of unexpected clarity to it, like bright flesh suddenly and shockingly revealed under a layer of skin ripped away. For months I had felt distant and separated from the world I

26

walked through; a patient behind a smooth, impenetrable glass wall. That morning I felt that I could reach out and touch whatever I saw. I was acutely aware of the pavement underneath my feet, pressing up against the soles of my shoes. When I reached the shop and raised my head to look up at its purple painted sign, the letters flashed at me, winking crazily. I closed my eyes briefly, and I could still see them — *Belle's Boutique*, written in luminous script across the darkness.

I pushed the door open, listening to the sharp tangle of sound that pealed from the bell above. Catherine was already there, her platinum head bent over a glossy magazine. As always, she was sipping from a huge mug of tea, cradled in her tiny hands with their vixen-painted fingernails. When she saw me she set it down and gave me a brief friendly nod of acknowledgement. Catherine was twenty-two and blessed with the prettiness of a pixie. She had been away from the village for the past three years at a London fashion college, and I suspected that she would soon be gone again. Today she was wearing a linen smock covered with green and crimson flowers and a pair of high-heeled, strappy emerald sandals. In my first few weeks she had tried her best to make friends, but I had been unable to rouse myself to reciprocate and as a result we had fallen into an uneasy truce, two strangers brought together by a common setting. That morning I tried to smile in a way that would tell her that something had changed, even if I wasn't quite sure what, but her face gave no sign that she had understood.

'Sorry I'm late,' I said, glancing at the clock. The extra lingering on my way in had cost me ten minutes.

'Doesn't matter,' Catherine said, shrugging. We rarely got any customers before eleven. 'Good day yesterday?'

'Yes, thanks,' I said, finding that it was at least partly true. Looking back on it now, the drive to the airport had lost its nightmarish quality. I felt expanded, like an animal let out of a cage into the open air.

'You were picking up your dad, weren't you?' she asked.

I stared at her. She wasn't looking at me, still thumbing through the magazine and drinking her tea. A sudden bolt of vertigo hit me. For just a second, the whole shop lifted itself and shook before settling back into place. I opened my mouth to speak and the words came out. 'Actually, he's not my father.'

Catherine looked up now, her face

quizzical and alert. 'Oh, right — sorry,' she said. 'I just assumed he was — I mean, well, because you live with him, and . . . ' *And because you always call him Dad,* her frown finished silently.

I sat down opposite her at the till. My heart was beating very fast, with excitement or fear. I wanted to giggle. 'I know,' I said. 'He and Laura are actually my parents-in-law. I married their son, Jonathan, a couple of years ago.' The truth slipped easily from my lips then, and I wondered why it had stayed locked up for so long. Catherine was staring across at me, red-painted lips parted in blank surprise. I could see her tussling with questions, selecting one almost at random.

'How old are you?' she asked bluntly.

'I'm twenty-one next month,' I said. 'I married young.'

Catherine was alive with shock now; I could feel it buzzing, crackling off her. 'That's amazing!' she shrieked, reaching out and grabbing my hand hotly in hers. 'I can't believe I've been working with you all this time, and I never even knew you were married! God, I don't know anyone who's even in a serious relationship, let alone . . . it's so romantic.' All of a sudden she looked down, as if her hand were telling her something. She examined mine, turned it over. 'You don't wear a ring?' she asked. For a second her face dropped with disappointed suspicion.

'I do,' I said quickly, hating her doubting me. 'I just wear it around my neck, see?' I fumbled for the long, thin white gold chain beneath my shirt and drew it out. The platinum-and-diamond ring sparkled wickedly in the light, swaying back and forth like a dowser's pendulum beneath my hand.

'I see,' said Catherine slowly, reaching out a finger to touch it. 'Why do you do that?'

I drew in breath to speak, and found that this was harder. I fought past the sudden sickness in my throat: I had come this far. 'Jonathan died last October,' I said. 'I didn't want to get rid of the ring, but it feels wrong to wear it on my wedding finger now. I don't know why.'

She leant in towards me, her hands clasped tightly together now as if she were praying. Her face was flooded with sympathy. '*Oh my God.*' She was looking at me as if I were someone entirely different from the girl she had thought she had known — a curiosity, a rare discovery to be treasured and explored.

'You're the first person I've spoken to about it.' I corrected myself. 'The first person who didn't already know.'

Catherine bowed her head, as if sensible of

the honour, simultaneously gratified and unworthy. When she shook her head in disbelief, her long beaded glass earrings leapt and jangled prettily against her neck, casting pale shadows against her skin. For a few moments, stupidly, I couldn't tear my eyes away from them. I felt the hairs on my arms stand on end and prickle against my sleeves; despite the heat of the day, I was cold, and shivering with what felt like delayed shock. Now that I had told her, the glee had drained out of me. I wanted the words back, wanted them swallowed back up into the back depths of my head.

I heard her voice, tentative but insistent, come to me from somewhere. 'How did it happen?'

'It was an accident,' I said, and in the same instant heard the bell go. A group of young girls poured into the shop, chatting and screaming with laughter. Catherine looked swiftly across at them, then back at me, frozen into silence. *Excuse me, excuse me,* one of the girls was bleating, holding up a skirt, *do you have this in a size ten? She means a twelve,* another cut in. Whoops of laughter. *You cheeky cow. Oh, come on — you're never a ten.* Their words rolled around the walls like marbles. I watched Catherine rise reluctantly from her seat and move towards them. I could still feel my pulse beating hard and fast, thumping in my eardrums. I slipped the chain back inside my shirt. For the rest of the shift, I could feel the cool, perfect circle of the ring against my skin, always there, reminding me, branding me.

★ ★ ★

We stay away from the office for the next two days, holed up together in Jonathan's penthouse flat, leaving only to buy food, which we eat mostly in bed. On Friday morning he sleeps in until twelve, and I spend over an hour just lying there looking at him. His lips are slightly parted, showing a flash of white pointed teeth that gives me a sick, shifting pang of lust deep inside my stomach. His eyes move mysteriously under closed lids, rolling and flickering. I want to peel them back and step into his dreams.

When he wakes he reaches for me reflexively. 'Good morning,' he murmurs.

'Good morning,' I repeat. He must catch something different in my voice, because he sits up sharply.

'What's up?' he says. 'Are you hungry? Do you want me to get you something to eat?'

'No,' I say. 'It's just . . . I'll have to go soon.'

Jonathan shakes his head, more in confusion than disagreement, as if he simply cannot believe what he is hearing. 'Go where?' he asks. 'What for?'

I spread my hands helplessly. 'I'm going to Manchester tomorrow,' I say. 'To start university. You know that.'

He frowns a little, lines creasing the smooth beauty of his forehead. 'You can't do that,' he says. When I don't reply, he repeats it, louder this time. 'You can't do that. You'll have to cancel.'

Even though I can hardly bear the thought of leaving him, a laugh rises unwillingly in my throat. 'You can't just cancel university. I have to go.'

'No,' he says, grabbing my hand, pulling me against him. We are so close that I can't even focus on him any more, but I can still feel his eyes boring through me. 'You have to stay. Here with me. If you go to Manchester, it's over.'

His words land like a punch and I gasp. This conversation is moving too fast, making me dizzy. If I've thought about it at all in the haze of the past two days, I have vaguely assumed that we will manage, no matter how far apart we are; visits at weekends, long stretches of time together in the holidays. I love him, and although he hasn't yet said so, I know he loves me too. This is what love is about: enduring separation, believing that we can surmount all obstacles. I tell him as much, but he thumps his hand impatiently down on the bed, making me flinch.

'No, Violet,' he barks. His face is aflame with anger and outrage. 'Love is about being together. I want you, and it's now or it's not at all — I won't wait for you.' It should sound hard and unfeeling, but somehow it doesn't. It sounds like exactly what I've dreamt of hearing all my life. Someone who needs me, who's desperate for me, so desperate that he can't even bear me to be out of his sight.

'I can't,' I say again, but the conviction has gone from my voice.

He leaps up and pulls on a robe; grabbing the phone from the bedside table, he strides back and brandishes it in front of me. 'Of course you can,' he says. 'You can call them right now and tell them you're not coming.' Suddenly, he smiles wickedly, and the warmth of it soaks right through my skin to my bones. As I take the phone I'm laughing and shaking my head, because it's all so ridiculous, because the truth of it is that I barely know him, because it would be crazy to throw the future I've planned for months away with one phone call, and because I know that this is it, suddenly there's no other option — he's the one and I'm going to do it.

The woman at the admissions office on the other end of the line is silent for a long while, and then asks to speak to my parents. My mouth opens and words fall out: I tell her she can't, because they are both dead. I have not crafted my thoughts or moulded them into speech — they have just happened to me, used me as a vessel. As the woman flounders and gropes for a response, I press the button and cut her off. I'm laughing like a madwoman as I jump into Jonathan's arms. He hugs me back, but I can feel the tension in his shoulders. Sure enough, after a few seconds he grips me by my arms and pushes me back slightly, frowning at me.

'Was that true?' he asks.

'No,' I say, even though an inner voice is telling me to stick to my story. To do otherwise looks crazy, unreliable, but I can't help myself. *Anyone else I can lie to*, I think, *but not you, not you.*

He tips his head back sharply for an instant, as if to throw his thoughts together into a heap. 'Why did you say it, then?' he asks. I can't know, at this point, that denying his parents' existence would seem to him the worst kind of sacrilege.

I shrug, looking at him steadily, straight on. This is who I am, and if he can't accept it then he is not who I think he is. 'I had to say something,' I say. 'I'm doing this for you.'

For a split second, uncertainty pulses across his face and I feel something curl coldly between us; a sudden distance, a moment of clarity. We're facing each other, both our bodies tensed. His face spells out his thoughts as plainly as if he has shouted them into the silent room. He's wondering what the hell he is doing, if he is right to have pushed me to make that call, if it's too late to backtrack. He's wondering whether I am worth his time. Just as he begins to speak, his mobile rings, shrilling and flashing insistently from the bedroom cabinet. His head snaps instantly towards it, and he strides across the room to pick it up. Facing away from me, he murmurs a hello. I watch his back straighten; he moves towards the balcony, pushing the glass doors open and pulling them to again behind him. I'm left alone in the bedroom. I stare down at my hands; they are clenched and shaking, blurring in front of me. I feel as if I have narrowly avoided a disaster. In the past two days I have discovered something so strong and so powerful that it comes as a shock to find that it could also be so fragile. I can't let him take this away from me, from us. I will have to fight for him.

Dimly, I become aware of his voice outside

on the balcony, seeping in through the tiny gap where the door has not quite closed. He's saying that there is nothing to worry about, that he has everything under control and that he will be back in the office on Monday. He sounds deferential, stumbling over his words in a way I have never heard before. After a minute's taut silence, he says, '*Yes — yes, she is.*' Another silence, and then a short, relieved laugh.

'OK,' he says, and as he does so he pushes the door open again and steps back inside the room. 'I will. Lunchtime tomorrow at the club? Got it. I'll see you then.' He disconnects the call and tosses the phone on to the bed, breathing deeply. He glances at me and I am surprised and relieved to see a flirtatious spark in his eyes. 'That was my father,' he says. 'Wondering why I've been playing hooky from the office. He's a clever old devil, I'll give him that — he worked out that you must be with me, and he's intrigued. He wants to meet you — us — for lunch tomorrow with him and my mother. Fancy it?'

I blink, unsure of what has just happened. The thought of lunch with Jonathan's parents both exhilarates and terrifies me. I stare at him, running the tip of my tongue nervously along my bottom lip. 'Yes,' I say, because there seems to be nothing else to say, nothing else that will keep us on this course.

He comes to sit beside me on the bed and puts his arm around me, and with that one gesture my doubts dissolve and I want to weep with relief. 'I'm sorry this is all so fast,' he whispers into my neck. 'But I don't want to lose you. I know that already.' He kisses my collarbone, a soft, long kiss that makes me close my eyes. 'You'd better go home later,' he says. 'Explain things to those parents of yours. Maybe leave out the part about them being dead.' A low snort of amusement against my neck lets me know that he's teasing me, repainting what initially seemed bizarre and disturbing in a kinder, more indulgent light.

'We're not close,' I say. I'm trying to justify myself to him, but he doesn't seem interested in hearing me. He's running his hands slowly over me from top to toe, as if he has just noticed that I am naked. He mutters something that I can't catch, and soon enough I don't want to talk any more. He attacks my body with a passion that half frightens me, so roughly at times that I can feel the pain stabbing at me through the haze of pleasure, and more than once I almost scream at him to stop, but he seems to read my thoughts and softens his touch at the crucial moment every time. Soon enough I will reflect that things are much the same out of bed as they are in it. Some people have a knack for bringing you to the brink again and again, pushing you right to the limit of your endurance until you think you cannot take any more, but never quite tipping you over the edge and out of love.

★ ★ ★

Laura was in the garden when I returned from the shop, tying lengths of pale green and lilac crêpe paper in bows around the back of each chair in turn. I stood and watched her from the kitchen window. When she had tied each bow, she stepped back, shaded her eyes against the sun and tipped her head a little to one side, as if expecting the chair to speak to her. Several times she came forward again and readjusted the crêpe paper, fluffing it primly and precisely into place until she was satisfied. There must have been fifty or sixty chairs in total, huddled in groups around spindly metal tables dotted across the sweep of lawn. A pile of bunting was stacked up by one of the tables — multicoloured flags strung together on a pale yellow cord, stirring slightly with the summer wind. As I leaned out of the window, peering closer, I could see tiny sparkling dots nestling in the grass, winking and glimmering like jewels. Rose petals perhaps, or some kind of confetti. As I stared at them, Laura looked up and saw me, gave me a little wave. I came out into the garden to join her.

'How was the shop?' she asked when I was close enough to pick up the soft, low register of her voice.

Briefly, I considered telling her the truth. *I told Catherine about Jonathan today. She treated me differently all afternoon, and before I left she asked me whether I wanted to talk any more about it. I said no, but now I'm not so sure. I think I might, and soon.* 'This all looks great,' I said instead, gesticulating to take in the whole lawn. 'Better hope it doesn't rain overnight.'

'Oh, it won't rain.' A hint of Laura's old imperiousness surfaced. 'I wanted to get everything ready today, so that I could concentrate on the food tomorrow. We've got almost sixty coming, you know.'

There was pride in her words. I stared out across the lawn, shading my eyes against the evening sun, trying to imagine it filled with people intent on celebrating Harvey's sixty-fourth birthday. It was an arbitrary number to be making such a fuss over, but I suspected that the birthday itself was little but a device to kick-start Harvey's return to society. Last year, visitors had come and gone with a monotonous regularity that had rapidly thinned into nothingness when it became clear that none of us was inclined to put on a brave face and entertain company. I could tell that through his grief Harvey was still capable of being disappointed by the shoddy pretence of respect with which his erstwhile friends and colleagues had retreated — and contemptuous of it, too. All the same, the garden party had been his idea, perhaps to test the permanence of the situation. As the RSVPs had trickled back I had sensed a kind of cold satisfaction emanating from him, a growing confirmation that he had not been erased as swiftly as it had appeared. He had always known, as well as they did, that he was not the sort of person who was easily forgotten.

'It'll be strange,' I heard Laura say, as if half to herself. 'Seeing everyone again. It feels like such a long time since we've had this sort of gathering.' Her fingers plucked disconsolately at a thread of lilac crêpe, teasing it apart into long filmy strands. 'I hope Dad enjoys it.'

'I hope we all do,' I said, 'but there's no reason why we wouldn't.' Empty though the words were, they seemed to reassure her, and she nodded. I hesitated, and then put my hand over hers. Despite the heat of the day, her skin felt cold and faintly damp, as if she had just come in out of the rain.

'I think this will be good for you, Violet,' she said unexpectedly. 'You're too young to . . . ' She trailed off and, not wanting her to go on, I gripped her hand more tightly. The sudden smart of tears behind my eyes surprised me. Affection, even love, for Laura tended to strike me like that; randomly, as if unthought of ever before.

'I'm looking forward to it,' I said, as brightly as I could muster, and as I smiled at her I felt my spirits lift with the knowledge that I wasn't lying. The closest I had got to a party in the past nine months was a strained, abortive gathering with a few of Jonathan's old university friends — women ten years older than myself who wanted to drink cocktails, talk loudly about their own lives and subtly compete to give the impression that they themselves had been far more deeply touched and bruised by my husband's death than I could ever imagine. It was a mistake that I had never made again. There was something unsettling about the distance I felt from them, a sharp contrast to the easy friendliness with which they had seemed to welcome me when Jonathan and I were first married. Perhaps they had seen me as temporary. Now, in their eyes and mine, he would always belong to me, and they had not liked it.

'Really, I'm looking forward to it,' I said again, almost defiantly. Still smiling, I swung round to look back at the house, and saw Harvey there. He was standing motionless at the kitchen window. I raised my hand, but he gave no sign of having noticed me. He was staring out through the glass across the lawn, his face blank and remote, as if he were watching Rome burn.

I began to walk back towards the house. I didn't want to see the garden through his eyes, as I knew I would if I turned around again: the pointless little bunched-together groups of tables, the coloured bows fluttering emptily in the breeze. Harvey had a way of stripping back pretence, albeit without intent or volition. He simply saw the futility of things, and it bled out of him, tainting everything that it touched.

★ ★ ★

I heard them before I saw them: a rising and falling hubbub of voices outside the kitchen door, their words blurring into each other so that I could barely make sense of them. I kept my head down, piping cream into meringues in perfect circles, feeling heat spilling over me. Now that the guests were arriving I wanted them gone again. A painful shyness was spreading in my chest, making me gasp for breath. My fingers shook as I placed the strawberries one by one on top of each meringue, taking far longer than I needed, spinning out the task. Above the general hum I heard Harvey's coolly authoritative tones, inviting the guests to go out into the garden and exchanging niceties. Now and again, I thought I could hear Laura chiming in, palely echoing his words. Shadows moved across the work-surface as people passed outside, but I kept my back to the window. I collected the meringues on to their silver platter, then went to wash my hands. In my agitation I turned the tap on too hard and water sprayed out on to my dress, staining darkly against the red linen. I dabbed it ineffectually with a tea towel, feeling my heart beat faster, hearing the voices grow louder outside.

'And where is Violet?' I heard someone say, my name cutting through the babble of words. 'How *is* she?' I didn't recognise the woman's voice, but her tone was deferential, sympathetic, as if she were referring to an invalid. I couldn't catch Laura's reply, but the woman made a noise of ostentatious understanding in response. 'Of course, it's very hard on her,' I heard her say. 'On *all* of you.'

I snatched up a tray of quiches at random and made for the back door, gripping the tray tightly to cancel out my shaking. When I saw the lawn I stopped in my tracks and blinked, half dazzled; dozens of people, many of them women with bright, jewel-coloured hats and shoes that danced and sparkled jauntily in the sun. I had not meant to make an entrance, but as I appeared, conversations seemed to fade, heads turn sharply my way for an instant before whipping back into place. I came forward across the lawn, placed the tray carefully down on to the nearest table, then straightened up, searching for a face I recognised. Many of them stirred up vague memories: ex-colleagues from Harvey's law firm, their eyes alert and watchful. I couldn't remember a single one of their names.

I saw Laura and made my way towards her, forcing my lips into a smile. Next to her, a large matronly woman loomed, her hair teased up into tight little brown curls that clustered around her bovine face. I knew instinctively that it was her voice I had heard in the kitchen, but I had no idea who she was.

'Violet, I was just going to bring out some more of the food — but you remember Miranda,' Laura said, almost beseechingly, as if willing me to say yes. I looked closer, and with a shock I connected the name and the

45

face: Miranda Foster, Jonathan's godmother and an old family friend. All at once I could see her on our wedding day, bearing down on me and telling me how lucky I was and how Jonathan was like a son to her, before enfolding him lasciviously in a hug like no mother I had ever seen. The past eighteen months had not been kind to her; her face looked strained and stiff, as if it had been dipped in wax.

'Of course,' I said, holding out my hand, but Miranda made an impatient gesture and cast aside the sandwich she had been holding, pulling me against her voluptuous bosom into a forced embrace. I froze in shock, the sticky, cloying scent of her perfume flooding my nostrils.

'My poor child,' she whispered into my ear. 'What you must have been through!' As swiftly as she had drawn me towards her, she pushed me back, holding me by the shoulders to examine me. 'You look older,' she said, a little critically. 'I suppose it's to be expected.'

Yes, I almost said, *the passage of time tends to have that effect* — but I knew that was not what she meant. What she was trying to imply, not very subtly, was that grief had ravaged me, stolen the youthful bloom that she might once have envied and rendered me wholly unremarkable. She may well have been right, but I fiercely resented her assumption that she was entitled to say it. She was no one to me; had meant less than nothing to Jonathan, who had once told me that he wished the old harridan would stop undressing him with her eyes every time they met. For an instant I felt my colour rise and the words threatened to burst out of me.

'I suppose it is, yes — for all of us,' I contented myself with. 'I would hardly have recognised you.'

Miranda's brow wrinkled in suspicion and dismay, but before she could speak Harvey materialised at my side. He was wearing a crisp linen suit in pale grey, his silver hair drawn back from his forehead, and a necktie I had not seen before: an unusually flamboyant affair, apple-green silk shot through with metallic thread. When she saw him, Miranda's face softened into what I suspected she thought was coquettishness, and which indeed might have been in a woman half her age.

'Lovely to see you, so glad you could make it,' Harvey said smoothly. 'Violet, why don't you go and see if anyone would like a top-up? There's more champagne inside.'

Gratefully, I broke away. Harvey had an instinct for seeing when people needed to be rescued and an admirably self-sacrificing nature when it came to substituting himself into the firing line; it was something I had forgotten about him in these months of near-isolation. As I retreated, I stole a look back at him. He appeared relaxed, urbane and smiling. It was impossible to tell whether it was just an act.

I spent the next hour passing through the crowd, offering drinks and canapés, stopping here and there for a brief five minutes of small talk. Most of the guests had eyes that flooded with a mixture of pity and curiosity as they spoke to me, but at least, unlike Miranda, they had the good sense to keep their tongues in check and stuck to chatting about the weather. As time passed I felt myself begin to unwind, the tension relaxing from my muscles. A couple of Harvey's colleagues flirted gallantly and unthreateningly with me, making me roll my eyes and blush. I wondered whether I might be having fun. Standing there on the lawn in my red dress, tossing my hair over my shoulders and laughing, I caught a glimpse of the future opening up. It was not the future I had planned and not the kind of fun I had been accustomed to, but there was little prospect of that any more. Glancing into the crowd of guests, I tried to imagine Jonathan among them, moving with his old confident ease from group to group, and found that I could not. For so long I had carried him around with me like a dead weight, projecting him so vividly into every situation I found myself in that it sometimes seemed I had summoned his ghost. The thought felt disloyal, but if I had lost the knack, I was not sure that I wanted it back. I was tired of missing him, tired of living my life around someone who no longer existed. Any respite from it, no matter how temporary, made me giddily thankful.

I was helping Laura to collect some empty glasses when I saw Harvey stride across the lawn towards us. He put his arm lightly around Laura's waist, bending in towards her so that his mouth almost brushed her ear. 'What is that man doing here?' I heard him murmur, jerking his head to indicate who he meant. To anyone who knew him less, his voice would have sounded unruffled, but I caught a steely undertone to it, the merest hint of a threat.

Laura followed his gaze, narrowing her eyes in the sunlight, and I did the same. Underneath the low-spreading apple tree at the edge of the lawn, a little apart from the crowd, a man stood, smoking a cigarette and looking out across the grass, his face half turned away.

'It's Max Croft, isn't it?' Laura said. When Harvey did not reply, she turned her face up to his appealingly, searching for a clue as to what to say. 'I suppose his parents brought him,' she said finally.

'His parents?' Harvey repeated, a little bitingly. 'Couldn't they find a babysitter?' His voice threatened to become louder, and he took a full minute to compose himself, smoothing the flat of his hand slowly and repeatedly over the knot of his tie. I squinted harder at the man, but could make out little but the short, angry-seeming drags he was taking on his cigarette; hard, muscular movements.

'I didn't realise that you didn't want him here.' Laura fluttered, her hands making desperate shapes in the air now as she spoke. 'I mean, I didn't specifically tell Patricia and James that they couldn't bring him, I wouldn't really have thought of it — and after all, he did know Jonathan, I thought they were quite friendly once — '

'Actually,' Harvey cut in levelly, 'I don't think Jonathan liked him at all.'

'Oh dear . . . ' Laura began to flap, her eyes darting wildly back and forth between Harvey and the man underneath the apple tree. 'I'm not sure . . . I don't think I can . . . '

'Of course you can't,' Harvey said, so softly

that I could barely catch the words. 'All the same, next time, perhaps you could finalise the guest list with me.' His tone was perfectly pleasant, almost soothing. Before Laura had a chance to reply, he had turned and melted into the crowd, clapping yet another well-wisher on the back. Laura looked after him, wringing her hands, her face haunted. I knew that she would worry about the incident for the rest of the afternoon.

I drifted away from the central tables to get a better look at the man whose appearance had jolted Harvey's famous equilibrium. As I stood on the fringes of the group, staring across at him, he saw me and half raised his hand in a silent salute. Automatically, I waved back. He paused, stubbing out his cigarette against the tree, then beckoned me over. I hesitated, glancing back, but curiosity drove me forward; I walked slowly across the lawn, the pointed heels of my shoes sinking a little into the earth with each step. As I drew closer I realised that Harvey was right. This face had no business at his garden party. The features were bold, tough and cruel; brutal slashed cheekbones, a hard, unsmiling gangster's mouth. His dark hair was cropped close to his skull, bristling along the strong lines of his bones. His shoulders looked tensed for battle, and his body gave the impression of being hard-packed into a container a little too small for it, restraining its force. *If I ran into you in an alleyway*, I thought, *I would be terrified*. I could smell the powerful scent of nicotine and burnt smoke rising off him.

'All right,' he said when I halted a few feet away from him. His voice was every bit as harsh as his appearance, a faint rasping rattle running underneath the surface that made me want to clear my throat. When I didn't reply, he lit up another cigarette, keeping his eyes warily on me, cupping his hand secretively around his mouth.

'Hello,' I said at last.

'Max Croft,' he said, thrusting his hand out so that I had no choice but to take it. He crushed mine for a few painful seconds before throwing it back. 'I think you work with my sister.'

It took me a beat to understand who he meant. I looked more closely at him, and could see no trace of Catherine's elfin prettiness in his face. 'Really?' I said.

He gave a grin more like a sneer, showing even, regular teeth. 'Well, you tell me,' he said. 'Do you or don't you?'

'If you mean Catherine,' I said, 'then yes.'

'That's the one.' He was silent for a few moments, leaning back against the apple tree and smoking, his lips sucking on the cigarette in a way that made my skin prickle with revulsion and fascination. 'Nice do,' he said eventually, jerking his head in the direction of the clustered guests. His voice was lightly laced with irony.

'For those who were invited,' I said. His mocking tone had set off a small fire of protectiveness in me, and I folded my arms. 'Harvey didn't seem to think you were one of those.'

Max raised his eyebrows, looking at me speculatively. 'Come to kick me out, then?' he asked. I was silent. 'Look,' he said after a few more drags, 'I don't want to cause any trouble. I don't think your old man likes me very much, but it's not down to anything I've done. I liked Jonathan — we didn't have a lot in common, granted, but he was a good guy. We played a few games of pool, hung out a few times. If your old man doesn't think I was a suitable friend, then that's his problem.'

I frowned, trying to remember. As far as I could recall, Jonathan had never mentioned this man. I had certainly never seen him before. I thought of Harvey's quiet words to Laura: *Actually, I don't think Jonathan liked him at all.* There was no way of telling who was right. The silence threatened to stifle me. 'He's not my old man,' I said.

Max shrugged. 'Yeah,' he said. 'Obviously.

53

He might as well be, though. Seems you've been well and truly welcomed into the family bosom. Just shows what an untimely death can do, eh? But for that you might still be knocking on the back door pleading to be let in.' His voice had dropped, taking on a nasty, sarcastic quality.

A bright flush of anger swept over me. This man was being insufferably rude, and he had no business saying these knowing things to me, as if he knew more about me and my family — for family they were, in a way — than I did myself. I drew in a sharp breath and turned to go. In the same instant, he had leant forward and caught me easily by the wrist, the tips of two fingers still holding his cigarette, burnt down to the stub now, sending heat coursing across my skin.

'I'm sorry,' he said, looking straight into my eyes, and I felt my whole body jolt with something strange and dark. 'I shouldn't have said that. It just makes me angry to see a girl like you shut away with those two. They're not so bad, don't get me wrong, but they've got no life to them. You're, what? Twenty? Twenty-one? You should get out more.' Incredibly, I thought I saw his left eye briefly flicker in a wink. He dropped my arm, still staring at me. 'I'll see you,' he said, making it sound like a promise and a threat. I backed away from him, breathing hard. My heart was thumping in my chest, as if he had pulled a knife on me.

The next few hours slipped by like minutes. I watched, as I might have watched a scene in a dream, as Harvey commanded everyone's attention and made a short speech, thanking all the guests for coming and saying how pleased he was that he was able to celebrate his birthday with so many of his friends and family. The polite smattering of applause fell into my ears like rain. As people gradually started to peel away, the sky above began to darken. I helped to find coats, showed departing guests to the exit. The wind was picking up, shaking the green and lilac crêpe paper tied to the chairs, setting up a low insistent rustle across the lawn. Drinks were finished, glasses cast aside, presents left in the hallway. I stood smiling and thanking people for coming, saying the same lines over and over, kissing and shaking hands with what might as well have been so many brightly dressed puppets. '*I saw you talking to Max Croft earlier*,' Miranda whispered as she left, intent on imparting one final sting, '*he's not our sort, not our sort at all.*' As I waved off the last of them, a light drizzle began to slash against the windowpanes.

I went back out into the empty garden,

feeling the rain soaking into my skin, collecting coldly in my hair. Far in the distance, I could see Laura, sitting still on a bench by the rose garden. I walked down towards her, my shoes sucking and sticking to the damp earth. She was gazing at the yellow rose bush, the one she had planted in memory of Jonathan. I remembered her digging the cold ground, her head bent down, shoving the spade in with such violence that it shook her whole body, sending gravel spraying in a fountain around her, muddying her dress. The roses were in bloom now; huge, gorgeous blooms the colour of sunshine, trembling with fat drops of rain. I sat down beside her, and for a long while we didn't speak. Her face was set and distant, as if she were sorting through her memories and finding nothing new there.

'Do you ever wonder?' I said. 'Do you ever wonder what happened?'

Laura raised her head slowly, searchingly; didn't speak.

'I don't mean . . . I know that we know what happened,' I said. 'But . . . ' I didn't know how to continue. All at once, and without warning, I felt the old familiar grief and incomprehension rising to the surface, sending a shiver of nausea the length of my body. As we sat there, I began to cry as I hadn't done in weeks, huge ugly sobs that shook the air around us. I wanted these feelings gone — wanted them out of me. It seemed that they were here to stay; that however much I wanted it and however much I might fool myself that I was moving on, they wouldn't ever leave me.

★　★　★

I unlock the door and push it open as quietly as I can, feeling it snag and scrape against loose carpet. As I slip into the dark hallway, I hear the low static noise of the television coming from the sitting room. I move towards it, the familiar smell of must and musk flooding my nose and mouth as I do so. If I stay in this house too long, it starts to cling to my hair and my clothes, infecting everywhere I go. It's the same with the mess; even when I'm not here, I can see it in the back of my mind, weighing me down. Now, coming from Jonathan's immaculate flat, it hits me even harder: boxes piled up against the hallway wall containing God knows what, stacks of old yellowing newspapers, a heap of ironing that never seems to get done. I have long since passed the stage of seeing these things as charmingly bohemian.

I creep to the sitting room door and stand

there, peeping through the chink. The room is dark but for the television, light bristling off it like an eerie aquarium, and a small floor lamp throwing dim shadows against the back wall. The backs of my parents' heads are there, popped up above the sofa and framing the television, motionless. I know they will have heard me come in, despite my efforts to be quiet, but they don't turn around. I push the door open and come into the room, go and sit opposite them on an armchair that sighs and whines when I settle myself down on it.

'Nice of you to join us,' grunts my father, and for a few moments we're just sitting there silently, all of us together, our eyes trained on whichever stupid quiz show they've been watching for however many minutes or hours or days. The pictures dance in front of me, blurring meaninglessly into blobs of coloured light. I think of Jonathan, the hot sharp smell of sweat and sex in his bedroom. Already I can't wait to see him again.

'Are you all packed, dear?' my mother asks idly. I have told them that I have been staying with a friend, Gemma, for the past few days. It seems they haven't bothered to check. From anyone else this question might be barbed — if she had bothered to set foot in my room, my mother would know that no packing had been done — but from her, it

58

denotes nothing but ignorance. I look at her, her calm and indifferent face. In a minute I will make that mask crack. I can feel my hands growing hot and damp; I wipe them slowly against my skirt.

'No,' I say. 'I haven't packed, because I'm not going to Manchester.'

The change, in my mother at least, is instant. Her head jerks up and she shoots a sharp glance at my father. He just stays slumped in his seat, watching the television, looking bored and faintly contemptuous. He has heard this before, of course, but he doesn't know what has changed.

'We've been through this, Violet,' my mother says in a voice that might be meant to be compassionate, but just sounds hard and impatient to my ears. 'It's difficult going to university at first, but you'll be fine. You'll make friends. You'll manage with the work.'

'I've met someone,' I say. 'We're in love.' Saying the truth here, in this faded room with its threadbare rug and peeling walls, makes it sound totally unreal, a little girl's fantasy. I dig my fingernails into my palms and will myself to remember. I won't let these pedestrian surroundings crowd him out. Still, the echo of my words around the room sounds hollow even to my ears. Quietly, my father snickers, a low, unimpressed chuckle that makes me so angry I have to close my eyes briefly, seeing bursts of red pumping across the dark.

'Oh, Violet,' my mother says, her tone exasperated and brittle. 'You'll meet plenty of boys in Manchester.'

I picture them: spotty youths with stripy scarves and flat Northern drawls. 'He's not a *boy*,' I spit out. 'He's a thirty-year-old man with his own flat. And I love him, and I'm not leaving him. Some things are more important than — ' I stop. I want to say 'than education', but it sounds wrong. It's not a question of importance, but one of necessity. I can't leave him. The thought twists a fist in my stomach, tensing my whole body in desperation.

'Oh, Violet,' my mother says again. She clasps her hands in front of her, and I see the ancient engagement ring glinting on her finger. When I was younger I had thought it was the most beautiful ring in the world, but now it looks dulled and tarnished, just like everything else in this house. 'This sounds like a crush to me. We've all had them, but really, a thirty-year-old man is not going to be interested in a young girl like you.'

I feel a surprised bark of laughter rise in my throat. How can she be so naive? 'I think you'll find he's very interested in me,' I say, my voice shrill and loud, battling against the television's merry clatter. 'I've been with him for the past three days, not that you'd care.' For a wild moment, I want to shock her further, push her over the edge, tell her every detail of what we have done. Forbidden words crowd into my mind, making me breathless.

'What?' my mother says, louder now. 'But this . . . this is outrageous. I don't know what's been going on here, but whatever it is, it's ridiculous. You need to go and pack. We'll be leaving at ten a.m. tomorrow.'

'You're right,' I shout. I am on my feet now, towering over her on the sofa, my fists clenched impotently with rage. 'You *don't* know what's been going on — you never have. I love him, and I'm not going. I phoned the admissions office today and told them, so there!' The last two words slip out, and I want to bite them back; even to me they sound silly and childish, but I stand my ground, glaring.

For the first time, my father raises his head and looks at me. He seems faintly puzzled, grooves of confusion etched into his brow. 'You did what?' he asks gruffly.

'I phoned them up and told them I'm not coming,' I repeat. I find that I'm shivering with adrenalin.

My father wipes a hand slowly and

61

deliberately across his mouth before rising to his feet. He's not a tall man, barely a few inches above me in his socked feet, but right now I have to fight the temptation to shrink before him. He puts one hand on my shoulder, but not in comfort. I feel my muscles tense, wanting to shrug him off, but I keep still. He peers forward, into my eyes, as if he is searching for the person he wants to see inside them. But she's not there. I have never been his vision of me. I am somebody else, and all at once she is fighting to get out.

'You have a choice here,' he says. 'Either we call up the admissions office first thing tomorrow and we forget about all this and we take you to Manchester, or you get out of this house and don't come back.'

'David . . . ' I hear my mother say behind him, floating there worriedly like a ghost. I can sense her there, but I can't look at her. My eyes are fixed on my father's.

'No, Jessica,' he interrupts. 'We've done everything for this girl. Everything for *you*,' he says to me. 'If you don't like it, you're not welcome here.'

For a second I am rigid with shock; then I move back, out of his force field, my arms folded across my chest. The hurt and disbelief that wash over me feel strangely familiar, as if they are already a part of me. 'OK,' I say, just to fill the silence. I turn his words over in my head. All I can feel is confusion, incomprehension at how he can believe that eighteen years of what has sometimes felt like near-total indifference amounts to doing everything for me. My mother's face swims into view, her mouth half opened in shock or indecision. She's no better; some days can barely rouse herself enough to care whether I'm dead or alive, for all her protestations when it suits her. I have tried for too long now to pretend that this is how things should be — to be content with this hollow parody of a family. I feel fury rise inside me again, making me heady and nauseous, but I don't speak.

I turn on my heel and leave the room, pounding up the stairs to my bedroom. I let the door swing open, revealing the tatty single bed, the piles of books scattered around it, the childhood knick-knacks that I haven't used in years crowding the dressing table, leaving no inch of space. I step forward and pull my largest suitcase out from under the bed. My blood is pumping in my head. I am not sure what I am doing, and I don't want to stop and think. Quickly, my hands shaking, I start stuffing things into it, almost at random. I force myself to make a list in my head. Clothes, make-up, a few favourite books, the charger for my mobile phone. I zip the bag up easily; it's only half full. There must be something else I need. I look around the room, my eyes darting from corner to corner, taking in the piled-up possessions that don't even feel like mine any more. There's nothing.

I run back down the stairs, dragging the case behind me. They're waiting for me in the hallway. I see my mother's eyes narrow in uncertainty, wondering whether I have been packing for Manchester, or for somewhere else.

'I'm going,' I say, and through my anger, to my own shock, I hear my voice crack even though my eyes are dry. 'Thanks for . . . for *everything*.' I sound hard and bitter, but I don't care. My father's face is stern and set, betraying no emotion. I've seen him more animated in front of the TV.

'There's really no need for this, Violet. This isn't like you,' my mother says. I am silent. Again she looks to my father, and finds no encouragement. I see her grasping for words. 'Perhaps a couple of days away will help you get things in perspective,' she says. 'When you've calmed down, then . . . Well, be in touch soon in any case, won't you? Let us know where you're staying.' She sounds as if I'm going on holiday. Already I can tell that she's reframing the incident in her mind, trying to force it within the bounds of acceptability, unable to cope with the reality of what is happening. She has always been a coward. I won't turn out that way, not if I can help it. This is my chance to stop it happening.

I move towards the door, put my hand on the latch, hesitate for an instant. Now that I am on the point of leaving, it feels so surreal that I almost laugh. The fight threatens to drain out of me as I stand there. How much easier it would be to do as they want. I glance back and see my parents' faces, and for a second they seem different, older. I look at the tiny wrinkles around my mother's eyes, the sprinkling of grey in my father's hair, and my heart contracts unthinkingly, taking me back to a time when I loved them so much that I couldn't bear them to be out of my sight. It's so long ago, but I can barely understand how we have got from there to here. I want to scream with the unfairness of it. I want those people back — not these two painted dolls who no longer know anything about me. It seems that in the past few years we've peeled apart so subtly that I'm no longer sure where the threads between us are, and now it's far too late to stitch us back together, ever again. I have spent eighteen years following in their footsteps, and somehow I know that unless I act now, I will spend the next eighteen doing the same.

Sometimes the biggest decisions are made in a split second. In the half-light of the hall, I think I see my father's face start to change and sag with sorrow, and I can't watch. I open the door into the dark and pull it shut behind me. A light drizzle is beating down on to the ground beyond the porch, splattering wetly on to the gravel. I step out into it and start to walk. In fifteen minutes I will be on a train to London; in a little over an hour I will be with Jonathan again. Unless he offers me one, I no longer have a home.

Already I can feel my memories sealing over. If I am not to regret this decision and go crawling back out of weakness, I must put my parents in a box where no one can find them but me, and I'll only open it when I'm ready. It's a vow that I will keep to, and while they're there, locked and trapped somewhere I don't want to reach, I find that I don't miss them much. I barely miss them at all.

★　★　★

I put on my best dress — black, dotted all over with tiny indigo violets. I hope that Jonathan will pick up on the violet reference, and find it endearing rather than trite. In front of his floor-length mirror, I brush my hair slowly and luxuriously, drawing out the crackling of static. I have spent almost twenty minutes doing my make-up, anxious to strike the right note. The tension between the sex symbol I want to be for Jonathan and the homemaker I want to seem to his parents still shows itself on my face, in the battle between my heavily kohl-lined eyes and the neutral, subdued gloss of my mouth. In the mirror I see him approaching behind me, buttoning a white shirt, naked but for boxer shorts from the waist down. He's sizing me up, his eyes running carefully from top to toe. What he sees seems to please him; he comes closer and slips his hands round my waist, encircling me.

'Stunning,' he says into my hair, and I see his eyes flick up to look at us together in the reflection. 'My father ought to like it anyway, randy old devil.'

'Jonathan!' I twist round in his arms. 'He's not really like that, is he?'

'Ah, no,' Jonathan says dismissively, loosening his hold on me. 'Not really. We'd better get going — I said we'd be there by one.'

'Better put some trousers on,' I suggest, heading for the door. Nervous though I am, happiness floods me. Quickly, I run back through the events of the night before in my head: turning up at Jonathan's door, finding him eager and unquestioning, not caring about what has happened with my parents or why, just pulling me into bed and making love to me until I was sore with exhilaration and exhaustion. Later, he did ask, but when I told him that I had moved out, it seemed to be taken for granted that I would stay on with him. Amazingly, this flat already feels like home. I love it, its slickly painted walls and gleaming polished floorboards, its tasteful array of ornaments and clean gleaming gadgets. Compared to what I have come from, it feels like a palace, and although I know it is disloyal to think so, I feel that it suits me. I should have been born to this.

Outside it is raining again. The harsh smells of diesel and damp ground press in on me as we step into the road. Jonathan hails a cab effortlessly, seeming to only briefly raise one hand for it to do his bidding and screech to a halt. I climb into the back and listen to him ask for the Sherbourne Club, reel off an address I don't recognise. I barely know London at all. As we drive, I see the city rushing past the window: a jumble of streets and houses and towering industrial blocks, parks and roundabouts, all so unfamiliar that the instant they are out of sight I forget them again.

'It'll be fine, don't worry,' I hear Jonathan murmur next to me, and I realise that I am shaking. I look at him. In his casual suit, his blond hair just brushing the edge of his collar, he looks so beautiful and desirable that I can hardly bear it. His blue eyes are full of kindness and concern; a tenderness that I have never seen in them before.

'I love you,' I blurt out, and as I say the words I realise that I have still not heard them from him, not exactly, not in as many words. I hold my breath.

He just looks back at me, smiling. 'Here we are,' he says, moving across me to release the catch. It is almost as if he has not heard me. I force down my panic and follow him out of the taxi. On the pavement he takes my hand and squeezes it, and I remind myself that it is actions which count. Holding on to his hand, I let myself be drawn into the building's lobby. Everything is panelled in luxurious dark oak, giving it a secret, cloistered feel. A long, low, green baize desk stretches out across one wall; an immaculately dressed receptionist sits behind it, her shining blonde helmet of hair dazzling my eyes. She smiles at Jonathan as if she knows him. Her eyes don't move from his face. She knows who is in control here. For a perverse moment I almost want to stamp my feet and draw attention to myself.

'We're lunching in the club,' Jonathan says. 'Is my father here yet?'

'Yes, Mr Blackwood and his wife took his table a few minutes ago,' the receptionist says. 'Mr Blackwood senior, that is.' She laughs prettily, revealing teeth like polished pearls, narrowing her eyes so that her lashes sweep across them. She's flirting with him. I steal a glance at Jonathan; he's smiling back as if she has made the best joke in the world. I have to fight to keep all the muscles in my face under control.

'Thanks, Alice,' Jonathan says. 'We'll head through now, then. Oh . . . ' He stops, glancing at me. 'This is Violet, by the way.' He doesn't put a label on me: my girlfriend, my lover — but it doesn't matter. I smile genuinely at Alice now, but I know that my eyes are sending her a warning.

'Lovely to meet you,' says Alice sweetly. Her complexion is perfect and smooth, as if it has been painted on. For an instant I imagine that perfection reproduced all over her neat slim body. She lowers her head, as if engrossed in her appointments book, dismissing me.

'Do you know her well?' I ask Jonathan as he steers me through the hallway and into the restaurant. My voice sounds appropriately light and curious to my ears, but I can feel the early stirrings of jealousy prickling my skin.

He snorts, his shoulder rising and falling lazily in a shrug. 'As well as you know anyone you see three times a week and exchange a couple of sentences with,' he says. 'Look, there they are.'

I follow his pointing finger. There, across the banks of heavy wooden tables, I see a corner banquette, tucked tastefully on to a slightly raised level, allowing those seated there to have a view of the whole restaurant. The best seat in the house. Seated at the banquette, talking privately to each other, are two figures; my vision suddenly blurred by panic, I can't take in anything about them. I move forward, guided by Jonathan's hand. When we're up closer his father lays the menu aside and stands up. He must be around sixty, but he's extraordinarily well preserved, as if he's been kept on ice for a decade or more. His silver hair is smooth and immaculate, and for a moment I find myself wondering whether it is a wig and have to drag my eyes away. His face is alert and aquiline, a sharpened version of Jonathan's. Immediately I can sense that same hardness in him; the hint of a threat that fascinated me so much when I first saw his son. With his father, though, it's more than a hint. I sense straight away that it runs right through him like fault lines through rock.

'You must be Violet,' he says to me, piercing me with imperturbable blue eyes. 'I must say, this is the first time that a summer secretary has made quite such an impression.' He smiles genuinely enough, despite the dismissive undercurrent to his words. For a brief moment I shake his hand; firm, dry and enclosing.

'This is my father, Harvey,' Jonathan says, ignoring the snub, if snub it was. 'I expect you've seen him around the offices, anyway.'

I nod, but the truth is that I have never seen this man before. I am sure I would have remembered. I have heard his name, of course — whispered deferentially and fearfully by administrators, cited lordly over the telephone to clients. Now that I can put a face to it, I realise that there is no other face that could fit.

'And this is my mother, Laura,' Jonathan continues, indicating the woman sat next to Harvey. I look at her for the first time. She has the palest skin I have ever seen, stretched tight like cling film over a finely modelled face. Her straw-coloured hair is tied in a chignon at the back of her neck. She wears an understated black dress, but her fingers are heavy with gold and sapphire rings, which she is twisting round and round automatically. She raises her eyes to mine and nods. Before, I never would have expected anyone to rise when they greeted me, but now it feels strange that she has remained seated. I sit down myself, slipping quickly into the nearest chair. For a full twenty seconds there is absolute silence as they all peruse the menu. I glance down at it, but the words jump before my eyes, shaking themselves together like dice so that I can barely make them out. Unfamiliar French phrases leap out at me: *filet mignon, sole meunière.* Underneath the table, I can feel my legs twitching. For an instant, the thought of sitting here with these people for another hour or more is almost too much for me, and I shift in my seat, glancing at the exit. Jonathan doesn't look at me, but he puts out his hand under the table and rests it on my thigh.

'So, are you thinking of pursuing the law?' Laura asks. Her voice is such a soft drawl that I have to bend forward to hear it, and yet she doesn't seem shy, just very confident that what she says deserves to be heard.

Harvey and Jonathan both snort with laughter, glancing at each other with easy complicity. 'Rather a strange way of putting it,' Harvey remarks, pouring the wine. I have never been a big drinker, but I let him fill my glass up to the brim. I don't want to do anything that calls attention to myself, or to my youth. Tentatively, I smile too, trying to share in the joke. Laura seems unmoved. Her eyebrows are still raised in polite enquiry.

'Well, I wouldn't rule it out for the future,' I say, and am almost instantly conscious that somehow it has been the wrong thing to say. It isn't even true: I've never thought about law as a potential career path. At Manchester, I was going to study philosophy. I'm not sure what career options might have arisen from that — probably none. 'But no, I doubt it,' I backtrack, taking a large gulp of white wine. It tastes bitter and dry, raping the back of my throat.

'Violet is more of a homemaker,' Jonathan says. 'She wants to settle down and get married and have lots of babies.' His light tone tells me that he is teasing me, and yet there is a flicker of hopeful sincerity in his eyes. I suddenly can't think of anything better than to do those things, and with him. I smile radiantly across at him, and see Harvey watching me, and slowly nodding.

'Right.' Harvey snaps his menu shut, and within seconds a waiter is hovering attentively at his side. 'I'll have the sweet-breads, and my wife will take the sole, please.'

Jonathan glances at me. 'The sole, too, please,' I whisper almost at random. Was I supposed to have somehow made him aware of my choice in advance, as Laura has obviously done? Or perhaps Harvey has simply chosen for her, and I should have kept quiet and allowed Jonathan to do the same. I feel my cheeks warm and know that I am blushing, stare down at the table. This is not the world I have been used to.

'It's very good here,' I hear Laura say, rather kindly. I force myself to look up and smile. I have never felt so shy, and it doesn't feel like me at all.

The wait for our meals passes in a blur; Harvey and Jonathan talk briskly about office matters, sharing details of some case. I vaguely remember the main players' names from a letter I typed under Jonathan's dictation several days ago, but the niceties of the matter completely elude me. Laura is quiet, but watchful. She tops up Harvey's glass when it is empty, passes him the butter when he splits open his roll. I take note, marking down her little gestures as ones that I could replicate with Jonathan, some other time.

'We should stop talking shop,' says Jonathan as our lunch arrives. A huge sole is placed in front of me, its eye gleaming blankly up at me. I force my gaze away from it. 'Violet is probably bored stiff,' he elaborates unnecessarily, grinning.

'Quite right,' says Harvey smoothly, looking at me. 'Tell us about you.'

My mind empties. There is nothing to say, nothing that could possibly be of interest to him. I think of the things that, up until a matter of weeks ago, occupied my time. Hanging around the local shopping centre with my school-friends, going to the multiplex and eating popcorn noisily in the dark, dressing up and going to our town's excuse for a nightclub, where we would sip lurid fizzy cocktails and dance unenthusiastically with slurring teenage boys. I have always felt mature for my age, but looking back at these things now, they horrify me. Harvey would think I was nothing but a child.

The silence threatens to become uncomfortable. I take another large gulp of wine to buy myself a few more seconds. 'I come from Sussex,' I say. 'I'm an only child. I like art a lot.' This is even worse — extracts from a primary school essay.

'Looking at it, or creating it?' Harvey asks.

'Well, both.' I search for words. 'I sometimes go up to galleries — the Tate, the National. But I like painting in my spare time.' Harvey waits. 'Modern stuff, mostly,' I say. 'Abstract.'

'Yes,' Harvey says thoughtfully. His cool blue eyes sweep my face. 'Well, it's always nice to have a hobby.'

I put a forkful of sole into my mouth and swallow. A tiny bone rakes the roof of my mouth, bringing a smart of pain to my eyes.

'And what about your parents?' Harvey continues. 'What do they do?'

I contemplate inventing something, turning my family into something other than what they are. As I run through the possibilities swiftly in my head, I feel suddenly defiant. I will tell them the truth. 'My father works in a garage as a mechanic,' I say. 'My mother used to work in a shop, but she stopped that a few months ago.'

'An honest crust,' says Jonathan, seemingly to fill the silence. He is looking at me with new eyes. Of course, he knows nothing about my background — why should he? Perhaps he has assumed that because I landed up in his law firm for the summer, I must have sprung from suitable soil. Opposite, Harvey and Laura are exchanging eloquent glances, saying nothing.

'Excuse me for a minute,' I say, standing up. I walk shakily away from the table, unsure as to where I am going. A waiter steers me confidently back, pointing at a small gold door set into the back wall. I nod and thank him, slip into the cloakroom and lock myself into the nearest cubicle. I lean my back against the wall, closing my eyes. The air conditioning blasts down on me, making me shiver. I feel humiliated and furious. I don't care what they think of me — I only care about Jonathan. I don't want them to colour his opinion of me, to make him see me as a laughable mistake. I curl my hands into tight fists. Already I can feel it happening.

I unlock the cubicle and push my way out, going to the mirror. I glare at my reflection, gold-lit and soft-focused. I will not be made a fool of. I will go back in there and show them just how contemptuous I am of them and everyone like them. Jonathan will take my side, and if he doesn't . . . I draw in breath sharply and wheel around, fighting my way through the heavy gold door. I walk slowly and deliberately back to the table, approaching it from behind. They cannot see me, but as I draw nearer, I can hear their voices. I stop, momentarily frozen. *She's very pretty*, I hear Laura saying, and there is a general murmur of assent. *And she has spirit*, Harvey says. *She's very young, of course, but that's all right. If anything, it's a good thing.* His voice drops lower, and I can't hear what he is saying, but I can hear his tone: purring, warm and approving. Now and again, Jonathan makes some eager interjection. *She's very special*, I think I hear him say.

I can feel my whole body glowing, pulsing with delight and excitement. All at once my scorn withers up into nothing, and my heart feels light and empty, as if the hurt were never there. Now that I have heard them praising me, I realise that it is what I have wanted all along. I don't hate these people. I want them, need them, to love me. As I walk back to the table, my head held high now, I can barely stop myself from laughing out loud with relief.

Later, outside the restaurant, Jonathan embraces me in the rain and pulls me closely against him, planting kisses in my hair. *They like you*, he murmurs. *I knew they would.* He kisses me long and hard, then strokes the damp hair back from my face, holding it in his cupped hands, studying me as if I am a rare and thrilling discovery. 'I love you,' he says. When I hear him say it, I start to cry, tears spilling from my eyes and dissolving into the rain, and I have never, never been like this — so luminous with happiness that it is raging and burning inside me, and I can't control it, I can't contain it, it feels as if nothing can extinguish it ever again.

★ ★ ★

Catherine was good with customers. She always seemed to know exactly what to say to them, when to compliment and when to offer a tactful alternative, how to close a sale and leave them feeling proud and boosted by their purchases. Behind the till, I sat and watched her. Head cocked prettily to one side, Catherine admired the girl as she came out of the changing room and did a self-conscious twirl, glancing at her reflection in the mirror. The jeans were slightly too small for her, cutting into her flesh and sending a faint red line running across her back. I tried to think of what I would say if I were in Catherine's place. *Sorry, I think you need the next size up?* I wouldn't be able to do it. I would lie and tell her that they looked great, and then when she got home she would try them on again at more leisure in a less flattering light, and wonder what I had really thought.

'Lovely!' Catherine said. 'Why don't you try these with them, though?' She handed the girl a wide blue belt and a pair of tan high heels. As the girl fastened the belt around her and slipped her feet into the shoes, I saw her transform before my eyes. The belt hid the tightness of the jeans at her waist, the heels elongating her legs and making her look elegant and almost willowy. From the look on her face, she was seeing the same thing. Ten minutes later she was loading her purchases on to the counter and pulling out her card. I rang the sale through, smiling at Catherine over the girl's shoulder. She was clearly glowing with her success, eyes bright and eager. What would it be like to have that kind of talent for something, that kind of satisfaction in what life had given to you?

'So how was the party?' she asked when the girl had bounced out of the shop, bags jauntily in hand. Her voice was light, but she was looking at me with the same thinly veiled expression of curiosity and sympathy that she had worn since I had told her about my marriage. 'Did Harvey enjoy it?'

This seemed to be everyone's primary concern. 'I think so,' I said. 'Everything went smoothly, anyway. Well, except — ' I broke off. I felt unaccountably shy about mentioning Max — perhaps because to the best of my recollection she had never mentioned him herself. A flash of his dark, scowling face came to me; the rough, earthy smell of smoke that had risen off him as he grabbed my wrist and leant in towards me. The previous night, I had dreamt about him. In my dream he had been cutting down the old apple tree in the garden after dark, naked from the waist up, bare muscular arms swinging with contained power as he hacked with a gleaming silver saw at its trunk. I went forward to greet him, but he acted as if he could not see me, his black eyes burning through me with ferocious concentration, wide and oblivious to the sparks of wood that flew all around us and stung the air. I had woken in a sweat, my heart thumping as if an intruder had slid into something far more threatening than my dreams.

'I think you met my brother, didn't you?' Catherine said, as if she had read my mind. She was watching me very intently now, as if searching my thoughts.

'Yes — yes, I did,' I stammered. 'You don't look alike, at all.'

'Everyone says that,' said Catherine, shrugging. 'I think we do.'

I almost laughed, looking at her fragile prettiness; the white-blonde hair feathered around her face, the pert nose and full pink lips. 'Maybe if I saw you together,' I said.

'Well, you'll get your chance,' she said. 'He said he was going to pop in here around midday, so he should be here soon.'

'What? Why would he do that?' I asked sharply. I saw Catherine's face crease in confusion, and bit my lip. The echo of my voice, unnaturally and unnecessarily harsh, hung between us. I knew that I was being ridiculous, but the thought of seeing Max again frightened me. I felt an instinctive wariness, the prickling of a sixth sense running over me from top to toe.

'I wondered that myself,' Catherine said. 'He never has before. But maybe it's not me he's coming to see.' Her voice was teasing, but there was anxiety in her eyes. 'Only joking — I think he just wants to catch up. He moved out from our parents' a few years ago, so we don't see each other so much these days. But if there's a problem — I could call him and tell him not to bother, if you like.'

I hesitated; it would be easy to say yes, but I didn't want any awkwardness to develop between myself and Catherine, not so soon after I had finally begun to sense the potential for a friendship between us. 'No, no, of course not,' I said, softening my voice to compensate for my outburst. 'I'm sorry. To be honest, I'm just a bit cautious around men these days. I know it's silly, but since Jonathan, I don't have much to do with them — well, except Harvey, of course.' I was speaking without consideration, almost at random, but as I did so I realised that there was more than a grain of truth in what I was saying, and it comforted me a little.

Catherine looked indecisive, her fingers agitatedly running back and forth along the long strands of green glass beads she wore around her neck. 'Of course,' she echoed. 'I didn't think.'

I sensed her automatic deference to a situation she knew nothing about, and felt guilty. 'Honestly, it's fine,' I said, more firmly this time. 'I can't hide away for ever.' These words had been said to me many times over the past few months, mostly in the form of unanswered voicemails from my former school-friends that had graded from sympathy to worry to sulkiness, and eventually through to silence. I had always hated the sentiment: I wasn't hiding away, just had no desire to see them or anyone else. Now, though, I discovered that it could be a useful panacea — and when I was the one saying it, I found that I didn't mind it so much.

'Well, that's good,' said Catherine, breaking away and giggling nervously, 'because speak of the devil . . . '

. . . *And he'll draw near*, I thought. The bell above the shop door jangled with brittle force as Max pushed the door open and came in. Hands in pockets, he surveyed the shop for a few seconds, as if it were some curious new world. He was wearing a charcoal-coloured T-shirt that hugged the tops of his arms tightly, outlining the muscle beneath. Seeing him again, I noticed anew the brutally close cut of his hair against his skull, and how tall he was — taller than Jonathan, maybe by three inches or more. He didn't take off his sunglasses, and it was impossible to tell exactly where he was looking. I found it unsettling.

'All right, Catherine,' he said, striding forward and slinging one arm around her neck briefly to kiss her cheek. With a shock, I saw that although I could still see nothing of her in him, there was something of him in her — warped, softened and feminised, but unmistakable. He must have felt me staring, because he wheeled round and directed the blank dark glare of his glasses towards me. 'Hello,' he said.

'Hello.' I was determined to be polite, but all the same I could think of nothing more to say. Now that we were face to face, all I could feel was humiliation at our last meeting — my childish protestations that he had not been invited to Harvey's garden party. 'I could make you some tea, if you like.' I clutched at the idea with relief. It had felt like the right thing to say, but as soon as the words were out, I wished I had kept quiet: it sounded like an absurdly middle-class offer. I felt as embarrassed as if I had suggested that we should all sit out on the lawn together in Edwardian dress, drinking out of bone-china cups and eating scones with jam.

'Tea,' Max repeated. 'Yeah, well, why not.' He spoke the words in a flat monotone that to my ears was tinged with sarcasm, as if he was doing me a favour rather than the other way around, but all the same I was grateful for the acceptance. I ducked into the back room, pulling the door shut behind me to drown out their voices. I put the kettle on, lined the mugs up with trembling hands. I felt totally out of control of my own body. For a second I screwed my eyes tight shut, breathing deeply, but when I opened them again everything looked eerie and unreal, brightly coloured and two-dimensional. I gritted my teeth; it was ridiculous to be so nervous, nervous at nothing. I bent down and took the milk out of the fridge, then realised that I had no idea whether or not Max took it, or sugar for that matter. The thought of going back in to ask paralysed me. I tapped my fingers against the mugs, willing myself to think. Jonathan had taken milk and one sugar; I would give Max the same. The logic made no sense, but I didn't care. I filled the mugs with exaggerated care and put them on to a tray. Briefly I considered adding some biscuits, but thought better of it; I didn't want to seem like an overeager housewife. I pushed my way through the door, tray in hand. Max and Catherine were talking by the counter, their heads close together in a way that suggested something more than idle chit-chat.

'Tea!' I said brightly, brandishing the tray. Catherine sprang apart from Max, coming towards me. For a fraction of a second, like a trick of the light, her beaming face looked false and untrustworthy.

I handed Max his mug and watched as he raised it to his lips. From the wince that passed over his face, I assumed that I had been wrong about the sugar, but he continued to drink without comment; it gave me a perverse sort of satisfaction. Silence fell. We made a strange little tableau: Catherine perched on the counter, bright watchful eyes on her brother as she sipped, myself and Max standing a couple of feet apart in front of her. I felt a dizzy, vertiginous sense of rising and falling — as if I had been plucked out of the scene, surveying it from a great height, then returned to earth again.

'Do you get a lunch break?' Max asked suddenly. I thought at first that the question was directed at Catherine, but she just looked steadily back at me, awaiting my answer. As I floundered in shock, Max pushed the sunglasses up on to his forehead and his unsmiling eyes met mine. With the contact, I felt my heart twitch, not understanding why.

'Yes,' I said. 'I usually just go to the café across the road.'

'Let's go, then.' He put down his mug, still half full. The set of his shoulders was challenging, tensed for combat. I swallowed, tasting an acrid tang behind the sweetness of the tea. My eyes flicked to Catherine again. What exactly was happening here? The thought that I was somehow being set up, pimped out to this ridiculously unsuitable man, was so incredible that I could barely give it credence, and yet what other explanation could there be? Catherine's face was tentatively eager, urging me on, but she looked so innocent, as if there was nothing here to worry about or be afraid of. Perhaps she thought that I needed a male friend. If so, I wished she had alighted on a less threatening candidate. I took a deep breath, straightened my shoulders. I was an adult — I had no obligation to waste my lunch hour with a complete stranger.

I opened my mouth to say that I was busy, but in the brief pulse between the decision and the words, something happened. Slowly and deliberately, Max held out his arm, as if to encourage me to slip mine through his — an exaggerated pantomime of a polite

Victorian gentleman. The gesture looked so ludicrous on him that a sharp peal of laughter burst from me. I glanced up and saw that he was smiling too, teeth glinting wickedly in the dark cavern of his mouth. On impulse, I picked up my handbag and moved towards him. It was only a lunch, after all. There could be no harm in this.

'I'll be back by one,' I told Catherine.

'No worries — I've got sandwiches here, anyway,' she said airily. 'I'll see you at Mum and Dad's next week, Max?'

'Yeah, maybe,' Max threw back over his shoulder as he pushed the door open. I had been used to chivalry, but all the same I was surprised when he held it open for me to go through. I did so, blinking as light flooded my eyes. The heat of the day had intensified over the morning, and now everything looked faintly sticky and glistening. I could feel the heat of the pavement through the thin soles of my sandals. I pulled my cardigan off, leaving my shoulders bare to the sun, and I thought I saw Max's eyes flick there, a quick reflexive action that was over almost as soon as it had begun. We walked in silence to the café. A few people passed us as we went, and I thought I saw something in their eyes: wariness, perhaps, or concern. Watching Max stride along the street, I could understand why.

He walked with controlled force, as if he were on a mission that would not end well. Staring straight ahead, he seemed to dismiss everything around him. *He doesn't fit this quiet town*, I thought, *or its people.*

Inside the café he barked out an imperious order for a toasted sandwich and a cup of coffee, black, with no sugar — as if to ram the point home that I had offered, and chosen, wrongly. I ordered the same, smiling appeasingly at the sweet elderly woman behind the counter. I knew her well, came in almost every day that I was at the shop, but she was looking at me now as if I had betrayed her. Her permed hair quivered with distress, and behind her glasses her white eyelashes fluttered like moths. As she turned to make the coffee, disapproval and dismay radiated from her hunched shoulders. You're not who I thought you were, her back said.

'You don't seem very popular,' I ventured when Max and I had settled at a little table by the window.

He gave me a quick glance of surprise. 'You don't mince your words, do you?' he said. 'No. I don't suppose I am.' He looked as if he were about to continue, then took a bite of his sandwich instead, chewing hard and energetically, his brow furrowed in thought. 'I've had a bad year,' he said eventually.

'Well, I can understand that,' I said. 'It hasn't been the best for me either.' I waited for an apology, some kind of acknowledgement that the pain of what I had been through surpassed anything that he himself might have suffered, but none came.

'The problem with people round here . . .' he said, as if embarking on a long and well-trodden path of thought. Whatever it was, it would remain private. 'You don't need to worry,' he added. 'It's not like I killed anyone's kids. I just . . . I've made my presence felt.' I looked at his darkly scowling face, the tough lines of his mouth. I didn't want to think about what making his presence felt might entail.

'Why would I worry?' I asked instead. 'I barely know you.'

'You might worry,' he said. 'If you wanted to get to know me better.' His directness momentarily silenced me. I sipped my coffee, feeling its heat rise on to my cheeks, keeping my eyes on the red-and-white checked tablecloth with its silly lace frill fluting the edges. Above our heads, speakers were spilling out a pretty little pan-piped tune. The conversation felt incongruous — the sort that you might have in a seedy nightclub or a backstreet doorway, after dark and under your breath.

'Why would you want me to?' I asked at last, and far back in my head I was nauseously conscious that this was the sort of question that could be interpreted as flirtatious, fishing for a compliment.

'Just a hunch,' Max said, spreading his hands out across the tabletop. 'I think we might have a lot in common.' He glanced around, fishing in his pocket. 'Can you smoke in here?'

'You can't smoke in anywhere,' I said dully. I had a sudden heavy sense of weariness; it seemed that this conversation should be taking place somewhere different, with someone else. I felt myself closing up. This man had no right to presume that we had anything in common — that I had anything in common with anyone. I had grown used to not fitting in with the world around me.

'Oh yeah,' Max said. 'I still forget.' He grinned, and for a moment I caught a glimpse of something new; a kind of easy charm that I sensed could be devastating when it was applied with intent. 'Come outside, then.'

It wasn't a question. I thought about challenging him, but it seemed easier to stand and follow him out of the tearoom, shooting a last furtive glance at the elderly waitress as I went. She gave me a small concessionary wave, but her eyes looked sad, blinking manically behind their glass cages. I turned my back on her and stepped out on to the street. The air was close and expectant, a tangible presence. Max leant against the wall, pulling out a cigarette, the muted crackle of the lighter as it sparked up instantly swallowed up into the dense heat. He jerked the packet towards me; I shook my head and he smoked in silence for a while, blowing a thin steady stream up into the bright blue canopy above us. I leant back on the wall beside him. My legs didn't feel strong enough to stand unsupported; I was still struggling with the lingering sense of desolation that had overtaken me in the café, the feeling that I might as well not be here for all the good it was doing me, and yet that at the same time I might as well be here as anywhere.

'You know,' he said after a while, 'I meant what I said to you at the party. You should get out more. Why are you still living with his parents?' He didn't mention Jonathan by name, as one usually might the first time one brought someone up in conversation; he didn't need to. It seemed that he was standing right there between us, elusive but inescapable.

I paused, unsure how to answer the question. At times I barely knew myself why after Jonathan's death I had not remained with Harvey and Laura for a few much-needed weeks, then moved a discreet distance away, thanking them for their hospitality and getting on with my life. Perhaps it was because it didn't often seem like hospitality at all. They needed me just as I needed them, and we fed off each other, off what we had shared with him. Once, several months ago, I had secretly visited a flat for rent, and spending five minutes in its white memory-less template had been enough for me to curl back up into my cocoon — joyless, maybe, but full of a meaning of which I was not ready to let go. Trying to communicate this to Max was useless. 'They've been good to me,' I said. 'Besides, I've got nowhere else to go.' Briefly, I thought of my own parents; the polite, stilted letters that still came three or four times a year from another world.

Max swivelled slightly against the wall, angling his body towards me. When he spoke, a thin wisp of smoke escaped from between his lips, curling into my face. 'You call him Dad,' he said. 'I heard you.'

I shrugged. 'Yes. I always did, after we were married. He expected it.' This time I deliberately didn't attach a name to the pronoun. It had been Jonathan, really, who had expected it, as much as Harvey himself, and this perhaps was why I had clung to the tradition.

'It's sick,' Max said, glaring at me with a sudden quick anger that made my breath catch in my throat. 'I bet he loves it, dirty old man.'

His words felt eerily familiar; on and off over the course of our marriage, Jonathan had made reference, oblique and blatant by turns, to Harvey as some kind of sexual predator, whether of me or others. It seemed an accepted view that behind his cool exterior lurked a rampant Casanova, but the truth was that I had never caught so much as a whiff of sexuality in the admittedly intense attention that he gave me. He was devoted but detached, the same way that you might be with a prized inanimate possession. 'He's not like that,' I said, but I didn't expect Max to believe me.

It was his turn to shrug, tapping the glowing cigarette butt out against the heel of his shoe as he did so, then flicking it to the ground and grinding it into the gravel in one swift movement. 'Whatever,' he said. 'The point is, it's not doing you any good being there. Even I can see that. Catherine used to talk about you as if you were a tragic deaf mute or something. You've worked together, what, four months? — and from what I can make out, it's only in the past week that you've even started talking to each other. I

95

assumed you were a dud, a cold fish. But when I saw you, I knew I'd got it wrong. There's a lot inside you. It just needs to come out.' He was talking very low, so that I had to lean in a little to hear him, his eyes fixed steadily on mine. 'Why don't you come and stay with me? Just for a couple of days, if you like. See what you've been missing.'

All at once I became aware of how close we were, the side of my face only inches from his. In my agitation, I backed off, rubbing reflexively at my ear with my hand, and as I did so I felt my fingers catch against my earring, send it spiralling to the ground. I started forward to retrieve it, but he stopped me, his eyes sending me a warning. Slowly, he bent down. His fingers closed around the sparkling metal in the dirt; a long silver hook, translucent mauve beads dangling from its post. When he brought it up, I saw the dirt cling to his fingertips. Deliberately, he brushed them off, blowing softly on the silver to clear the dust. I reached my hand out to take it, but he shook his head. With his free hand, he pushed the hair back from my ear, and as he touched me I felt my whole body jolt, a strange premonitory shiver that left me holding my breath. I stayed completely still, letting him turn my head. His hand felt hot and dry, his touch rough yet gentle, his

96

thumb cupping underneath my chin, his fingers buried in my hair. Slowly he brought the earring up, his eyes seeking the hole intently. I felt the cold tip of metal probe and penetrate, felt him push it into place. I couldn't hear either of us breathing, and as he smoothed my hair over again, for an instant my vision blurred and fuzzed, his face shrinking out of focus. When I blinked he was back. I could feel the earring there, hanging secretly, out of view.

'Will you?' he said quietly, and I had to stop myself from spilling over into sudden crazy desperation: *yes, yes, yes I will, yes.* I nodded, not trusting myself.

'Good,' he said. 'Meet me tomorrow evening at half seven, outside the church. My house isn't far from there.' Without waiting for confirmation, he swung away from me, the distance between us abruptly spreading and thinning the air. I watched him walk away, knowing that he would not look back and yet willing him to, willing myself to have some sort of influence.

That afternoon I told Catherine all I knew about how Jonathan had died. That his body had been found down by the lake two miles out of town; that his injuries had been consistent with slipping and falling against the rocks that lined the waterside; that the post-mortem had revealed that he had been drinking heavily; that I had no idea why he had been there or what he had been doing. I didn't explain why I was telling her, but I thought she knew. I had to purge these things. I had to get them out of me and into the open. Without that I would never be able to think about letting go of them; I would never be able to move on.

★　★　★

Finding the right time to tell Harvey and Laura that I would be away for a couple of days was like playing Russian roulette; there was no way of discerning whether any given hour would be more or less loaded than another. Several times I told myself that now was the moment — over a near-silent dinner as the windows darkened and the lamps flickered; watching an old film on television before bed in the living room; after breakfast the next morning as I helped to clear the crockery away. Each time I pulled myself cravenly back from the brink. Soon enough, the antique clock in the hallway was crawling round to six, the black metallic hands accusingly bisecting its spherical face. In an hour I would have to set out to walk to the church. Even at that stage I knew that there was no possibility of going back on my promise to Max. The thought of escaping this house, even if only for a couple of nights, made me feel more alive than I had done in months.

I took a breath and went into the living room. Harvey was listening to the radio, some classical station, eyes closed, head raised attentively to the music. On the other sofa, Laura sat knitting, her tiny hands flying over the stitches like fluttering bats. As I watched them, I was overcome by an irrational rush of love, almost painful in its force.

'Mum, Dad,' I began, queasily aware that I might as well start well, if I had to finish badly, 'I'm going out soon. I may be gone for a couple of days — I'm going to stay with a friend.'

Laura raised her head from the knitting, her face hurt and startled like that of a deer faced with the hunt. I saw her look to Harvey. His eyes had snapped open. He didn't move, as if awaiting further information. I had none to give; none that I wanted to share with him, at any rate. Seeing that the onus was on her, Laura turned to me. 'This is a bit sudden, dear,' she quavered. 'Who is this friend?'

'It's Catherine,' I said, 'from the shop. I'm sorry I didn't let you know before — we only sorted it out yesterday.'

There was a silence as Laura struggled to process this new information, and to somehow forgive the obvious; that there had been twenty-four intervening hours or more in which I could have made her aware of the situation. As she raised her eyes to mine, I saw something more in them — confusion, incomprehension. As far as she had been aware, I had no friends, or at least not the kind of friends with whom I would choose to spend two days away from home. Less than a week ago, a three-hour round trip to the airport to collect Harvey had kept me awake for two anxious nights in succession. She had been there as I paced my bedroom at 3 a.m., unsure of my ability to perform this simple task. She knew me, and she wanted to know what had changed.

'Of course, you are free to see whoever you want,' she said slowly, glancing again at Harvey for confirmation. 'As I said, it's just a little sudden. You'll have your mobile, of course? We can contact you if we need to? And you'll be back by Wednesday?' I nodded again and again, seeking to somehow suck the poison from the heart of the situation: that for the first time in nine months I was choosing to leave her, leave them, on their own. 'Well, then,' she said at last, a little sadly. 'I hope you have a nice time.'

'Thank you,' I said. 'I'd better go and pack some things.' I began to back slowly out of the room, sure that at the last moment Harvey would stop me and start to issue an inquisition, but as I slipped out of the door I could see his silver head still motionless and unchanging. My heart thumping, I ran up the stairs. I started to pack clothes into a case, and as I did so I was hit by a sense of déjà vu — a strange knowledge that I had done this before. For an instant I was back in that shabby house, surrounded by my childhood things, my parents — my real parents — seething downstairs. I shook my head to rid it of the image, and felt the blood pound in my ears. Wrenching back control, I folded the clothes more carefully, smoothing them into neat piles. I added make-up, cleansers, a book. I had no idea what to expect; I felt as if I were packing for a mystery break, the destination of which I would not know until the tickets were placed in my hands. I closed the case, tugging the buckles tight shut, and as I did so, I heard it: the sound of footsteps on the wooden landing outside, slow and regular. I listened as they drew closer, each one echoing in the emptiness of the hallway. When Harvey appeared at the door I moved aside to let him through. The thought of doing otherwise was futile.

He came into the room, sat down on the bed. His face was stern and remote, a Roman god overseeing a scene of carnage. When he spoke, his voice sounded dispassionate, and yet I could tell that it cost him a lot to say the words. 'I need to ask you, Violet,' he said, 'if this has anything to do with that man. With the Croft man,' he added after a pause, as if to leave no room in my silence for doubt.

Part of me was not surprised; after all, it was Harvey's habit to infer a sordid purpose in any contact I had with any man who was not him, and I knew that his sharp eyes would not have missed me talking to Max at the garden party over by the apple tree. Ninety-nine times out of a hundred his suspicions would have been entirely without cause. In this instance, I sensed that a denial would only further provoke his instinct that he was being lied to, and yet I shrank back from telling him the truth, unclear as it still was to me. 'Catherine is his sister,' I said instead, struggling to find a middle ground, 'so I suppose it is possible that I will see him.'

From Harvey's reaction, I might as well have said that we intended to marry. His head jerked up sharply, and I saw his throat convulse as he swallowed — whether with rage or with sorrow, I was unsure. When he looked at me again, his eyes were blue ice. He spoke calmly, spacing out each word. 'I hoped not to have to tell you this,' he said, 'but the history between that man and our family is not a happy one. More specifically, the history between him and your husband.' I shivered; the way that Harvey spoke of Jonathan made it sound as if he were in the next room, living and breathing and judging me. 'I don't deny that they were once friends, of a sort,' he continued, 'but it soon became clear that friendship, and honour, were not high on that man's list of priorities. As you know, Jonathan was always too trusting. He liked to see the good in people. Once, I believe he lent him money. Of course, it couldn't continue, and when asked again he naturally refused. Suffice it to say that your new friend took this badly. He became threatening and abusive; there was a public altercation. He made things very oppressive for Jonathan, for a time — I don't know the exact details, but I am convinced that there were attempts at blackmail . . . That kind of man tends to expect to find mud even when there is none to find,' he added scornfully. 'In the end, of course, they avoided each other altogether. But make no mistake, Violet, he is an unpleasant character. I would even go as far as to say that his behaviour was in no small way responsible for Jonathan's state of mind shortly before he died.'

He stopped abruptly, as if conscious he had said enough. His last words crept into the back of my mind, a lurking grenade, ready for an unpredictable explosion. I couldn't think straight, each line of argument or enquiry crumbling up into a jumble of nonsense as soon as it came to me. My hand was still resting on the buckle of my case, and I could feel it trembling. A flash of Max came to me: the ruthless cut of his jaw, the hands that I sensed could strike as easily as they could touch.

'But why did I never know any of this?' I asked.

Harvey looked impatient, as if my question was stupid and superfluous. 'Jonathan would never have wanted to worry you with such things,' he said.

No, I thought, *he wouldn't, and as a result, I have no way of knowing whether you are lying to me.* I looked at Harvey's profile, turned to the light that streamed through my bedroom window, and fury shot through me like electricity. He was a jailer, intent on keeping me locked up in his own prison, never able to let me go. It would be just like him to invent a story designed to paralyse me with guilt, to keep me away from another man's influence. And yet, a voice niggled at the back of my head, he had never lied to me before, not that I knew of — lying was not his style, it was beneath him. I felt tears start to my eyes. As if beyond my control, my hand went to the earring still hanging from my left ear, feeling for the place that Max had touched. I could talk to him, tell him what Harvey had said. I would be able to see the truth.

'I may not even see him,' I said, ducking my head down, picking up my case and heading for the door. I had to leave this instant, before he had another chance to change my mind. All of a sudden Harvey was barring my way, quick as a flash at the door before me, his eyes burning down on mine. Frozen in shock, I stared back at him. For a brief incredulous moment, I thought he would hit me. Then, inch by inch, as if slowed by disappointment and scorn, he moved aside and let me pass.

★   ★   ★

We marry two days before Christmas, in a hastily booked hotel ballroom filled with Jonathan's family and friends. I have asked no one, not even my parents, despite writing them an invitation which I never quite posted. I will write and tell them after the event, when it is too late. I could not have faced the shock and disapproval; it would have soured the day, and this is a new start for me, nothing less than a rebirth. In my pure white dress I float like an angel, transported and ethereal, the diamonds that Jonathan bought me shining on my finger, around my neck, in my ears. The reception hall is flanked with scented candles; the air thick with the aromas of mulled wine and fir trees. Above our heads, strings of tiny sparkling fairy lights thread their way across the ceiling, sending shimmers all around the room. It is three months since our first kiss. If anyone thinks that we are rushing things, they don't dare to say so, not today. I know that there is nothing to worry about. When everything is right, there is no need to wait before taking what you know is yours.

When we say our vows, Jonathan's voice cracks and I see him staring at me in such a way that the violence of my love for him threatens to overwhelm me, to drown us both. At the reception he is never far from my side. He helps me to negotiate my way through the thicket of well-wishers, murmuring introductions into my ear. *My cousin Stephanie. My colleague and his wife, Paul and Jacqueline. My godmother Miranda.* I'm safe, sanctioned by him. When it is finally time to go, I throw my bouquet of deep red winter roses high into the air behind me and listen to the shouts and squeals as it is caught. When I turn, I see that one of Jonathan's cousins is the lucky one — a fresh-faced teenage girl, probably no more than a year or two younger than I am. I smile at her, to let her know that it can happen to her, as it has happened to me. As we leave, to a chorus of goodbyes and well-wishes, Harvey appears at my side, resting his hand lightly on my shoulder. 'Welcome to the family,' he says.

We spend two weeks in St Petersburg, roaming the Christmas markets after dark, walking in the snow, lying in front of the log fire in our luxury suite. Jonathan says that all the women in the city look as if they could be related to me. *Your bones are Russian*, he says to me as we travel through the lit-up streets in a quaint little carriage, rubbing his finger along my cheekbone, and as I laugh, freezing air rushes into my lungs and makes me gasp and exhale, the steam from my breath curling perfectly and brightly in front of me. I tell him that I have heard that there is somewhere on earth — the name of the place escapes me — where it is so cold that when you breathe out your breath turns to ice and shatters at your feet. He laughs and tells me that one day we will go there, wherever it is. We never do.

When we return from our honeymoon things move fast, as they always do with us. We move our possessions out of Jonathan's penthouse London flat, and transport them down to Brenchley, the little village where his parents live. When he had first made it clear to me, several weeks before the wedding, that a move was desirable, I was a little surprised, even dismayed. I already loved the penthouse flat; felt myself at home there in a way I had never experienced before. We would keep it on, Jonathan reassured me, perhaps rent it out for the time being, but a cottage had come up mere streets from Harvey and Laura, and the chance was too good to miss. The village was less than three miles from the nearest station, which had a swift route in to London — eminently commutable to the law firm; indeed, Harvey did it every day. The move to be near the Blackwoods seemed to be taken as a matter of course by all concerned. Although the thought seemed strange, it was almost as if it had been arranged before Jonathan and I had even met. I did not protest — it didn't matter enough to me, as long as we were together — but I wondered at the wiseness of the plan. Now that it is happening, though, I can feel myself coming around to his point of view. It's a fresh start for us, a house without residual memories attached of other times — perhaps, for him, other lovers about whom I know nothing.

We settle quickly into the new cottage, and week by week I begin to fill it with new possessions, things we choose together, things with our stamp on them. I learn to cook; I even make jam. Jonathan works hard, but he always comes home at the end of the day with a bunch of flowers, a box of chocolates, a magazine he thinks I might like, or some other little token. I soon learn the art of being ready for him: the dinner baking away in the oven, my hair and make-up done, a calm and smiling exterior even if half an hour earlier I've been tearing my hair out with rage because I can't follow a recipe. I know that I am acting out a parody of a 1950s housewife, but I don't care. This is all new to me, and it is the way I want things. Dimly, when I think of the future, I see a time when I will go out to work — either that or throw myself into a different kind of endeavour altogether. But for now, it doesn't matter how much of a bland domestic goddess I paint myself as, because Jonathan and I both know that I am more than that too.

I grow closer to Harvey and Laura — I

have plenty of opportunity. We see them perhaps three times a week; a Sunday roast almost without fail, a couple of evening drinks or Saturday afternoon tea in their conservatory. They live five minutes' walk up the road, in a huge rustic mansion that both intimidates and fascinates me. 'This house is beautiful, but I wouldn't like to live here,' I say to Jonathan once. 'When I walk along the corridors I feel like I'm being watched.'

Laura is an unlikely mother figure — often remote and distant, wrapped up in her own world — but I soon uncover flashes of warmth in her. She sometimes sits with me after lunch, chatting quietly about her day or offering recipes that she thinks I might like. I find myself wanting to please her, to make her smile, as it seems to happen so seldom. It is clear that she adores Harvey, defers to him unthinkingly. She has everything she might want, and often says so. Nevertheless she has a subtle air of tragedy to her, as if behind the easy perfection of her lifestyle she is carrying some kind of secret sorrow. I suspect that this is simply part of her; that there is no source to it but her own essence. Once I catch her staring blankly out of the kitchen windows, the tap running into the sink with her hand stock still underneath it, as if she is checking that the water is running cold. She's frozen in the moment, lost to it. When she shakes herself out of her reverie, she slots back into her task without a beat.

When we marry, Harvey is on the point of retiring from the law firm, acclimatising to the thought of being absent from work and all that it means. It seems that he is searching for a substitute. In the first few months that I know him, he takes up golf, joins the Neighbourhood Watch scheme, even buys a book on birdwatching. All these pursuits are laid aside without comment shortly afterwards. He prefers to travel, taking the occasional break away from home alone. When he is gone, I am surprised to find that I miss him. He has a sly sense of humour, delivered in that characteristic British dead-pan tone, and while he never quite ceases to remind me of a particularly awe-inspiring headmaster, being noticed by him — liked by him — feels special. It is an accepted joke among us that I am his pet project, and indeed he does take notice of me, watches me when he thinks I am not looking. I don't feel worried by it; there is nothing sexual in his inscrutable gaze. I soak up his attention like a sponge, because I recognise and value what it means.

Slowly, Jonathan starts to introduce me more to his friends, whom he has neglected a little since we met. I accompany him to sophisticated cocktail parties in Soho bars, tiny expensive dinners in understated restaurants. On one occasion, some six months after our marriage, we go out with a group of his university friends, including a girl who has been on an exotic sabbatical in Thailand and whom he has not seen for some time — Susanna. I hate her on sight: her aristocratically curled lip, her aggressively platinum hairdo, her shrill voice that could cut through glass. All through the evening she holds court, talking about old events that I have not been privy to. She laughs at her own jokes, which are mostly designed to strike to the heart of others' failings, leading the ripples of amusement from all around the table. This much I could bear, but the glare of her disdain soon turns on me. When we are first introduced, she calls me a 'pretty little thing' and kisses the air several inches from my ear. All through the dinner she makes little barbed comments, the sort that are almost, but not quite, lost in conversation. She asks where I went to school, and when I tell her, says that from little acorns huge oaks sometimes grow. She makes oblique allusion to university escapades, implicates Jonathan in all sorts of unedifying seeming scenarios, making me gulp down my drink so fast that stars swim at the back of my vision. She asks me how old I am, and laughs when she finds out — just a laugh, but imbued with such incredulous condescension that I can feel my blood boiling underneath my skin.

Jonathan says nothing all night; barely seems to notice Susanna's behaviour. If anything, he is especially attentive to her, laughing at her sallies and keeping her glass attentively topped up. By the time we finally, blessedly leave the restaurant, my throat aches with the effort not to cry. As we walk along the street outside towards the tube, my sense of betrayal is so great that I can't look at him, and I keep my eyes on the ground. As we reach the entrance to the station, he says, almost as an afterthought, 'We won't be seeing her again.' His face is troubled and hurt. All at once I see that his earlier actions have been nothing but damage limitation. I throw myself on his neck in relief, babbling out my thanks, breathing in the heady scent of his aftershave, sandalwood and spice. I take it as an indication of how much I mean to him. Later, though, I am to reflect that it is also the first example of how ruthless he can be — instinctively able to cut people cleanly and smoothly out of his life, without a backward glance.

★ ★ ★

I can pinpoint the exact day on which my perfect husband begins to transform into something different. It's our first wedding anniversary. I have set the table, placed two long-stemmed roses by our plates, dimmed the lights and put on a new dress — black silk, with underwear to match. When I hear his key in the lock I go to greet him, smiling. He smiles back tightly, giving me a perfunctory kiss, then strides through the hallway, throwing his rain-soaked jacket carelessly on to the back of a chair as he enters the kitchen. Irritation radiates from him. Of course, it is not the first time that he has returned from work frazzled and ground down by the pressures of the day. I wait for him to relax and embrace me, but instead he wheels round, snatching a newspaper as he does so, and walks angrily through to the lounge, setting himself down in his armchair with a thump.

Uncertainly, I hover, conscious that the dinner will be burning. 'Shall I dish up?' I ask. He doesn't respond, viciously turning the pages of his paper, his brow creased in concentration. I sidle up to him, placing my hand on the back of his collar and running my fingers lightly through the blond hair at the nape of his neck, but he swats me off as if my touch is an irritant too great for him to bear. I bite my lip and try again. 'Dinner is ready,' I say. 'I made something nice, for our anniversary.'

Jonathan looks up at me blankly, for all the world as if he has forgotten the day, forgotten the huge bunch of roses he gave me just hours earlier before he left for work and the gilt-edged card in which he had written how happy I had made him. 'Sorry,' he says, in a tone that makes it sound as much an accusation as an apology. 'I'm not hungry.'

His words are like a slap, but I turn them frantically over in my head, trying to knock some good out of them, something that can salvage the evening. 'OK,' I say. 'I'll turn the oven down, maybe we can have it later. Perhaps we should just go to bed?' I move round to face him, smoothing my hands down my new dress, which is almost sheer at the base, outlining my thighs in translucent silk. I have chosen it with care, knowing that he loves to be tantalised, but not too much.

A look of intense weariness passes over Jonathan's face, as if he has been bitterly disillusioned with life and everything in it. 'Is that all you think about?' he says cuttingly.

I gasp, feeling my body flush hotly under the new dress. His words feel like sacrilege. Ever since we have been together, our sex life has been a source of near-constant delight to me — to us both; we are always ready for each other, always able to click our chemistry smoothly into gear. This at any rate is what I have always thought. Now, standing in front of him, I have a horrible flash of an alternative scenario: a bored husband fulfilling his conjugal rights with a woman whose novelty has long since faded. I force it underground, pressing my hands to the side of my head as I do so. There is something badly wrong. There must be. Jonathan would never speak to me like this otherwise. 'What's the matter? Has something happened at work?' I ask, fighting to keep my voice under control.

He leaps up, throwing the paper furiously to one side. 'No,' he thunders, 'nothing has happened at work. Nothing is the matter. Does there have to be another reason for me not to want to sleep with you?' Leaving me speechless, he storms from the room and stamps up the stairs, slamming the bedroom door shut behind him with a crash that reverberates all the way along the beams of the ceiling below.

Hours later he creeps down to find me on the sofa, my eyes red and sore from crying, my limbs shaking as if I have a fever. He kneels humbly by my side in the low-lit room, putting his arms around me, murmuring regrets into my ears. His hands move across the black silk of my underwear, and suddenly he's pulling it to one side and pushing me back on to the sofa, face down, crushing me against the cushions so that I can barely breathe, his body suddenly hot and urgent against mine. At first it hurts, but I will the tension out of me, force myself to relax and give myself up to him. Afterwards he holds me so tenderly that I can't stop shaking, and he tells me that he will never treat me like that again, and I believe him, because I have to, I have to.

For the most part, he keeps his promise. He is frequently sweet and attentive, still bringing me presents and assuring me that he loves me. And yet after that night I suddenly start to see little cracks appearing everywhere I look — like multiple fissures spidering out in all directions from one tiny scratch on a sheet of glass. Sometimes it seems as if I would only have to press my thumb, once and hard, against the centre for it all to cave and shatter into a million pieces. At first this knowledge feels dark and uncertain, a nightmare glimpsed out of the corner of my eye. Slowly, it grows and grows. He works late and comes home at nine, ten, sometimes close to midnight. When I call him, he doesn't always answer, and when he does he sounds tense and strained. Sometimes he returns smelling different — not of another woman's perfume, nothing so crass; simply not like himself. He clicks his mobile shut when I come into the room and casts it aside, as if to disassociate himself from whatever is contained within it. When we make love his eyes are elsewhere. He is having an affair.

Once the thought has dropped into my head I can't get it out. Over the next few weeks it rots there, infecting everything it touches. There can be no other explanation for this sudden distance I feel from him. I even think I know who it is. Alice, the blonde receptionist from the Sherbourne club. I still go there with him, maybe once a fortnight, and I can tell from the way she greets him that she has seen him in my absence. Her prettily smiling red lips, her darkly fluttering eyelashes, seem made to entice; she uses them with the ease and confidence of one who has been born to this. There is an electricity between them that was never there before. I can feel it crackling across the space. Whenever I see her, I feel myself trembling with the force of having to hold myself back. I want to lean forward over the desk, grab her smooth shining hair in my hands and tear it from her scalp, shake her until her perfect teeth rattle in her head, scream at her to leave my husband alone. But of course I never do, and every time I smile politely and walk past her into the bar or the dining hall, I can feel Jonathan lingering behind me, reluctant to follow me, reluctant to leave her.

Of course, I confront him about my suspicions. The first time he is amused and dismissive, leaving me unsure as to whether I have spoken at all. The second time we are at the Blackwoods' house for tea. I blurt it out while Laura is making sandwiches in the kitchen, just yards away. It's not that I think it's the best time. It's more that I'm looking numbly at the bone-china teacups and the pretty lace tablecloth, and suddenly I feel the words rising uncontrollably up and out of me. *You're having an affair with her.* He looks up, seemingly totally confused as to where this has come from. If we were on our own in the house, he might well have said, 'With *who*?', or made some other little sidestep to show he had no idea what I was talking about, but now he knows he has to defuse this quickly. There is no time for false ignorance. He leans forward and takes my hands in his, roughly, across the tabletop.

'Violet, look at me,' he says in a low, urgent voice. 'I am not having an affair. Not with the little receptionist, not with anyone. You need to stop thinking these thoughts. They're dangerous. I love you, and I won't leave you. You are just going to have to believe me.' There is no way of telling whether he would have said more. Laura pushes open the door and comes in with a plate of sandwiches, her face briefly suffused by pleasure to see us holding hands. Once more, I bite my feelings back. I know that I won't be able to do it another time. Sooner or later, they will all come out.

The time comes a little under a fortnight later. I'm sitting up waiting for him to come home from work, watching the last of the light die over the treetops at the end of the garden. It is almost ten o'clock. I have called his office phone three times. Each time, I have sat listening to it ring, for so long that I can still hear it buzzing in my ears. When I hear his key in the lock I don't move. I just sit there, my eyes trained on the horizon as it slips from midnight blue to black. I hear his footsteps behind me.

'Hello,' he says. I don't speak or turn around. I know that if I look at him I will lose the courage for what I am about to say.

'You haven't been at work,' I say, quickly, before I can push it underground. 'I called you several times.'

I can see him shifting around at the edge of my field of vision, trying to make me look at him. 'Well, of course I wasn't,' he says. His voice sounds tender, puzzled. 'I was on my way home.' For a second I feel my certainty jolt, my mind scrambling back to think about the times I have called. I can't remember. 'It was a bit of a long journey — my train got delayed,' he continues. 'I'm exhausted.'

For some reason, his last words light a match to my anger; I feel it flaring up, consuming my whole body, impossible to put out. I leap to my feet. I'm not afraid to look at him now; I glare at him straight on, taking in his rumpled suit, the loosened collar, a button undone below his tie. Every tiny sign I see is more and more evidence, more and more ignition. 'I know,' I scream, and my voice comes out strained and harsh, barely recognisable. 'I'm not surprised. Of course you're exhausted, because you've been screwing another woman all evening.' I see him open his mouth in protest and cut him off, raising my voice even further so that it rings through the room, bouncing off the walls, stunning him into silence. 'You think I'm stupid, but I'm not. I know what's going on, I have done for weeks. How could you do this to me?' I'm crying hard now, tears spilling fast down my face, my eyes and head and throat aching with the force of my misery. I know what I must look like to him: ugly, mad, out of control. I don't care. My own words are there in my brain, knives digging sharply into my skull. I move towards him and hit out, my fists connecting with his chest. He steps back, as if in surprise, and for a second I freeze.

'Please, calm down,' he says. His voice is strangely sad. He's looking at me as if I am truly insane, as if he is concerned for my safety. His eyes are bright and wet and I can't help seeing how beautiful they are — so beautiful, so precious, and the thought physically hurts me, deep in my chest — I'm losing him, and I can't bear it, it can't happen. 'I'm worried about you, darling,' he says. 'You're not yourself. Deep down, you must know that what you're saying is crazy. Please, Violet. Let's sit down and talk, or have some dinner. Please.'

His hands are stroking my face softly, smoothing the damp hair back from my forehead, his fingers brushing my eyelashes, stiff and wet with tears. And for a minute I feel myself begin to droop and give in, dropping my head against his chest. But there in the back of my mind a thought buzzes — he's not denying it, not this time. I summon all my rage and push him away from me.

'No,' I scream, and the shock on his face is coldly gratifying. 'I know what you think. You think that you can be nice to me and it will all go away, but it won't. I know what you've been doing with that little slut, that horrible, *evil* woman, and I won't let it go, I won't — I won't let you treat me like a doormat, because I'm worth more than this, I won't — '

All at once I run out of steam and gasp for breath in the sudden silence. Jonathan looks harder now. He shoots me a glance of such undistilled contempt that I shiver. 'I married a fucking child,' he says, as clear as day, even though later he will swear that he said no such thing, that I must have misheard him, that I must be crazy.

★ ★ ★

I took the long route towards the church and into the village. As well as speed, the other route had something else on its side; it avoided the cottage where Jonathan and I had once lived. In the long first weeks after it had been sold, I used to linger palely outside, searching for some clue as to who now lived there, but its windows were always expressionless and blank. Soon enough I had started feeling like a stranger to the house, and that hurt me so much that I had vowed to stay away. Now, though, my enforced absence seemed silly and unnecessary, just another way of sanctifying the past.

I turned my steps towards our road, familiarity soaking through me in a rush as I approached the cottage gate. I remembered Jonathan nudging it open and carrying me over the threshold, laughing and panting, shouting that we were home at last. That night, we had sat on one of the dozens of cardboard boxes that crowded the front room and eaten fish and chips, toasting our new home with lemonade. The taste of it came to me suddenly: warm and sweet, its fizz punching the back of my throat. Afterwards we had lain on the mattress upstairs and he had said that he knew we would be happy here, and that one day we would share the house with our children. Automatically, as I recalled his words, my eyes went to the little window in the eaves — the room we had always designated as the nursery. There was something hanging from the window frame which I thought could be a mobile; a bright swaying twirl of pink. So Jonathan had been right: there were children there now after all. Just not his, and not mine. The thought seemed poignant, designed to jerk tears, but the message didn't seem to be making it through to my heart. I felt nothing.

I became aware of the strap of my holdall, digging painfully into my shoulder. I heaved it back into place, wincing as I did so. There was no point staying here any longer. I barely knew myself why I had wanted to come; only that in the wake of Harvey's words I had needed some distraction, some other pain to take over. It had not worked. Everything he had said was still buzzing there in the back of my brain, demanding attention, and it took all my strength to push it back. I began to walk again, continuing the long circuit towards the high street. By the time I reached it, the sky above was darkening and the heat of the day was draining away, leaving me chilly. Ahead of me I saw the church, its arched windows glowing softly and warmly with honey-coloured light. As I walked closer, the strains of evensong drifted towards me, mournful and sweet on the air. The heavy wooden doors were shut tight, but light poured out from the cracks underneath, spilling in golden strands on to the stone tablets of the pathway outside. For a moment I caught a glimpse of how it would be to be swept up into this world — safe and protected, fuzzily cocooned. After Jonathan's death a priest had spoken to me, insinuating that if I found my faith, then this tragedy would be easier to accept and understand, and that I should train my thoughts towards the kingdom of heaven.

I had wanted to do as he said, but when I thought about the possibility of an afterlife my mind refused to do anything but fold into blankness. I had identified Jonathan's body. Looking at it in that cold antiseptic room, I had known with absolute clarity that the immortal soul had not simply departed for another plane. It had never been there, and to think otherwise was pointless and sad.

Hoisting myself up to sit on the stone wall that flanked the church, I let my bag drop to the ground. I was still early, but I had no energy left to walk farther. I listened to the hymns, humming the tunes under my breath. Their familiarity was strangely soothing, and slowly I felt the tension inside me ease and dissolve. By the time I heard footsteps behind me, Harvey's words felt far away and meaningless, entirely unconnected to me or to what I was doing here. I turned and saw Max there — a tall silhouette coming quickly towards me through the churchyard, backlit by the shining windows. As he passed in front of the wooden doors, the light caught his outline and shimmered there, casting a faint halo all around his body. For a moment it looked so strange and so perfect that I laughed.

'What's so funny?' he asked, striding over and frowning. I shook my head, not wanting to explain. He looked annoyed for a moment, then shrugged and broke into a smile. 'You escaped,' he said, and the sudden admiration in his tone was like a caress. Inches from mine, his eyes glittered in the dark. I could smell the aftershave on his skin, exotic yet familiar, infecting the air between us. 'Let's go. It's not far.' He swung away from me, ignoring the heavy bag at my feet. I picked it up and followed him back through the churchyard, stumbling over the uneven stones. As we moved away from the church the path ahead darkened, and I found myself walking as if blind, by instinct, brushing against trees and tombstones. I couldn't see Max ahead, and suddenly panic rose up inside me, making me light headed and dizzy.

'Please, wait,' I cried out, hearing my voice tremble plaintively like a child's.

In an instant I felt him at my side, hissing briefly with amusement through his teeth. 'Come on,' he said, and his hand grasped mine tightly, pulling me after him. The feel of his skin against mine sent a shiver of adrenalin through my body; rough fingertips scraping against my palm, then pressing hard against the pulse at my wrist. We walked in silence, out of the churchyard and away down streets I had barely known existed. The houses here were different, scuffed with age and neglect, stirring a faint unease in me. In some, through thin net curtains, I could see the inhabitants moving secretly, like fish in dark aquariums.

'Here,' Max said, turning abruptly into a close of four or five houses, clustered around a small paved courtyard. Here and there, weather-beaten shrubs broke the bleakness of its surface. I followed him to the house on the far left, glancing around me as I did so. Huddled in the corner, perched on a wall, I could see a teenage figure smoking a cigarette, eyes trained on us watchfully. Max unlocked the door, and I saw him look back over his shoulder for an instant, reflexively on guard, before he ushered me into the house and bolted the door behind us. Dropping my bag at my feet, I switched on the hall light and moved towards the front room. Two threadbare sofas flanked the walls, thrown into stark relief by an unshaded light bulb starkly burning in the corner of the room. All around, newspapers and empty cans lay abandoned in piles on the boarded floor. A low, scratched coffee table was propped like an afterthought against the far wall; when I went closer, I saw that cigarette ash was scattered all across its surface, blown in soft dark eddies against the pale wood. Without thinking, I put my fingertip to it and felt the ash collect on my skin.

Max was standing in the doorway, watching me. I found my voice. 'You shouldn't have.' It had been an old joke between Jonathan and myself in the early days; whenever one of us was selfish or rude, we reacted as if they had done us the greatest favour in the world. From Max's blank expression, he did not share in the joke. I sat down on one of the sofas, feeling the springs scrape coldly against my thighs. I knew that my face was smooth and calm, but I could feel my stomach twisting itself up in knots with the sudden consciousness that I should not have come here, that I had made the wrong choice.

Max crossed the room in two quick steps, and it struck me that the space was too small for him, as if he were a tiger fenced into a cage. Crouching down by the table, he pulled a bottle of red wine out from underneath, brandishing it in a way that suggested not so much an enquiry as an order. I watched him unscrew the top and take a swig, his lips closing around the bottleneck with savage suction. When he passed it to me, throwing himself down on the sofa next to me, my skin prickled for a moment with fastidious disgust, but I blocked the thought out and applied my lips to the wetness where his own had been. The wine was rough and sweet, bringing tears to my eyes as I swallowed. I searched for something to say, and found myself simply looking at him. Stubble had sprung up around his mouth, emphasising the crude sensuality of its lines. I wanted to look away, but at the same time part of me itched to run my tongue along the fullness of his lower lip, to bite down hard on it with my teeth. The thought gave me a sickly pang of desire. He was staring straight ahead, as if he were totally unaware of my gaze, but I could feel his hand at the back of my neck, his arm slung along the top of the sofa and brushing my shoulder. I felt drugged by the contact; my mind emptied. I could think of nothing but his presence. Dimly, I heard myself sigh.

He looked at me then, his head jerking swiftly in my direction as if I had shouted out loud. 'Better give you the guided tour,' he said. 'The others will be here soon.'

'The others?' I felt as if I had been plunged into cold water. 'Who? What do you mean?'

Max gave me a look of lazy appraisal,

making the echo of my words sound stupid and childish. 'Keep your knickers on,' he said, getting up and prowling back through the hallway as he talked, leaving me with no choice but to follow him. 'I've just got a couple of mates coming over. You know, to have a few drinks? Play some cards? Have a chat? *You know*,' he said unpleasantly, as if he knew that I knew no such thing. I gritted my teeth, feeling an anger that I had long since forgotten I had the capacity for bubbling up inside me. I stayed silent, biding my time. Max strolled into the next room, sweeping his arm around the near-empty space expansively. 'Kitchen,' he said. Retreating into the hallway, we repeated the performance. 'Bathroom.' He mounted the stairs, which creaked in protest at his step. 'Bedroom.' The room above was larger, but the ceiling ran down claustrophobically at an angle, cutting out light. In one corner stood a double bed, a quilt thrown carelessly across it. Elsewhere, empty space punctuated by an old guitar, a few books, a wardrobe with its doors swung open to reveal a monochrome collection of clothes. An image of Jonathan's dressing room swept into my mind: crisp pink and blue shirts, carefully pressed, plump silk ties, gold cufflinks in little velvet boxes. The memory froze me to the spot; I couldn't take my eyes off the wardrobe.

'Not quite what you've been used to,' I heard Max say, as if he had read my mind. 'This place,' he clarified when I did not reply. 'Bit of a far cry from Harvey's nice little palace.' I made some vague noise of assent, looking around the room more carefully. It stretched all across the top floor of the house, and there was no spare bed.

I sat down heavily on the edge of Max's own bed, for want of anywhere else to sit. 'Why did you invite me here?' I asked. The question sounded blunt to my ears, but I sensed this was the only kind of questioning he would respond to. 'So that I could fix your drinks while you hang out with your mates, and then sleep on the sofa and cook you breakfast in the morning?'

Max laughed, throwing back his head in what looked like genuine delight. 'So you wanted to spend some time alone with me?' he said mockingly, strolling over to stand in front of me. His hands were in his pockets, pulling the material of his jeans tightly across his crotch; I felt my eyes drawn to it magnetically, half repulsed. 'Well, I'm sure that can be arranged. I wanted you to meet some people — you know, *different* people, people who are less than forty years older than you are. Besides, it was my birthday

132

yesterday. Always nice to celebrate, eh?' I stayed silent, biting back the usual birthday platitudes. 'But they won't stay here for ever,' he continued. 'And after they leave, well . . . ' His voice dropped, became low and thoughtful. He crouched down in front of me, putting his hands palms down on the bed either side of me, trapping without touching. 'We'll just have to see, won't we?' His dark eyes gleamed as he stared straight into my own. Downstairs, the doorbell rang out. It was a full thirty seconds before he rose to his feet and went to answer. When I stood up to follow him, I found that my legs were shaking.

I lingered at the top of the stairs, peering down through the banisters, as Max unbolted the door and pulled it open on the chain. Whoever was outside was clearly friend rather than foe, as he swiftly undid it and ushered the guest in. I saw a small, slight man with a shock of sandy hair and a nervous, ferrety face, dressed in distressed jeans and a loose white shirt which looked to be splattered with dark drops of paint. He was shifting from foot to foot, scratching the back of his neck as if he had an itch. His eyes were darting around the hallway, and I knew it was only a matter of time before he looked up and noticed me. I came down the stairs, and with my tread the man swung around as if he had been stung.

When he saw me there, his face broke into an uncertain smile.

'Steve — Violet,' Max said, waving a hand vaguely between us. 'Violet is staying with me for a couple of days.'

Steve thrust out a hand for me to shake, all the time watching me through flickering, narrowed eyes, as if he was trying to place my face. 'Pleased to meet you,' he said, garbling the words so fast that I barely caught them. 'Aren't you, ah, aren't you — '

'Jonathan was her husband,' Max said. 'Jonathan Blackwood.' He spoke as if he would rather not have divulged the information, warily surveying us both.

Steve nodded fast, his face twitching with something else now — curiosity, perhaps, or confusion. 'Thought so. Saw you in the paper after it happened,' he said. There was a strange silence, one which people usually filled with condolences. Steve said nothing, but he didn't seem to want to tear his gaze away from me. His mouth moved faintly, as if struggling with words that couldn't quite reach the surface. It was Max who broke the silence, brusquely saying that we should go and sit down. As he did so, the doorbell rang again. Ushering us into the front room, he went to answer it. I could hear him murmuring urgently, inaudibly, to whoever was in the hallway.

Steve was pacing the floor, hands in pockets, looking at me as a scientist might survey a strange new species. 'So how do you know Max?' I asked, for want of any other connection between us.

He stopped abruptly in mid-step, seemingly considering the question. 'Always known him,' he said. 'How about you?'

He hadn't really answered my question, but I played ball anyway. 'I work with his sister, Catherine,' I said. 'Do you know her?'

Steve shrugged one shoulder, a forced, asymmetric movement that made him look as if he were shaking off a fly. 'Not really. She don't come round here much.' Looking around again, I could see why. I tried and failed to imagine Catherine, always perfectly groomed and spotlessly clean, at home in this setting.

Max came back into the room, bringing two more men with him. The first was almost as tall as he was, with a cocky face and a muscular body barely hidden under a white vest top. The other was a smaller, less good-looking version of the first, and I realised at once that they must be brothers. They had obviously both been primed on my presence, as they didn't ask any questions, but simply nodded at me and smiled tightly.

'Chris,' barked the taller man. 'And Lee,' jerking his head in the direction of his brother. Lee didn't speak, just grinned, his gaze sweeping me from head to toe.

'Nice to meet you. I'm Violet,' I said, and with a shock I found that I was changing my voice, dropping the carefully cultivated vowels that I had thought had become a part of me, reverting to type.

Chris choked with amusement on the cigarette he was lighting. 'We know, baby,' he said, winking at me. 'We know.'

There was an uncomfortable silence. Max crossed the room and switched the stereo on, filling the room with music; hard thudding beats that made the walls buzz. Nodding his head, he swung around, gesturing at Steve, who fumbled in his pocket and passed him a small bag.

'Cheers, mate,' Max said, clapping him briefly on the back. He turned to the coffee table, crouched down, brushed the ash off its surface on to the floor. The others were chatting easily and quietly among themselves now, as if soothed by the start of a known ritual. I knew that they were looking at me, probably talking about me too, but my eyes were glued on Max. Although part of me had expected it, I still felt a jolt of panic when I saw him shake the white powder carefully out across the surface and form it into lines, tapping a credit card along their edges. Jonathan had been scathing about drugs, dismissing them as a teenage phase, and I had never been interested enough to investigate further, lapping up his words as if they were gospel.

I tasted something sour in my mouth, and swallowed it down. As I looked at the back of Max's head, the hair cut bristlingly close against his skull, it came to me with absolute clarity for the first time just how far apart we were. It had been Jonathan's air of danger which had first attracted me to him; a restrained brutality that was both an entice-ment and a warning. I saw now that without the privileged parents and the suitable career, this hint of cruelty would have frightened me, just as it did in Max. I felt hot and dizzy, the beats of the music boring through me. I was out of my depth.

With practised speed, Max rolled a note tightly in his fingers and bent his head quickly to the table. When he raised it again his face was bright and alert. Passing the note to Chris, he came and sat next to me on the sofa, slipping his arm around me, pulling me closely against him. I could feel the thud of his heart against mine, smell the sharp scent of him, and for a moment I thought I would pass out with the conflicting sensations that raged through me.

He applied his mouth to my ear and whispered, his voice crawling up into my head. 'Don't be scared,' he said. 'I'm here.' He gave a brief snort of amusement, almost as if he understood the contradiction in his words. 'I just want you to forget about everything for a while,' he continued, his breath stirring the hairs at the nape of my neck, blowing hot air on to my skin. 'I just want you to be happy.'

Although I knew they meant little, the words brought a lump to my throat. I couldn't remember the last time they had been said to me. Suddenly I thought of my school-friends — girls I had not seen for years, who had lived as I had in modest houses on council estates, who had already accepted that their lot in life would stay suspended at a certain level. I had thought that Jonathan had saved me. Now I saw where I could have been without him — in a house like this, with friends not unlike these, and perhaps it would not have been so bad, perhaps I would have been happier after all. I got up and went to the table, knelt down next to Steve. The note felt rough and cold in my fingers. Hovering over the table's surface, for a moment I felt incapable and tearful, like a child who does not know how to tie their shoelaces and doesn't want to try. An image of Harvey's face popped into my mind: stern, unsmiling, reproachful. I closed my eyes and acted on instinct, inhaling hard through my nose. I felt it hit instantly, a sharp burning sensation that made me gasp and blink. Looking around, I was surprised to find the room entirely unchanged. I rose to my feet unsteadily and went to sit by Max again. He was watching me expectantly, tapping his fingers in an energetic staccato rhythm on the arm of the sofa.

'Now that wasn't so bad, was it?' he crooned, stubbing out his cigarette in the ashtray balanced between us, then instantly flicking another to his lips and lighting it. The room was heavy with smoke, making my eyes sting and my throat sore.

I laughed, suddenly giddy with the thrill of the forbidden, of having crossed a boundary and emerged alive. 'It wasn't anything at all,' I said. 'I can't feel anything.'

Max laughed too, jumping to his feet without warning and making me start. 'You will,' he said.

Time passed; I wasn't sure how much. I found myself talking and talking to Chris and Lee, chatting about nothing, conversation spilling out of my memory as quickly as I poured it in. They were trying to teach me how to play poker, waving cards fast in front of my face, gabbling rules and showing me hands. When I fanned the cards out in my hand I giggled, seeing nothing but what was there to see — little red and black symbols dotted on white rectangles, and in the middle a lurking, secretive Queen of Spades popping her head out like a spy. I tossed down cards at random, not understanding, not caring, and after a length of time demanded that we play Snap instead, knowing I would win. Again and again I slammed my hand down hard on the pile, scattering cards everywhere, laughing at their astonished faces as they tried to compete, asking me to tell them the knack. The game descended slowly into chaos, none of us knowing what we were doing and why, and I found myself restless again, my hands moving like fireflies as I talked, my eyes darting from face to face, unable to focus for more than a few seconds on any one point. I could feel the music speeding up, and my pulse with it, thrumming like a motor under my skin, at my chest, my neck, my wrists, until it felt as if my whole body was jumping to the beat. As the music grew louder I found myself shouting to be heard, barely knowing what I was saying, but aware that I was charming these men, holding them captive in the palm of my hand, seeing their eyes moving from my breasts to my legs and back again, over and over like a stuck record. I felt glee trickling through me in a rush, a sense of everything in me coming together and fusing into perfect happiness. My eyes alighted on Chris's shoulder muscles, flexing as he reached for a drink, and suddenly I was touching them, feeling my eyes stretched wide open, marvelling at the way the muscle slid smoothly under the skin. All at once I thought of Max, and I wanted him, so much that I leapt up from the sofa and went to search for him. He and Steve had peeled away from the group; they were facing each other in the kitchen, talking intently, their voices buzzing off the walls.

'You know this is all wrong, man,' Steve was saying, his face twitching crazily now on one side, making him look insane. 'You shouldn't of brought her here, it's just taking the piss, she's a nice girl and I'm sorry for her, it ain't right . . . ' *I'll do what I like.* Max was snapping over his words, so that their voices blurred together and I was no longer sure who was saying what or why. *You don't know me, you don't know nothing about it. Have some compassion. Get the fuck out of my house.*

'Are you talking about me?' I shouted,

coming forward into the kitchen, blinking in the sudden bright fluorescent light and feeling the room spin around me, my heart thumping so hard that the sound of it threatened to deafen me. Max spun round, came towards me, and he was talking, but I couldn't concentrate on what he was saying, the words jumbling up into a pile of nonsense in my head. I could only look at him, and think how beautiful he was, not pretty like others I had known, but desirable as a man should be, sexy and uncomplicated, just a collection of bone and skin and muscle. I felt my paranoia drift, losing my grip on it. I was staring up into his face, reaching a hand up to stroke the side of his jaw, and all at once there was a stillness in the room, an absence of anyone or anything else, just me and him caught up together, and then it all snapped back in a rush and I gasped. He took my hand, pulling me after him into the hallway, telling me to wait for him. I saw him go into the front room again, shake another line out on to the table and snort it hard and fast.

He came back to find me and grabbed my hand again, holding it so tight that it hurt. 'Let's go,' he said, and he was dragging me up the stairs, my shoes clattering on the wood and setting off tiny disjointed sparks of noise. I reeled after him into the attic room, and it was cold in there and dark, but for a thin stream of light curling over the bed from a street lamp outside. I heard the rustle of cloth against skin as Max pulled his T-shirt over his head and threw it down, sending it skidding across the floor like a rat, and he came towards me, naked from the waist up, his eyes glittering in the dark like jewels. I felt the strength of him as he grasped me roughly around the waist with one hand, the other tearing at my clothes, ripping them away from me until I was stark naked but for my shoes. My hands were there, at the buckle of his belt, fumbling with the catch with fingers that spun and danced over the metal, unable to get a hold on it. He was touching me now, roughly exploring, and he pushed my hand out of the way and undid the belt himself, shoving the clothes to the floor. I tried to pull him over to the bed, to the light, but he pulled me back, dragging me to the farthest wall and slamming me against it, bruising my shoulder with the force, but I didn't care — I felt everything on fire, straining to be held and touched. I couldn't see a thing. His breath came hard and sharp in the darkness, and I heard my own matching it, both of us hot and urgent, feeling his mouth kissing and biting as if it were everywhere at once.

'Please,' I gasped, and although it was pitch

black I shut my eyes, reaching out for him. I had never done it like this; this was raw and dirty, something to be ashamed of, done by someone else, someone I would despise. I saw stars as he thrust into me, holding me back against the wall, moving hard and fast until the whole room seemed shaken up into chaos, and I felt the force of it rising up through me, and heard him cry out, a noise that sounded like a sob of rage and pain, before he went still. A moment later he was lifting me up, as pliant as a doll, into his arms, carrying me over to the bed and laying me down there. I stared up at the ceiling. In the corner of my eye I could see him doing up his trousers, pulling the T-shirt over his head. In the space of a blink, he vanished. I heard the door slam. I was alone and suddenly it was all over.

When I opened my eyes again dawn was breaking, soft grey light pouring into the attic and waking me. My body felt stiff and cold. The house was completely silent, so much so that when I swung my legs slowly down to the ground the sound of my shoes on the wood felt as if it could shatter the air. I went and pulled on my dress, sat back down on the bed. I felt an encroaching sorrow, a flat, blank sadness that seemed to be without boundaries. I sat listening to the silence, watching the clouds move bleakly, unfathomably, outside the skylight window.

I didn't know how long I sat there before Max appeared in the doorway, then came and sat beside me. He looked exhausted, mauve shadows staining the hollows underneath his eyes. His hair was damp and smelt faintly of peppermint shampoo; I could still see the water from the shower gleaming damply in droplets on his neck.

'Have you slept OK?' he asked, putting his hand into my lap. There was none of the violence of a few hours before; it lay there like a dead thing, suppliant and unthreatening.

'I must have done,' I said. 'How about you?' I felt drearily embarrassed, my mind shying away from what we had done. I didn't even want to look at him.

Max sighed, lying back on the bed and pillowing his head on his hands. 'I haven't been to bed,' he said. There was something mournful in his tone, faintly wistful, as if he were already regretting his choice. 'The others left a couple of hours ago, but I stayed up. I came to see you,' he added quickly, shooting me a glance from under hooded eyelids. 'But you were asleep.' I couldn't put my finger on it, but something in the way he said it told me that it was a lie. I couldn't be bothered to argue. Instead I lay down beside him, feeling any last scraps of energy draining from my body. He put one hand out, began to stroke my hair slowly and repeatedly, as if he was barely conscious of what he was doing. 'Tell me about Jonathan,' he said.

I felt a jolt of unreality. Of all the things I had expected him to say, this was the last. 'You knew him,' I said.

Max was silent a long time. 'Not like you did. I want to know how he was with you,' he said finally.

I tipped my head back to the ceiling, waiting for the desolation I felt stirring inside me to subside. 'Loving, most of the time,' I said. 'Attentive. He liked to pamper me, and himself. He indulged me a lot. He was charming and funny, sometimes. But he was distant . . . towards the end, especially. I could never tell what he was thinking or how he was feeling, the way I think you're supposed to be able to with someone you love. I used to think it was my fault. I'm not so sure now. Sometimes I think it was just that I didn't know him as well as I thought I did. I'm not sure he wanted me to know him.' As I spoke, I felt my insides twist dully with pain, but my eyes were dry. These thoughts were too familiar for tears.

Max kept his eyes on the skylight, watching the clouds intently. Light moved and shifted in waves across his face. 'It must be hard for you,' he said after a while.

Somewhere, I felt glad, but a larger part of me was angry that it had taken him so long to acknowledge it. 'No — really, it's great,' I said bitterly. 'This is exactly where I always hoped I would be.' Resentment, too often dampened down in recent months, built up in me. I wanted to scream with the unfairness of it, the way that my life had blown up in my own face and somehow led me to this place, in bed with a man who had practically raped me with my own consent, who so obviously despised me that I had lost sight of why I was even here.

As if he could sense what I was thinking, Max rolled over on to his side, propping himself up on one elbow. Close up, I could see that the shadows underneath his eyes ran a gauntlet of colours, from pale violet through to black, as if his skin had been bruised. He looked bizarrely vulnerable. He bent his head and mumbled words that I didn't catch, cleared his throat and spoke again. 'I don't think he would have liked it,' he said. 'I don't think he would have liked the way I treated you. I'm sorry.'

The apology seemed strange, made through the vehicle of a dead man, someone who could no longer have any say in how I was treated. I took it in, knowing that I deserved no apologies in any case. I had been compliant, drugged with sensation after so long without. Images from the night before ran dispassionately through my mind like film: I couldn't recapture the lust I had felt, the hot, swimming urgency of it. It seemed to have drained out of me. Looking at Max, slumped back against the wall now, I found that it had been replaced by something else — a strange tenderness, built on no solid foundation, as if in some mysterious way his actions had claimed me as his. I lay back, closed my eyes. 'That's OK,' I said. Once more, I felt bleakness roll over me.

'Do you believe what they said?' Max asked, and I knew exactly what he meant, but I stayed silent. 'That it was an accident,' he said finally, as if he knew that elaboration had been unnecessary.

I kept my eyes shut. Through my closed lids, I sensed the sun move across the skylight window, changing the quality of the darkness around me. 'I don't know,' I said. I meant to stop there, but suddenly the words came pouring out of me, words that had been there for so long that I spoke them on autopilot, not having to think them through. 'Sometimes I think he meant to do it. I try and think about him being that unhappy, unhappy enough to want to do something like that, and I can never quite imagine it, but how could I? I used to spend hours there, down by the lake where it happened, just trying to get a sense of what he was thinking, what he was doing. I had to stop in the end. I wasn't getting anywhere, and it frightened me being in that place. Sometimes when I was down there at night, I would think I saw his shadow. I felt him there, and it wasn't comforting. It was horrible.' I stopped, remembering.

'When was the last time you went?' I heard Max ask.

'God,' I said flatly. 'Months ago.'

There was silence for a moment. I felt Max shift, swing his legs across me on the bed. When I opened my eyes he was standing there, casting a shadow over me. His face was exhausted and intent. From his hand, a silver car key swung, light refracting off it in brittle sparks, dazzling me. '*Come on*,' he said.

★   ★   ★

Our last few weeks together are quieter, kinder. It is as if my outburst, inconclusive though it was, has purged some poison between us. We do things for each other, little household chores and favours, smoothing each other's trials. Jonathan is soft and understanding with me, and although he never refers to my accusations again, it feels as if he is trying to refute them, subtly, day by day. I no longer know what to believe. He still works late, still keeps his mobile phone hidden, still sometimes seems like a stranger who I cannot reach at all. But I have learned that my histrionics achieve nothing, except to push him farther away. I am seeing the value of not rocking the boat. He never argues with me, often tells me that he loves me, and I take what is offered, even though I sense that, like Snow White, if I bit down on to the apple I would find it riddled with poison.

The day he dies is a Saturday. It's October, and when I wake up it is to the quiet, rustling sound of leaves falling against the window-pane. I draw back the curtain and watch them, a cloud of burnt orange and pale yellow, drifting gently to the ground from the old oak tree and collecting in piles at its root. I try and remember the old wives' tale, that if you catch a falling leaf it brings you luck for . . . a day? A week? A lifetime? I imagine myself out there under the oak tree, my arms outstretched and gathering the leaves, capturing a charmed life. Beside me, Jonathan stirs, and I remind myself that I don't need any extra luck. I have got what I wanted. Stuck in a groove, my mind repeats the thought over and over until it feels empty and meaningless.

'Good morning,' he murmurs, and for a moment I sink back against him, feeling the warmth of his body against mine. I linger there, wondering whether he will kiss me, but he merely buries his face briefly in my neck before slipping away and out of bed. A few minutes later, he returns with coffee for me. He has put the china mug on a duck-egg-blue tray, with a little jug of milk and a thimble-sized bowl of sugar. Lying across the tray is a single freshly picked rose, and when I bend my head to smell it, I see that droplets of dew still cling to its dark red petals like tears.

We pass the morning quietly, and eat our lunch together. He has made some mushroom soup, earthy and rich. I spoon it down in silence, soaking hunks of fresh bread in its cloying juices. The taste of it seems new and extraordinary. I have no way of knowing that this will be the last time that mushrooms will pass my lips; that in years to come the slightest scent of them cooking will make me want to retch.

We have barely finished lunch when he stands up and tells me that he has to go out for a while. 'Just for a couple of hours.' He has errands to do, he says, things to buy. We are redoing the bathroom, and he may search for some suitable paint, a new cabinet or mirror. It is best if I stay at home. 'You weren't feeling well yesterday,' he says. It's true; my throat was sore and I thought I felt the beginnings of a cold stirring, but today it seems to have faded away again. 'You should get some rest,' he says.

He settles me in an armchair, brings me a favourite book, finds a rug for me to wrap myself up in if I am cold, lights the fire. As I watch him kneel and put a match to the kindling, his blond head bent in concentration, whipping his hand away as the first flames spark up, I think, *He is treating me like an invalid.* I don't know why, but the thought makes me uneasy. He stands up again, turns to face me and smiles. His blue eyes are shining. He comes and kisses me on the forehead, but some instinct makes me draw back and pull his head down lower, so that his lips meet mine. The kiss itself is brief, but when it ends he does not pull away, and for a few moments we stay there, his lips resting, unmoving, against mine.

'Don't be long,' I say, and something strange stirs in my chest, something close to panic or fear.

'I won't,' he says. 'You will be here when I get back, won't you?' Suddenly he looks like an anxious schoolboy, hanging on my reply.

'Of course,' I say. 'Why? Do you want to go out later?'

'No.' He pauses. 'I just want to talk to you.'

The words are innocent enough, but somewhere some subtext is lurking, enough to send an impulsive tremble running through my body. I ask him what he wants to talk about, and he doesn't reply. When I ask again, he says that it is nothing important. As he speaks, he tucks my hair back behind my ears, concentrating on the movement. He gets to his feet, and a moment of clarity comes to me, one which I will look back on again and again as a turning point, a crucial second where perhaps I might have changed things. I think, *I will ask him not to go.* I am still struggling with the words when he turns and leaves the room. I listen to the sound of him putting on his coat and shoes in the hallway. Moments later, I hear the front door slam. Through the window, I watch him getting into the car, pulling quickly out from the kerb. It is not that I have changed my mind about asking him to stay. My body simply feels out of step with my mind, creating a strange time delay, so that by the time I have risen to my feet he has long gone. In the sudden silence, I look around. My limbs are shaking and my forehead feels hot. Perhaps I am ill after all. I sit back down, reach for the remote control and turn the television on.

Four hours pass. It is five o'clock, and outside it is already dark. I go to the window and draw the curtains, but a moment later I open them again. I want to see the car approaching when he comes home. Slowly, I cross to the telephone and punch in his mobile number. As the ringing starts up, I hear another ring, higher and shriller, coming from somewhere behind me. I lay the receiver down on the table and go in search of the noise. His mobile is lying on the dining room table, lit up and vibrating crazily. I approach it slowly, and for a moment the sound of it in the silent house somehow seems malevolent, sinister. Just before I reach it, it stops. I think about the answerphone message it will be recording: dead silence, but for perhaps a faint far-off crackling of the logs on the fire. I pick the phone up. He never leaves it, barely lets it out of his sight. I know that to search through his messages is wrong, but as I flip it open, I know that I am going to do it. I press the menu key, but when I do so, a message flashes up on the screen. *Keypad locked. Enter PIN.* I tap in his birthday, then mine. I try the year that he was born. The first four numbers in sequence. A series of zeros. Each time, the message flashes smugly up at me. *PIN entered wrongly.* I try a random selection of numbers, again and again, my fingers shaking on the keys, but the little phone stays as impenetrable as a fortress. I think of all the secrets that could be locked up within it, and suddenly it seems like a living, breathing creature in my hand, knowing and evil. I return to the lounge, still holding it, and sit back down.

Time flows like oil, thick and insidious. Seven o'clock. Eight. The fire has burnt down to ash, but the room still feels unbearably hot. I go to the window and push it open, feeling the cold night air flood in. My head is numb and soft, as if it is made of cotton wool. It is almost nine o'clock when I see the headlights, approaching in the distance, down at the end of the road. They are moving slowly, cautiously, as if driving through landmines. It is him. It has to be. As the lights draw closer and stop outside the house, something lifts and clears inside me. I start to my feet, my heart lurching with sudden relief, and go to the front door, fling it open. And then I see that it is not Jonathan's car at all, and that it is not one man getting out of the car, but two. They are coming towards me with their hands clasped stiffly in front of them like puppets, and their faces are soaked in professional sorrow.

★ ★ ★

155

At the funeral everything is fuzzy and unfocused. I stand with ten or fifteen others, clustered like black vultures around a corpse. An early evening mist hangs over the churchyard, curling like smoke beneath my clothes. In my thin linen jacket and skirt, I can't remember ever having been so cold.

I listen to the vicar as he drones out his eulogy, keeping my eyes on the coffin. I don't want to look at it, but I feel frozen, as if I will never be able to turn away. It's smooth and dark, carved from shining mahogany, with a spray of white flowers laid across it like icicles. When it is lowered into the ground, I can feel Laura shaking next to me, like a sick animal that needs a swift blow to the head to put it out of its misery. My hand twitches towards hers for an instant, then pulls back. It's too much effort, sending an ache running all the way up my arm. I watch the coffin descend. A handful of earth falls on to its surface, spraying out across the mahogany like gunshot. I think of Jonathan, locked inside, opening his eyes and stretching out his hands, placing them on the cold dark wood in baffled shock and surprise. I have seen his body, but still the image has not crystallised into anything close to acceptance. Watching the earth rise, I think with a kind of detached horror, the words falling into my brain like raindrops, *You are in there, and I am doing nothing to help you. You are being buried alive, and I am watching it happen.*

It's over. When I turn away, I see that the mist has fallen lower, whitening the trees all around us, blanking out the path ahead. I feel someone's hand on my arm, but I don't turn around. I walk forward, hugging my jacket to my chest, shivering. I realise that my eyes are dry. So dry that they ache in their sockets. Blinking feels strange and unfamiliar, and I am conscious of every time my eyelids seesaw open and closed, like rusted joints. I strain to see ahead, the path unfolding a little more in front of me step by step as I move through the rows of tombstones. I have felt sadness before. I had not expected there to be so much difference between sorrow and grief. Whatever is moving through me feels like nothing that I can hope to tame and understand, like nothing human. It frightens me.

I have almost reached the gate when Harvey steps in front of me. His lips are white, etched coldly into his face like marble. He places both hands upon me, one on each shoulder, and the touch makes me stop in my tracks. When he speaks, the voice that reaches me sounds drained of emotion, and there is nothing to give colour to his words, but I know that he means them. *You will always have a home with us*, he says. When I don't reply, he says, *You are my daughter*. I look at him properly then, standing tall and straight in front of me, feeling his long narrow fingers gripping my shoulders so hard that it should hurt. It feels as if my own father belongs to another life. In that instant, through the haze, I know that Harvey and I share something that cannot be erased. Grief binds people together as often as it tears them apart, and as irreversibly. I belong to him, for ever, whether I want it or not.

★   ★   ★

It was not yet six in the morning, and the streets were deserted as Max drove us slowly through the village. The radio hummed in the background, crackling out some chirpy 1980s song. Already the heat was rising, and I wound down my window as we drove, letting my arm trail out and feel the faint breeze. Max's face was tense with tiredness and effort, as if he could barely keep his eyes open to negotiate the route. I didn't know why I had not refused to come. All I knew was that when he had stood there, the car keys dangling from his fingers, this journey had seemed inevitable, and not worth disputing.

Sitting in the passenger seat, breathing in the faint scent of cut grass, I felt as if I might not be awake at all. Everything around us looked two-dimensional and too bright, like props on a film set. As we drove away from the village centre and out towards the lake, I glanced at Max again. His lips were moving slightly, on autopilot, mouthing the words of the song on the radio. Sunlight splashed across his brow, making him narrow his eyes and pull the mirror down to shade his face. As we glided down the long tree-lined road, pale green light flickered through the leaves in staccato, hypnotic patterns, making my head swim.

The lake unfolded in front of us suddenly as we turned the corner, like a magic trick, appearing from nowhere. In the distance, I saw the water curving out, dark ink spilling over a page. Slowly, Max drove the car down a dirt track, searching for some place to pull over. When he found it, he switched the ignition off, and with it the radio, and for a few moments we sat in total silence. Familiarity was nudging at me as I opened the door and got out, staring across the lake. I remembered the cluster of lime trees at the bank, the scattered rocks at the water's edge. And yet it was more than this; as I took the first steps down towards the lake, I had the sense that I had made this exact journey before, on this exact day, and every step gave me a little jolt of déjà vu.

Max was just behind me; I could hear his footsteps like an echo of my own. As I reached the bank he caught me up. We stood there together, looking out across the water. When I glanced at him, I saw that his face was taut with emotion; whether for me, or in some way for himself, I could not tell. His hands were deep in his pockets, and one foot kicked softly, rhythmically, against a rock at the water's edge. I knew suddenly that this trip had not been wholly for my benefit. There was a reason why he, too, had wanted to come here. As we stood, I remembered what Harvey had said to me. *I would go as far as to say . . . that he was responsible for Jonathan's state of mind . . .* All at once, the words rose up within me and I felt the truth of them, felt a conviction in them that I had not before acknowledged, had not wanted to.

'What did you do to him?' I asked, and my voice sounded flat and drained of emotion, not like mine at all.

Max turned to me swiftly, as if he had been anticipating the question. 'I did nothing,' he said, low and intent, his eyes boring through me. 'I did nothing, Violet.'

I stayed silent, staring back at him. Harvey's words popped in my mind like

160

fireworks, each one scattering sparks, reverberations. Money. Blackmail. Abusive. Threatening. I barely knew the man in front of me, and yet somehow when he spoke I couldn't help but believe him. I sat down by the water and kicked off my shoes. So early in the morning, the water was still cold, and the shock of it curled my toes. I let my feet drift, making ripples, patterns in the shallows.

Max sat down next to me. 'Sometimes you get mixed up in things you're not prepared for,' he said. 'Things you aren't meant to be involved in. But once you know something, you can't stop knowing it.' His words were oblique, frustrating. They rolled around in my head like mercury, splitting and re-forming, sliding out of my comprehension.

'What are you trying to tell me? What is it that you know?' I said at last.

Max did not reply for a long while, and in the pause before he spoke, the silence grew so loud around us that I could feel it humming in my ears, building, dangerous. The sun was slowly rising over the lake, tinting the water in reflected shades of rose and gold, catching in sparkles that leapt out at my eyes in random patterns, coded with mysterious meaning. Around my feet, the water softly rose and fell, stirred by the breeze.

161

'I know he killed him,' he said, and once again I was struck with the dreamlike inevitability of the scene that was unfurling, the certainty of the words. 'His own father. His own father,' he whispered, as if he could not bear to speak Harvey's name. There had been no need for him to clarify. I had known almost before he spoke what he was going to say. There had been no other way that this could go.

I felt Max grab my hand, twist me round to face him. 'I can't tell you how I know,' he breathed, urgency making his voice quaver and crack, and for a moment he looked like a madman, a pathetic fantasist living in his own head. 'But I know. He's evil, a fucking evil, dangerous man. You've got to believe me. You've got to help me.' I could see tears shining brightly at the corners of his eyes. He was trembling; I felt his hand in mine, jumping and shivering crazily, as if he had a fever. There was no foundation for the things he was telling me. And yet, as the words soaked through me, I could not shake off the sense that they were eerily familiar, voicing something which I felt that somewhere too deep to reach I had always known, something beyond reason or explanation.

My mind shut off the reality of what he was saying. I must push this conversation to its

162

end, that was all. 'How could I help you?' I said.

As swiftly as blinking, Max's mood seemed to change. He let go of my hand and picked up a little stone from the bank. Stretching his arm back as far as it would go, he threw it with all his force out on to the water; I saw the muscles strain and flex under his skin, sensed the power he kept locked up inside him. He watched it land, a speck in the distance, barely causing a ripple. When he looked back at me again it appeared he might laugh at any moment, his mouth twitching with barely contained mirth and excitement. 'He needs to get what's coming to him,' he said. 'He deserves it all. You could help me, Violet. We could kill him.' His face had not caught up with his words. He was still smiling, and somehow this made it harmless and safe, but as I watched, I saw the smile fall away, inch by inch, moment by moment, until he was staring at me with nothing but grim, flat determination. Waiting for me to answer him.

PART TWO

Harvey

June–July
2008

Monday, 28 June

You must kill the dead, or they will kill you.
So at any rate it was said to me once, and
although I can no longer remember when or
who by, the words have taken on the certainty
of a mantra carved into stone. The dead in
my life refuse to lie down and dissolve meekly
into dust. To me, they often seem more alive
than those who pass in and out of my sphere
each day, and my thoughts are so full of them
and their loss that they still threaten to obsess
me, to drain from me what little vitality I have
left.

I do not know what writing will achieve;
only that perhaps the act of setting pen to
paper and making these thoughts concrete
will take away some of their malignant force.
For too long I have felt like a child afraid to
whisper a demon's name three times in front
of a mirror in case its shadow looms behind
me. I write for no one but myself and you, my

167

son, and yet I cannot shake the inherent sense of arrogance; that in the act of writing this story I somehow intimate that it is well worth telling, to anyone and everyone. This instinctive recoil has halted me for too long already, and it will do so no more.

I arrived here in Spain three days ago, at a resort that might as well be anywhere: towering pastel blocks built around the focal point of a shining, too-blue swimming pool, rows of candy-striped deckchairs glistening in the sun like sucked boiled sweets, a poolside bar with waiters and waitresses dressed down in shorts and bikinis. There is a restaurant here, with laminated menus on which the dishes are listed in Spanish, then translated below in larger, crudely capitalised letters. My fellow holidaymakers are mostly families. Overweight parents whose primary aim seems to be to loll in state and bake themselves to death, shrieking children splashing each other. The odd sullen teenager, too, misplaced and finding nothing of interest, except perhaps the evening cocktails and karaoke. This all suits me. It is not purgatory, or self-flagellation, but pure escape. Here I am anonymous, and of minimal interest. I have a fortnight here before my return and what lurks ahead in the shadows — my sixty-fourth birthday, the garden party hosted in my honour. I am not yet inclined to think about these things, but nor do I wish to fill my days with mindless activity. On my arrival here I flicked through the brochure that lay on my bed, crammed full of trips and excursions designed to whet the appetite of the timid traveller. Dolphin-watching, nature-walking, pub-crawling. As always, I felt possibilities briefly stir before casting the booklet aside.

When I had unpacked my clothes I went to the poolside bar and asked for a drink, a whisky and Coca-Cola. The tanned moronic barman misheard me and his hand went to the rum instead, the same brown-and-gold bottle that you used to favour. Sharply, I told him no, but I found that once I was settled in my deckchair with the whisky I had asked for, the memory of the slip kept returning to me, the image haunting me, making it hard to breathe. Who would have imagined that the simple act of reaching for one bottle rather than another could so entirely ruin a morning? That it could cause such incredible pain.

★ ★ ★

The roots of anything are by definition in its beginning, but as I remember little of mine, uncovering them has always been impossible.

Too many of the memories I have of the years before eighteen have blurred together in my mind, darting like dragonflies, only occasionally blundering into consciousness. Mine was a post-war childhood, presided over by parents upon whom life had smiled, but who would have thought it in the worst possible taste to flaunt the fact. Despite his money, my father had a natural affinity for the austerity of the age. He was a doctor, a Harley Street man, and the large Georgian house in Kensington where I grew up was solely the fruit of his labours; my mother never lifted her hand to do a stroke of work in her life. That house was always cold, with a solitary log fire crackling sombrely in the sitting room grate. I remember stepping in through the doorway out of the thick, swirling yellow fog that still descended on London in those days, and feeling no discernible change in the temperature, no homely sense of enveloping warmth.

Sometimes in those early days I would sit at an upstairs window and watch the local children playing outside with sticks and balls, listening to their cries and taunts floating up from the street below. My father was elitist by nature, and discouraged my mixing with others. From as early as I could remember I felt somehow separate, displaced in a strange

170

city whose past I knew little of beyond what was drilled into me at school, but which I felt had had more influence on our lives than I could understand. I recall that there was an overgrown bomb site not far from our house; my father's steps would always slow as we passed it. I could sense the air of sadness and decay that hung about the street corner. I suppose that my father had lost friends and relatives in the war. He never spoke about such things.

My mother was a spoilt, indolent woman, the kind who believes that an accident of prettiness is enough to see her through life's rougher waters, and yet this prettiness seemed to weigh heavily upon her. She would often stand in front of the mirror arranging jewels or furs, twisting this way and that to see the effect of her costume, her face petulant and critical. I remember that on her dressing table she kept a small tin of sweets; chocolate was still rationed at that time, and I believe now that she saw this small luxury as a mark of distinction. She was never satisfied, and terminally self-concerned to the point of narcissism. It gives me pain to write these words, but there is little point in sugar-coating obvious truths.

I often wondered whether my father regretted his choice. Despite everything, I believe not: he had a high tolerance for her ways, and in this she was an exception to his uncompromising view of others. I believe that doctors are often strong in compassion. Perhaps the old adage concerning a tailor's son never being properly clothed holds true here, but I certainly saw little of this milk of human kindness. My father had been bred to show little emotion, as was I. Every evening, he would return to the house as the gas lamps were lit down the road and dusk fell, carrying his shining black leather bag, locked up and bulging with secrets. As a child I learnt the story of Pandora's box, and became convinced that my father's bag was similarly portentous; that if I opened it, all the diseases he had encountered that day would flood out and swarm about the house, infecting us all. Despite this macabre conviction I spent many furtive hours trying to open the bag when my father was elsewhere, my fingers working at the lock in vain. I was curious as to what effect the unsettling of our dreary equilibrium would have upon the household, but I never found out.

At eight I was sent away to boarding school, of which I remember little but the regimented rows of desks, the distant voices of teachers cutting through the silent classrooms, and that pervasive, evocative smell of Jeyes fluid that hung around the dormitory and which would flood my nostrils each morning when I woke. I was a good student, and stayed out of harm's way. I believe I was beaten only once — the swift, sharp smart of the ruler across my knuckles is still with me now, but not what I had done to deserve it. I was not homesick, although I do recall the muffled sobs of my classmates after dark, the sound softly piercing the night air. Their emotion was another mark of difference. Already I felt self-sufficient, with no need for others to comfort or reassure me. What has never been had cannot be missed.

It was expected that when my education was complete I would follow my father into Harley Street — I believe that offices were already earmarked for my eventual use. The law was my small rebellion. At seventeen I realised that only one thing had stood out for me from the bland mass of education that had been dumped on me through my schooldays; I had a keen sense of injustice and morality, of what was right and wrong. In the summer holidays, I announced my intention to apply to Oxford to study law to my father over a near-silent dinner of lamb chops and gravy. (My mother was dead by this time; a nervous complaint had finally bubbled over into pneumonia. Hers was the first death of those around me, and the least mourned, but I find that she still arises regularly in my dreams, decked out in organza and rubies, wearing an expression of habitual scorn to let me know that she is displeased.) That evening I do remember, and clearly; the lamps flickering and casting intricate shadows on the table, the strains of Schubert winding sinuously from the gramophone as a backdrop to our meal. My father often liked to listen to music as we ate, probably to render conversation less necessary.

When I had announced my plan he put down his fork and frowned, tipping his head back in thought, before saying that he was not sure I could reasonably be expected to know my own mind. I assured him that I did. He remained silent for a while longer, absently massaging his temples with the same long fingers that probed and explored his patients' suppliant flesh. 'The law is a good profession,' he said finally. 'It is not one that has ever run in our family, but I see no reason why you could not make a success of it. If you really feel that medicine is not for you, it is not for me to say.' This was the extent of his discourse. I reshaped his words in my mind, giving them a tender, approving inflection, turning them into something different from what they were — a public expression of indifference.

I had not told him of the other reason why the medical life was out of the question for me: I was privately squeamish, unable to countenance the idea of foraging gamely among blood and bone, or even of placing my hands on the skin of strangers from day to day. Touch was an unfamiliar concept in our household — I do not believe that my father ever laid a finger upon me, until the day I left for Oxford, coldly triumphant in having achieved my goal, when his hand closed around mine for a sterile moment at the train station. It did not feel like affection, but more like the passing on of something; what, I could barely tell.

★　★　★

The Spanish maid who comes to tidy my room every morning at eleven is small and nervous, with black eyes shining like olives and a tight glossy bun tied up against the nape of her neck. When she came this morning, I was still here at the desk writing, and she gave me a brief curtsy before scurrying into the bathroom. It occurred to me that there was something of Laura about her manner, and it gave me a brief pang of distress. I am not always kind to your mother, I know. As I watched the maid scrubbing frantically at the basin I vowed that when I return I will be softer, more considerate. It is a thought I have had many times before, I admit; when back at home and living with her from day to day, it somehow feels harder to stick to.

This afternoon I took a stroll around the town, drifting in and out of the shops jangling with souvenirs that line the road. It is so hot here that my eyes itch and ache with the dust that swirls up from the pavement, and I can still feel the beads of sweat trickling down my neck, collecting in my collar. I bought a little alarm clock, fashioned in bright green and yellow plastic in the shape of a seashell. My desk drawer at home is full of such knick-knacks, of no use to anyone — they are simply markers in the sand, showing where I have been. Holding it in my hand, passing over the money to a sun-blackened man with sleazy, lazy eyes, I felt peculiarly light and insubstantial. Something is changing with the writing of this diary, this story — whatever you wish to call it. I feel as if I am pushing open a door that has been sealed up for years, blinking in the sudden light which streams through the gap, not knowing what might be beyond.

I went up to Oxford in 1963. It was a strange time; the heady, burgeoning optimism that was sweeping the nation sat uneasily with me, and I clung to that accustomed austerity which had become so much ingrained that I could see no way to disentangle myself from its clutches. The new crazes that gripped many of my peers left me cold. I could find no affinity with the music they listened to, no self-knowledge or new identity in the leather jackets and slicked-back hairdos they sported. I took refuge in the history and prestige of the college in which I found myself. Walking its beautiful, sombre stone corridors after dark, with the collar of my overcoat upturned in a way that it took me two years to realise was embarrassingly affected, I could feel the heritage of the place seeping into me. My surroundings engendered an unprecedented sense of self-importance — a conviction that my presence on the earth was in some way vital. It was, perhaps, an illusion peculiar and contagious to the Oxbridge environment, for it appeared that all my peers had it too.

As you know, I have never been overly fond of people in general. Even then, my instinctive preference was to immerse myself in work, and I could spend hours in the cool tranquillity of the library, light shining softly through its high arched windows on to my textbooks as I sat reading, lost to everything else around me. And yet despite this (or perhaps because of it), I quickly became a figure of curiosity around the college; someone worthy of knowing, and of being known to. Strangers would acknowledge me with briskly confident nods as we passed by chance in the quadrangle. I was never short of someone to speak to at breakfast, should I feel so inclined. When the time came to elect members of the student body to a college committee, my name was proposed. I declined the offer, but all the same it showed me how deep the misapprehension was among my compatriots. They believed that I was a leader, and more than this — that I was suitable for responsibility, for notoriety. I suspect that these perceptions were built on little but the most superficial of foundations: my authoritarian height, my old-fashioned ways, my single-mindedness when it came to study. All the same, I learned to capitalise on their perception of me.

I began to throw the occasional social gathering in my rooms, which were some of the largest in college. Socialising was never high on my father's list of priorities. I remember one excruciating evening when, after almost three hours of inexplicable and stony silence from their host, his guests were forced to amuse themselves timidly with backgammon and draughts. At Oxford, I learnt that making people happy was easy enough. It required no more than keeping their glasses topped up, laughing at their jokes, maintaining a level of conversation that entertained, but never monopolised. What could be simpler? If this was all it took to get ahead in the world, I reasoned, then there was no reason why I should not play the game.

And so I made friends. Not with the expansive bonhomie with which, years later, I was to watch you form your bonds with others, but by something close to osmosis; a subtle invisible merging of their thoughts, habits and beliefs with my own. It created, if not intimacy, at least familiarity. I was never part of the fashionable set — seeking out instead those men who, like myself, had come from wealthy and traditional families, and who felt no need to rebel against the hand that life had dealt them. Most of these friendships fell by the wayside many years ago. The drive to maintain them was simply not strong enough to ensure otherwise. There and then, however, they felt real and essential . . . if lacking in a certain emotional verve. If I were to name one unifying factor that bound these men together as a group, it would be my own attitude to them: a mild indifference of which the seeds were comfortably sown from the very first meeting. But to every rule there is an exception, and Roman Levitsky was mine.

For the first time since I began to write I am at a loss as to how to continue. To form the letters of his name in concrete print feels strange and foreign, almost eerie after all these years. I find myself halting, reading them over until they bounce back, nothing but empty echoes, devoid of meaning. This is not only my story. I am also a biographer, and there are some people who are more difficult to catalogue than others . . . some who defy categorisation. The facts, however, are easy enough to set down. Roman was of Polish descent, and came from a wealthy family. His parents had settled in London several years before his birth. A brilliant scholar, he excelled at school, gained his place at Oxford and came up to study law alongside me.

I first saw him in the college common room, sitting on the windowsill and smoking a cigarette, chatting to some pale companion. He stood out in a room, largely because of his striking appearance; he dressed in expensive, impractical clothes that seemed to belong to some long-bygone age. I remember that he wore a thin silk waistcoat that day, patterned with green and purple peacock feathers. His long slim hands made sweeping gesticulations in the air as he talked, but the way his narrowed, almond-shaped eyes flicked from side to side betrayed that his mind was not entirely on the conversation. I disliked him on sight. I remember vividly the harsh, visceral shiver that passed through me, an animal's hackles rising. It was something I had never experienced before, and only once since.

In the months that followed, as Roman and I grew closer, I reflected on how strange it was that such a powerful gut instinct had been mistaken. Now I know better. The body knows when it senses danger, and at that moment I believe that mine picked up on a faint warning that my conscious mind could not: a knowledge that any association with this man would end in pain, even disaster. Of course, I had been bred to trust logic above intuition. And so when his eyes alighted on me where I stood framed in the doorway and he gave a slight, imperious jerk of his head to summon me over and into the conversation, there seemed no logical reason why I should not walk towards him.

Tuesday, 29 June

I slept badly last night. There is evening entertainment here — a troupe of cabaret 'artists' with slicked-back hair and virulent mustard-coloured waistcoats. They belt out classics with little regard for tune, and dance as if electric shocks are being pumped through them. This I know because I looked down from my balcony at half past eleven and saw them still there, gyrating and twisting by the pool as they sang, spotlights pouring down upon their heads and casting them in desolate illumination. Slumped against the sunloungers in the shadows, a huddle of holidaymakers were watching with rapt, drunken fascination.

It was well past midnight when the troupe wound their performance to a close, and for long afterwards, muffled shouts and splashing floated up from the pool to where I lay. Later, much later, came the sounds of the mousy-looking girl next door returning. She was not alone. Low chatting, stifled laughter, and then the dull rhythmic thudding of the headboard, threatening to split the paper-thin wall between us. Usually I am adept at tuning out from my surroundings, but last night it was impossible. All my energy was focused inwards, keeping thoughts at bay. In the solitary dark of my rented bedroom, they felt dangerous. I lay there trembling, whispering to myself, my hands grasping the sheet. Even in that state, a cold, small part of me knew that if anyone were to see me they would think that I looked ridiculous. It was all that stopped me from screaming out loud.

Now that I am sitting out on the balcony in relative peace, sunlight streaming down and the pool deserted below, such hysterics seem contemptible. I am able to return to the story I have to tell, and to my friendship with Roman. I remember clearly the first words he said to me, sitting there with his head cocked to one side, smoke drifting exotically from his cigarette, appraising me. 'I've seen you in lectures, I believe,' he said. 'You seem like a man who knows what's what. Now, wouldn't you agree that Beethoven is far superior to Bach?'

Classical music was a subject with which I was reasonably familiar, owing to my father's own passion for much of the canon, and I made a suitably measured answer, weighted just enough to show that in fact I agreed with his analysis. I was soon to find out that Roman's own knowledge of music was minimal. He simply enjoyed debate, and would often take up an opposing position to his companion on almost any given matter for the sake of perpetuating an argument, regardless of what he really believed. He listened intently to my reply, then nodded and shot the man with whom he had originally been chatting a look of chastisement and glee. 'You see, Carter?' he said, with the tone of one who has laid a debate to rest for ever. 'This gentleman agrees. I'm afraid I don't know your name.' With these last words he swung back to me, viper-like. For the first time his eyes met mine directly. I noticed that they were an unusual shade of pale green, and hard like diamonds. I told him my name. 'Levitsky,' he said in turn. 'Roman Levitsky. Have you lunched yet?'

Despite my instinctive recoil from the man, a streak of perversity and a lack of any other plans told me to accept his offer of lunch. We went out to a little restaurant a mile from college, the sort of place that advertises its expense so discreetly that it could almost be overlooked, but for the bill at the end of the meal. The patron seemed to know Roman, and fussed around him like a maiden aunt as he showed us to a table. When he noticed me, he asked whether we were brothers. I covered my embarrassment with a laugh, and yet the question shifted something in my mind, pushed me to consider Roman as something more than a stranger. We were of similar height and build, and his hair was as fair as my own.

'Don't mind him,' Roman said when our orders had been taken. 'He says that to all the men I lunch here with.' He accompanied this with a brittle smile to show that he was joking, but I caught what I thought was an implied snub, a warning not to think that I was special. My dislike intensified, and continued to do so throughout the meal. The impression I gained of him was one of controlled flamboyance. He was given to extravagant gestures and haughty expressions, but there was something in his manner that told me there was nothing spontaneous about any of them. His face could snap from shocked disdain to thoughtful dreaminess and back again in a matter of moments. He could click his fingers to summon a waiter with the imperious haste of a lord summoning a faceless courtier, then bestow a radiant smile on him that spoke of affection and even deference. *The man is insincere*, I thought as I thanked him politely for lunch and we parted at the college gates. *An amusing talker, but little else.* I watched his tall back recede across the quadrangle, his coat-tails flapping out behind him like dark flames.

That night I sought out the company of two friends — quiet, pleasant men from a similar background with whom I had spent several amiable evenings in my rooms, drinking and playing cards. There was nothing noticeably different about the scenario that unfolded over the next few hours, but I found myself bored and restless. The wine tasted sour, and my companions seemed colourless and two-dimensional, like pencil sketches. I found it hard to concentrate on their talk. When they left I went directly to bed, but I could not sleep, my mind working tirelessly, rubbing away at random long-forgotten memories until my body tingled with exhaustion. The next day I found myself lingering after lectures, and when Roman came walking towards me, smiling, it seemed only natural that I should shake him by the hand in greeting, and follow him out of the hall.

★ ★ ★

It is difficult to pinpoint the moment at which a friendship takes root, when it transforms from a pleasurable diversion into something that feels vital and permanent. Roman and I became close with deceptive speed. Despite our differences of character, we shared that sense of dislocation — the feeling of belonging to some fast-disappearing age

186

— that bound us together more effectively than a shared background or a liking for rock music could have done. Roman had no interest in following a crowd, or in aligning himself with any tribe, and I liked this in him. Within a few weeks we had settled into a routine of breakfasting together in the college dining room before walking to lectures, having lunch afterwards at a venue usually of his choosing, and separating to study for a few hours before meeting again in the evening. I quickly learnt the power of being one of two — the invincibility that such a friendship gives. If I had been respected before, I was doubly so with Roman by my side. We were, if not universally liked, then known, and given our due by our peers. With flattering heartlessness, Roman had dropped Carter, who I understood had previously been his comrade of choice. As for my other friends, I had no wish to be cruel, but I found myself growing distant from them. It was not that I had grown to dislike them; more that in their presence I felt somehow less myself, like a spectre that casts no shadow.

I have never considered myself to be the sort of person who is unduly influenced by others, but it is true to say that in Roman's company I discovered a side of myself that I had been unaware of before. He was not shallow, as I had at first thought, but there was something playful and capricious in his manner — an unwillingness to be dampened down by the more serious sides of life. I found myself enjoying this, and in turn I began to cast off some of the shackles that had dogged me, it sometimes seemed, since birth. I remember one sunny afternoon, the two of us rowing together on the river, when on impulse Roman drove the oar hard towards the boat, sending a glittering shower of cold water over us both, soaking my shirt and his. My instinctive reaction was to chastise him in disgust for such a pointless act, but as I looked at him, and saw the way that he was laughing, wringing out his shirt and alive with energy and delight, I found myself laughing too. It was a moment of release — one that I cherished — and in the months to come I became more and more sensible of the power he had to unlock this capability in me; a capability, perhaps, for nothing more noble than fun, but nevertheless one that I have been unable to recapture in later life, and probably never shall now.

To list a person's good qualities seems trite and simplistic, but I will say, too, that Roman was characterised by his generosity. The lunch he had paid for on our first day together was merely the tip of the iceberg

— he would often come back from town with something for me, be it a new textbook, a scarf or a bottle of wine. Once, in his rooms, I protested against these gifts. I had a nasty, niggling suspicion that my friendship was being bought, a strategy that would be not only unnecessary but verging on offensive. I can see now his look of hurt surprise as he wheeled round from the window, hands reaching out suppliantly, green eyes wide and uncomprehending. 'So you don't like them?' he asked, referring, I believe, to the gloves that had been his latest purchase. 'Then there's an end to it,' he said upon my inevitable demurral. 'My parents have a great deal of money, too much for me to waste on myself. I like buying things for other people. For *you*.'

I remember another evening, halfway through our second year. We had attended a cocktail party, and rolled back to college in the early hours. Roman was very drunk, as indeed he often was in those days. From time to time I wondered whether his fondness for alcohol extended beyond the usual student predilections, but any attempt at concern would result in a sharp request for me to mind my own business. That night he had drunk an inordinate quantity of cheap vodka, and spent a good five minutes fumbling with the lock before stumbling headlong into his room and throwing himself down upon the bed. One hand placed palm down on his forehead, the other flung out across the covers, he was a picture of desolation. Roman was not always a happy drunk, having a tendency to descend into maudlin depression after some incalculable but generally inevitable tipping point. I remember that as he lay there, he reached out and feebly turned on the gramophone, flipping a disc on and weakly manoeuvring the needle into position. The notes of something filled the room, but try as I can I cannot recall the music, only the feeling that it gave; a strained, bleak melancholy that seeped through the air.

I asked him whether he wanted a glass of water, fetching him one before he had the chance to reply. I sat watching him sip, struggling to a semi-prone position on the bed, his elbow shakily propping him up. His hair, normally perfectly and smoothly coiffed in a way I had almost unconsciously grown to imitate, was ruffled and tangled, sticking up in random angles across his scalp. His tie — a gorgeous affair as usual, crimson silk shot through with golden threads — was loosened around his collar. He was struggling to focus on me, his eyes slipping on to and away from mine.

'Pretty girl you were talking to earlier,' he said at last. He meant Helen, a third-year student from St Hilda's College, who had been paying me a few attentions at the cocktail party. Before I left, we had arranged to meet the next week for drinks. She had indeed been pretty, but at Roman's words I found myself struggling to recall her face. Dark brown hair, I thought, and a pert, mischievous look; heavy, flicked-out eyeliner and a bright purple miniskirt after the fashion of the day. In truth, I had agreed to the drink more out of a vague sense of duty than anything else. Romance was not high on my list of priorities in those days. I always intended to marry, of course, but I saw no need to hasten the process. I made some non-committal noise of agreement, but it seemed that Roman did not want to leave the subject alone. 'I'm not sure you should meet her again, mind,' he said, pointing a shaking finger at me in a manner that seemed to accuse. I asked him why not. He did not at first respond, but instead slumped back against the headboard, closing his eyes. I remember the way that the light from the bedside lamp danced across his eyelashes as they quivered. They were dark blond, and curled like a woman's.

'I can't always be telling you things,' he said flatly. 'There are some things you have to work out for yourself, Harvey.'

The use of my first name jolted me; we were still in the fad of using surnames, along with the rest of college. I opened my mouth to ask him to explain, but something stopped me; some nebulous sense that to do so would be to bring more trouble than was necessary upon myself. Besides, Roman's eyes had closed again, and his head was lolling to one side. Quietly I rose to my feet and left him there, letting myself out. As I crossed the dark quadrangle to my own rooms, the air was so cold that I felt my bones rattling under my overcoat, jumping and jolting like sparks under the skin.

I mention these things simply to show that I was a fool. Looking back on them now, it is easy enough to see that they were warning flags, popping up stark and scarlet against the relatively calm backdrop of our friendship. It was not that at the time I had no conception of this at all; worse, I chose to ignore it. I have always been good at blinding myself to the obvious . . . although to tell you that feels redundant, like pointing out that the sun rises in the east. No one knew my weaknesses better than you.

★   ★   ★

As our third year drew to a close, shortly before our final examinations, Roman disappeared. At first I assumed that he was merely exerting some discipline and shutting himself away to study, something which he did all too little of in general. By the third day, however, I was starting to worry. I passed by his rooms two or three times a day to knock, but was always met with silence. I was spending my own days largely in the library, concentrating on my texts but keeping one watchful eye on the door. He never came. On the fourth day I went to the college porter and explained that Levitsky had not been seen for some time and that I was a little concerned. The porter came with me to his rooms, bringing the spare key. We stood and knocked for what felt like hours before he deigned to unlock the door. The room was empty and dark. On the bed, books lay scattered and opened; as I went closer, I saw Roman's jagged writing scribbled in their margins — brief cryptic notations. For some reason, the sight of that writing gave me a pang of fear. The room smelt faintly of nicotine, mildew and little else, as if it not been inhabited for some time.

I saw that the porter did not know what to say, turning from side to side as if at any moment the errant Levitsky might pop out from behind the curtains or inside the wardrobe. Curtly, I thanked him, ushering him out and saying that it was probable that Roman had gone to visit his parents. Privately I believed this was impossible. I knew that money flowed more freely than love in his family, and the concept of Roman choosing to spend these last few precious days at college with them was unlikely in the extreme. At any rate it was not a hypothesis I could test. I had never been given his parents' address.

I spent the next two days in a state of high agitation. The examinations were fast approaching, and I had a multitude of revisions still to do, but whenever I sat down at my desk or at the window-seat in the library, my texts might as well have been written in ancient Greek for all the sense they made to me. I could feel my hands shaking as I turned the pages, tightness in my throat making it hard to breathe. I had never suffered from any kind of nervous complaint, but in those days I had a queasy, unpleasant sense of what it would be like to be so at the mercy of one's emotions. It took all the force of my will to push my fears to one side and get some modicum of work done, but I managed it, and in the midst of my angst I felt triumphant. I had not studied for years to fall at the final hurdle. I could see my future unfurling in front of me like bright silk; a suitable London practice, a rising through the ranks, a respected position and a salary to match. No one had the right to take these things away from me, and I began to feel angry with Roman. Wherever he was, he must know that I would worry. This kind of emotional sabotage was unforgivable.

The night before the first examination I was sitting up in my room, looking out across the quadrangle at the sweep of windows opposite, some darkened, some lit and popping out from the night like burning beacons. I knew Roman's window, of course; it had stayed obstinately secretive and dark for over a week. It had become a habit to watch it, but all the same, when the light came on I could barely believe it. I counted the windows again — four along, three rows up. I had not been mistaken. A faint reddish glow was shining out from the glass. The bedside lamp, I thought, the one with the crimson shade. Before I knew it I was on my feet, starting from my seat. I ran down the staircase, on to the quadrangle. I tried to calm myself, to walk like an adult, but my body would not listen, and I found myself running faster than before, clattering up his staircase, my breath coming in short gasps, hammering on his door. I counted five long seconds before it swung open. Roman was standing there, his hand still on the door handle. He looked exhausted, his face drained of colour, somehow thinner, shadows hollowing out his cheekbones. But he was smiling faintly, as if through pain, a soldier returned from the war. Before he could speak I fell upon him and embraced him. I felt his heartbeat thud against mine, and in that moment I realised that it was the closest we had ever been; more than this, the closest I had ever been to anyone, man or woman. Slowly, I drew back. He was looking at me intently, his pale green eyes boring into my own in a way that shook and disturbed me.

'I'm sorry I disappeared,' he said, and even his voice sounded different, older. 'These examinations are troubling me.'

At his words, I felt something of my anger flooding back. As I stood there opposite him, having seen and felt the incontrovertible evidence of his being alive rather than dead and broken in a ditch somewhere as my fevered imagination had feared, all my worry seemed futile. A waste of time. We were all troubled by examinations; it was natural, no reason to up and abandon life on a whim. 'Is that all?' I snapped.

My anger was contagious — I saw his chin lift and his eyes grow rapidly cold. For a moment he looked at me as if he hated me.

'No,' he said, almost shouted, 'no, that's not all,' and before I knew it, he was reaching out for me and pulling me against him, his breath hot on my skin, and his hands were moving my face against his own and changing something for ever, leaving me with no choice.

Wednesday, 30 June

A bad night again last night. I rose in the early hours and let myself out into the poolside gardens. Dawn was just breaking, and as I walked I could smell the sweet scents of jasmine and mimosa, mingling with the sharp salty air that blew in from the coast. In the half-light and the silence, for a few moments the resort looked oddly beautiful and serene. It took the dampness of the dew on the grass soaking through my skin to make me realise that I had come out barefoot. Turning back towards my room, I felt an intense emptiness. Thoughts of that night in Oxford, and the weeks that followed, have been laid to rest for so long that to awaken them again only throws the here and now into stark relief. What is left to me sometimes feels like nothing more than an imitation of life — like nothing at all.

I remember little of the week of my examinations. I pulled away from Roman and left that night without a word, ignoring his cries for me to stop and talk. The feelings that pulsed through me were too strong to dissect or explain. As I crossed the quadrangle again, back to my own sanctum, I felt a sudden and unstoppable revulsion for myself, of such violence that it almost blinded me. It made me stupid, unable to think. Unlocking the door, and locking it again behind me, my fingers were stiff with shame. I lay staring at the ceiling, unblinking.

I moved through the week with grim determination. Every morning I rose at eight and dressed in my suit and gown, averting my eyes from the mirror. I remember nothing else, except sitting in the draughty examination hall, staring at the question paper — a scene that played itself out six times, the feeling of déjà vu growing greater every day. I wrote. I wrote. Even as I did so, I knew that I was doing well. My knowledge flowed out on autopilot, unable to be stopped. Only once did my pen press so hard against the paper that it tore the surface, sending black ink pooling across the page. I crumpled the sheet in my hand and set it aside, reached for another, began to write once more.

On the day of the last examination, when I

had marked the final full stop on my paper, I allowed myself to look across the hall. I saw him there, diagonally across from me, towards the front of the bank of desks to my right. His blond head was bent low over the page, unmoving. I wanted to look away, but something froze me there. I must have spent ten minutes staring at that bright blond speck, thinking of nothing, or nothing that I could have formed into conscious words. Five minutes before the final bell rang out, I saw him stand, throw his paper down on to the desk and turn. He walked from the hall, down the aisle that split our two banks of desks. I saw his face as he approached. He looked haunted, ill. As he drew closer I looked back down at my paper, staring so hard at the letters I had printed that my eyes began to ache and water with the strain of keeping my gaze trained there. When I raised my head again he had passed by, and the aisle was empty.

I went out that night and got recklessly drunk, in the company of a group of fellow lawyers with whom I had once been friendly. Their uncomplicated chatter freed my mind for a few hours, and I bought champagne, pouring it down my throat with such abandon that by eleven I could barely see my own hand in front of my face. Now and then,

I caught snatches of conversation, standing out from the blackness, not meant for me to hear. *What's happened to Levitsky?* I heard one man whisper. *Have he and Blackwood fallen out?* I cannot recall, or do not choose to, the other's reply. I reeled through the next few hours, lurching from public house to members' club; more champagne, the heat and light of fireside tables, mindless banter. Then a back-street entrance, a little room with darkly patterned walls, purple spotlights, girls dancing and languorously peeling off clothes; feeling nothing, feeling nothing. My companions' faces bright and hungry. The smell of sweat. I stumbled back through lamplit streets at 3 a.m. alone, finding the college by instinct, surprised when the entrance loomed giddily above me. My eyes were brimming with unfamiliar tears. I turned left instead of right, floated up the staircase, hammered on the door. When he opened it his face was full of something I did not want to understand. I did not want to, but I could not help it. *Harvey, I've missed you, I've missed you.* And then just the two of us. The cover of darkness, and the rising heat of the air. Nothing else.

The next morning I rose before he woke, packed my things and caught the first train back to my father's house in London. I said goodbye to nobody.

★   ★   ★

Returning to the Kensington house after so long felt strange and regressive; I had spent the majority of my vacations in Oxford, reasoning that if my father wanted to see me, he would ask. When I arrived unexpectedly that day, he welcomed me with a cold handshake and asked me how the examinations had gone. I told him they had been satisfactory. He nodded and returned to his paper. I picked up a paper myself, settled myself in the armchair opposite him and read. Later we had a dinner of cold meats and mashed potatoes, served in the sterile depression of the dining room, which seemed to have changed not a jot since I had been away. The next day, things unfolded much the same, and the next after that. I planned to look for a job when the summer ended. Until then, I wanted nothing more than this dull familiarity. I felt the bleakness of my surroundings wrapping itself around me like insulation, felt my heart hardening.

It was, I think, on the sixth day that our maid came to the drawing room and told me that I had a visitor. My father raised his head in polite enquiry, no doubt wondering who could possibly want to be visiting me. I knew at once, of course, but I remained in the chair, listening with studied indifference. My father must see nothing in my face, if there was anything to see. A gentleman from Oxford, the maid told us, a gentleman who did not wish to give his name. I excused myself and went to the front door. Roman was waiting on the step, dressed in a pearl-grey suit and a white silk shirt loosened at the collar, giving him the look of a dandy or a cosmopolitan playboy. His face did not seem to know whether to scowl or smile. He was awkwardly holding a parcel, tied up in brown paper and string.

I was conscious of the maid still hovering behind me, and turned to her. 'It's all right, Mary,' I said. 'I know this gentleman. We'll take a walk in the park, I think.' I had no wish to walk with Roman, but nor did I want to cause any upheaval, and every fibre in my being wanted him away from my father's house. We walked to the park in silence, barely glancing at each other. As we went, I found myself looking at the open, uncomplicated faces of the people that milled around us. I had never wished to be anything other than myself; now I would happily have changed places with any one of them. When we reached the park I chose a spot underneath the trees, shaded and hidden from view. I remember that it was a warm day, the light summer breeze stirring the grass where we sat. I wanted to take off my jacket, but something stopped me; an instinct that formality was what was needed here, the only thing that would get me through the next few minutes. Roman removed his, rolling up his shirtsleeves. His forearms were studded with strong fair hairs that gleamed in the sun.

'I had a speech prepared,' he said at last, 'but it seems rather futile now. I hope you aren't too angry at my coming here. I had to see you.' He shot me a cautious look from under hooded eyelids. I kept my face impassive. 'This is difficult for both of us,' he continued, and for an instant a note of petulance crept into his voice. 'I hope that at least we can talk honestly.' I was silent, and he sighed. 'The honesty will begin with me, then,' he said. 'Harvey, what has happened between us is not what I would have chosen for myself, but I cannot ignore it. I am aware that the nature of our relationship is not something that is yet legalised in British society, for all this talk of freedom' — and how well I remember the faint world-weary scorn with which he spoke those words — 'but that is the way of things. All I can say is that I believe our feelings are the same.'

Still I found myself unable to speak. My mind was closing down, shutting out the conversation, these unthinkable words. I felt almost peripheral to the situation, like a figure passing through a dream sequence. I stared out across the park, gazing at the lush foliage that wound its way alongside the path.

Roman moved closer in, stretching his hand out to cover mine. I snatched it away as if he had branded me, glancing around instinctively to make sure that no one had seen. He saw the glance, and expelled a fierce angry breath, throwing his head back for an instant. 'Enough of this,' he said, his voice quiet and controlled, but with an intensity that cut to the heart of me. 'I want us to go away together. We can live somewhere, out of the public eye. Perhaps it won't be what we had planned, but we will be together, and that's what I want. You want it too, I know that. Take a risk for once in your life, Harvey, and come away with me.'

'You are mistaken. And you will never get what you want,' I said. I hesitated only for an instant before I spoke, but that instant was enough to plague me for years after; enough to threaten to topple the whole rotten edifice around me. For the first time, I looked at him straight on. I took in what there was to see, and I remembered it; the beautiful, moulded cheekbones, those pale eyes like emeralds in the pallor of his face, the curve of his parted lips. Thoughts raged inside me, but I kept them there. I knew that he saw nothing of them.

Sure enough, I saw hurt and bitterness swim across his face. 'You know,' he said, 'it's amazing how closely your love resembles contempt.'

'It is contempt,' I said. The words came more easily this time, and I did not have to turn away.

He half smiled for an instant. 'In that case,' he said, 'it's amazing how closely your contempt resembles love.'

Roman had an instinct for an exit line, but at that moment neither of us knew just how final an exit it was to be. I watched him rise to his feet and walk away across the park, his tall back ramrod straight and yet somehow defenceless, heartbreakingly vulnerable. It was some time before I saw the brown paper package lying next to me on the grass. I took it in my hand. Slowly, I untied the knots in the string, ran my finger underneath the seal. Inside I caught a flash of bright material — apple green shot through with silver. It was a necktie, beautiful supple silk, flowing over my hand like a caress. As I held it, regret shifted painfully inside me. I was struck with a horrible realisation, so stark that it physically hurt me in my chest — the knowledge that I had acted too rashly, that I was denying something so deep within myself that I was not sure I could ever dig it out of me, that if I let him walk away I would never be happy. I watched his back, still receding in the distance. *He will turn around, I thought, and when he does, I will go to him.* I kept my gaze there, until I was no longer sure which of the bobbing specks on the horizon I was watching.

★ ★ ★

Three months later I sat in a café with a pot of tea, opened the morning paper and saw his face staring up at me. The photograph was one that I had taken with his own camera — a close-up shot down by the Isis, towards the end of our second year. Roman was wearing an open-necked shirt, his head turned towards the camera, laughing, his hair caught by the wind. Below the photograph, black printed letters shouted out their story. OXFORD GRADUATE FOUND DEAD.

The shock of it was such that I could not at once make sense of the words. A shiver passed coldly down my spine; I blinked to clear my vision. A short printed paragraph ran beneath the headline. *The body of Roman Levitsky, 22, was found last night at his parental home. Mr Levitsky, a recent Law graduate from St John's College, Oxford University, is thought to have suffered from depression, and had been disappointed in the recent results of his examinations, in which he gained a lower second-class degree. A provisional verdict of suicide has been recorded.* I read the paragraph over, twice, three times. I thought, *It doesn't even say how he died.*

I sat there until the tea had cooled in the pot and customers around me had come and gone. I found that I was shaking, not from cold, but from something internal that I could not still. I raised my head and looked around the café, then back down at Roman's photograph. For a crazy instant, I wanted to pick up the paper and show it to the strangers around me. You see this man? We could have been happy together. I loved him. I loved him.

I read the paragraph again, and shamefully I felt a swift shard of relief pierce the fog. There was no mention of me — no mention that his death might have been caused by anything more than a pitiable overreaction to a poor examination result. Instinctively I knew better. In the intervening months there had been two letters; the first hopeful and passionate, the second desolate and bleak. I had replied to neither. I had known that he needed me, and I had done nothing. And with the knowledge my relief dissolved again, and left something so dark and powerful in its place that I had to screw my eyes shut tight. When I opened them again, nothing had changed. Slowly, I stood up, still holding the paper in my two hands. I folded it in half and placed it in my briefcase, but it made no difference. The picture and the writing beneath still swam before my eyes, so vividly that I could not banish them. I left the café, and when I stepped out on to the street and saw all of life passing by, untouched by tragedy, I felt my heart tighten with such grief that I genuinely thought for a moment that it would kill me.

How strange to tell these secrets to you, in death as I could never have done in life; these things which could have explained so much, and which are so useless now.

* * *

I am not superstitious by nature, but I always believed that tragedy came in threes. My mother's death had not been much mourned by me, but nonetheless I felt its significance; the sudden void where a role model and protector should be. Her end had come sooner than any of us had foreseen, but all the same, one expects one's parents to die before oneself — it is in the natural order of things. It was only after Roman's suicide that I began to realise that tragedy is unpredictable. It can strike at any time, upon anyone, with devastating, random violence.

In the years that followed, I often thought of the two deaths as gleaming, sinister pillars in parallel, silently awaiting a third to form the topmost point of the triangle. I expected the pain, when it came, to be lesser. I believed Roman had bled all the emotion out of me that I had to give; that I would never feel as much again. After you were born, I began to see that I was wrong, and it gave me a strange, nebulous sense of unease. As if by tempting my own fate I had somehow written yours in the stars. As if in the act of creating someone I could love, I had cursed them too.

Thursday, 1 July

After I had finished writing last night, I went to dine in the restaurant here. I felt the need to be surrounded by people, even if I did not speak a word to anyone. I ate an indifferent meal: some kind of bowdlerised paella, large rubbery prawns and tendrils of squid with hard bullets of rice in a luminous orange sauce. All around me, families chattered and squawked. Occasionally I felt their eyes on me, as is wont to happen in these places — wondering who I was and why I have come here, when I am so plainly out of place. I ate in silence, listening to the rise and fall of their conversation, the badly played guitar of a musician serenading a group of giggling girls at the table next to mine. I thought of Roman, and strangely the pain came as something of a relief. It is a change, at least, from the dull ache of loss that I have felt ever since your death — somehow sharper and cleaner, without the insulation of delayed shock and denial that haunt me still whenever I think of you. After my meal I sat out by the pool for what felt like hours, watching shadows swim across its turquoise surface, remembering him.

I am not stupid, or at least I have some self-knowledge, and I know that the tragedy of his death has sanctified him in my mind. If he were alive today, he might well be bloated and dissolute, his former charm hardened into arrogance. As it is, he is trapped there; twenty-two and beautiful, still possessed of the same magnetic and compelling presence, and my own feelings have been trapped too, unable to develop or fade. At the darkest times, I have wondered whether this was somehow what he had intended. To punish me. To show me how wrong I had been in turning him away. Of course, these thoughts are ridiculous. One does not give up one's life to make another person sorry. And yet still, from time to time, they persist.

I spent the years that followed building the life that I had chosen. I had got the first that Roman had deserved, and with it I gained myself entry to a large and respected firm of solicitors in the City. I found myself accepted there. The atmosphere of calm austerity that pervaded the offices was one with which I felt at home, and my colleagues were mostly dull, serious men not given to flights of fancy. I let my work consume me. To my colleagues it appeared as if I had a passion for the job, and I suppose that in a way their assumptions were correct. Poring over cases at my desk, or meeting with clients in ancient oak-panelled rooms, I felt safe. There was nothing for me to fear within the office walls. I began to feel a sense of achievement in the quick progress that I made, and if something within me knew that I was confusing success with happiness, I did not care.

Eighteen months later, I had saved enough to move out of my father's house and into a small place of my own in

Islington. My father travelled to the new place with me and took me out for a joyless dinner, then left me on Upper Street with a handshake and a promise to be in touch soon. When, within a year or two, our contact dwindled to birthday and Christmas cards, I was neither surprised nor grieved. I could not rid myself of his influence; I felt that he was embedded under my skin, like a splinter constantly evading the surface. To see him was unnecessary. In any case, I had been unable to enter the Kensington house without remembering Roman hovering hopefully on the doorstep, an inconvenient image that would flash upon me without warning whenever I crossed the threshold. I had no wish to go back there.

In the summer of 1967, a bill legalising homosexuality passed through its final stages in the House of Commons. It was impossible to hear the news without thinking of Roman and of what his reaction would have been; impossible to see the unbridled celebrations in some of London's less salubrious haunts without experiencing a pang of some sick irony. The law could do nothing to change what had passed between myself and Roman, and it could do nothing to change my own feelings. The sense of shame I felt when I

212

considered the past was enough for me to turn my back on what the future could have brought. I forced these thoughts down.

★   ★   ★

Some three years after I had joined the firm, one of the elder solicitors invited me out to lunch. His name was Charles Mason — a bluff, robust-looking gentleman with bristling whiskers and reddened cheeks. We had always been on cordial terms, but there was nothing social in our association; we talked of our work and little else. When the invitation came, I scarcely knew what to say. Seeing my indecision, Mason explained. His daughter was in town, and he had promised to show her something of London. She had just turned nineteen. 'I have no idea of the sorts of things that young people might like to see,' I remember him saying, as he fiddled with the chain of his glasses, suddenly displaying an agreeable ineptitude that clashed with the measured professionalism he was wont to display at all times. 'I thought perhaps at least you might be able to recommend some sights to her, and suggest a place where we could find a bite to eat. That is, if you're not too busy?'

I was busy, of course, but also flattered. I

scarcely thought of myself as young, despite the fact that I was not yet twenty-five; life had already aged me beyond my years. The thought of being selected as a suitable guide for a young girl touched me somehow in a way I could not explain. I agreed to the lunch, and so we set out the next day for Constable's, an expensive but affable brasserie near by.

Mason's daughter was late, and we had already smoked two cigars and worked our way through half a bottle of claret before she was shown to the table. I had expected a buxom milkmaid of a girl with her father's complexion, but I was struck at once by her fragility — ash-coloured hair piled against a long slender neck, spindly mascaraed eye-lashes, bare narrow shoulders, a slight, boyish frame under a short shift dress. When I rose to greet her, after a moment's hesitation she stretched out her hand, and a jewelled bracelet slid down her arm, resting against a wrist-bone I could have encircled with a finger. She told me that her name was Laura, and her voice was soft and hesitant, as if she had only just learned the power of speech. When we sat down, I saw that Mason was watching us through bright attentive eyes, rubbing his hands together, and a flash of insight came to me that he thought I might be a suitable match. When the realisation dawned I almost laughed, but somehow it did not offend or aggravate me in the way that it had done in similar situations in the past. I could not tell what was different. I knew only that as I began to make polite conversation, slipping easily and automatically into the role that was expected of me, there was something about this girl that drew me.

Laura ate little and talked less, but when she did it was to a purpose. I found her intelligent and incisive, surprisingly so in a girl her age. Over coffee, she accepted a cigarette, and I watched her slim fingers fumble with the lighter, blue veins standing out translucently beneath the skin of her hands. I reached across and lit the cigarette for her, and she smiled her thanks. She was innocent, demonstrably so. I could see it in the way she looked at me as I flicked the lighter, the lack of pretence in her gaze. And yet there was something beneath the surface that told me she was no fool, and that she understood the games played between man and woman. The contrast intrigued me.

As we left the restaurant, she hesitated at the doorway. 'You've been very kind, Mr Blackwood,' she said, and then, so quietly that I could barely catch the words, 'I hope you were not here on sufferance.' Before I had a chance to reply, she turned to her father and embraced him. 'Thank you for lunch, Daddy,' she said. 'Mr Blackwood has given me plenty of ideas to help me occupy myself during my stay. I think I will go to the Tower tomorrow.'

Mason nodded feverishly, like a man possessed, shooting me a look of such blatant enquiry that I felt embarrassed for him. I turned back to Laura. By her sides, her tiny hands had clenched into fists, and the colour had crept up into her cheeks, staining the porcelain skin. 'If you would like a companion,' I began, 'I'd be glad to take you to the Tower. If you were to come to our offices, I could finish at half past four.' She glanced up at me, seeming barely able to meet my gaze for more than a second at a time, and almost imperceptibly, she nodded.

'Oh-ho, you are honoured,' Mason burst out, clasping his hands together in glee. 'We hardly ever see Harvey leave his desk before seven. I hope you are sensible of the compliment, my dear.' He carried on much in this vein for some time, seemingly oblivious to his daughter's mortification. When we finally took our leave from her, I could feel the tension in her hand, as if all the sinews were straining against the skin. I did not know then, although she was to tell me months after, that she had already decided,

with the quiet determination that characterised her, that I was to be the one. She was an
unlikely type of woman to fall in love at first
sight, and I an unlikely recipient of her love,
but there is little rhyme or reason to these
things. *I knew I loved you, Harvey,* she would
say to me, *long before I told you, and I
prayed that you would love me too.
Sometimes, praying for a thing that much can
make it happen, can't it? What further proof
do you need?* I was not sure that I believed in
the power of prayer, but I told her that I
agreed.

When we met the next day she had made
her face up with care, and she was dressed in
a long purple coat and dress, wearing golden
jewellery. She looked like a queen in waiting,
and at the Tower, as we stood in front of the
crown jewels, I joked that she would soon
have them for her own. Her face was rapt and
dreamlike, reflected in the smooth glass screen
that housed the gems. I watched her eyes rove
over the clusters of rubies and sapphires, and
I realised that she was someone who loved
beautiful things, who felt instinctively that she
had a right to them. That much I would be
able to give her. I pretended to be as absorbed
as she was, but in reality my eyes were on that
shadowy reflection in the glass. It softened her
features, made them mysterious and alluring.

She was attractive, quietly so, in a way that did not at first strike you, but rather crept in under the skin.

Outside, as dusk was falling and the lamps lit up, casting the streets in a soft romantic glow, we walked towards the river. We strolled along the bank in silence, barely knowing where we were going. At last, I took Laura's hand and drew her against me. Her body felt cold and insubstantial, as if she were made of glass. As I looked down at her sharply drawn face, the hints of fear and desire that I saw there gave me a pang of something undiscovered in my heart; a need to protect, to guard against harm. I put my fingers underneath her chin and tilted her head, as suppliant as a reed, up to mine. I kissed her, and felt the coldness of her lips against my own. It was only a matter of seconds before she pulled back, blinking as if startled.

'Harvey,' she said. 'I must tell you — I'm not sure if you know this already, but I am a Catholic. I don't . . . I mean, before I am married, I . . . I can't . . . ' She spoke as if she were forcing the words out one by one, and soon trailed off, staring down at her feet. I sensed the effort that had gone into the half-finished speech before I truly appreciated what it meant. I looked at the small gold cross glinting around her neck. My mind felt slow and stupid, fumbling for comprehension. When it dawned, the swift stab of relief came before I could halt it. I took her hands in mine and told her it did not matter, and the thankful liberation that flooded her eyes made my heart stop for an instant. If there was ever a moment when I might have doubted my course of action, when I might have stopped and asked myself whether I could love her in the way she needed to be loved, it was then. Asking the question was futile, however. I could not answer myself then, and am not sure that I can now.

★ ★ ★

Our wedding day shines out in my memory like a star amid the fog of the years around it — Laura, on the cusp of twenty-two, myself just turned twenty-seven. A beautiful day, sunlight pouring over us like molten honey as we left the church, confetti thrown by the guests clustered around us and raining down in pink and white petals. Her dress, spun from lace as light and intricate as a spider's web, spinning out whenever she turned, then settling back against her fine narrow bones. Myself in starched morning dress, buttoned up to the neck. The feeling of warmth — of nothing less than love — spilling out from everyone around us, colouring everything it touched.

I had feared the day before it came. The night before, I had stayed up until dawn, watching the sun break over the city, my nerves alert and buzzing, filled with an indistinct foreboding. In the pure bright light surrounding us, these fears seemed childish and empty. The day passed in flashes, each one a vignette of memory in the making. My father shaking me by the hand with more affection than I could ever recall him doing so before, something in his eyes I could not interpret. The knife coming down and slicing through gleaming white sugar icing, sending shards scattering across the tabletop. The fizz and spark of champagne on my lips as I make my toast. The crowd of guests waving us off at the reception gates. The blaze of the cab's headlamps lighting up the road ahead, the road to our hotel, and my instinct that all was right with the world, and all would be well, that I had acted as I should have and that the past could not hurt me as it once had, that I could be happy.

In the dimly lit hotel room Laura stood before the old oak bed and undressed slowly and deliberately in front of me, without shame. I did the same, and then I held her and found that what I had thought of as an

220

impossibility was possible after all. My body took over, acting on instinct. It was the first of many such times. Our union was simple, uncomplicated and quiet. And if my mind was not always with her — if it was not always her face and her body of which I thought as we lay together — was there any harm in it, and if so, to whom was the harm done, myself or her?

Friday, 2 July

A different maid came to clean the room this morning — this one cocky and brash, her curled hair tightly tied in a ponytail and bouncing at the nape of her neck as she stripped the bed. I was out on the balcony, a newspaper laid out in front of me. Through the patio doors, I saw her fold my clothes and lay them upon the chair, then hesitate and glance around. She sidled towards the dressing table, and I thought I saw her gaze stray towards the drawer that held this notebook, her hand stretch out to the handle. In an instant I was on my feet, striding back into the room. I nodded at her curtly, dismissing her, and she went, but not without a resentful pout and a toss of her hair. Of course, she could have no conception of this diary; was most likely in search of stray coins or valuables. All the same, the thought of her laying her hands upon it — of anyone doing so — was enough to make me shudder with panic. It is a foolish thing that I am doing, laying these thoughts down in print, but I cannot stop now.

My marriage to Laura served to cement my position in the firm. Mason was set to make partner within a few years, and although I was skilled enough at my job to have no need for nepotism, my tie to him cast me in a new light in the eyes of others. I noticed a new deference in my colleagues' attitudes towards me, and as I inched up the ranks, I began to be talked of as something of a leading light within the firm. It was what I had always wanted, and Laura supported my ambitions. In some strange way, despite her fragility, she was a rock to me. She soaked up tension like a sponge, so that when times at work were difficult, I could return home and she would somehow absorb my irritation, leaving me calmed and relaxed. She rarely made her opinions felt, but when she chose, she could give a well-judged comment that would suck the poison from a wound and lay my worries to rest. I suppose that one can ask for nothing more in a wife than this sort of loyalty and devotion.

The qualities that shone through in those early years are still there, I know, even if grief has dulled them. I have always known that Laura adores me. Hard to write, without appearing self-aggrandising, but nonetheless it is the truth. Even now, I sometimes catch her looking at me, lost in contemplation. She believes herself lucky to be my wife, and because of this, she has endured more than perhaps she should have done. I know, and I regret, that love for me has not made her happy.

In those early days I was still attentive and affectionate, as much as I knew how to be. They were not traits that had been bred in me, but ones that I had to pull out of myself, from somewhere deep and instinctual. I grew to understand her need for a swift caress and kiss as I came through the door at the end of the day, or a touch of the hand as we talked. I learnt slowly, but well. To my surprise I myself found some comfort in these small rituals. They became the glue that held together our marriage, the daily reminders that we were bound to one another for life. I did not regret my choice. Of all the women I could have chosen to marry, I believed that none could have fitted into my life as smoothly as Laura — I believe that still.

Soon after we were married, we moved out

of London and down to Brenchley, a small village in rural Kent, commutable to the office by train. The choice of Brenchley was random, but a happy one, in the way that such choices often are. In our first weeks there, I spent much time patrolling the surrounding orchards, feeling the freshness of the air clearing my head and cleansing my soul. I had never lived so close to nature, and something in me responded to the simple call of trees and fields in a way that surprised me. There I could find solitude, and a modicum of peace. I grew to love, too, the village high street, with its quaint array of shops and houses, and the beautiful old church, set back from the road. The village was quiet and serene, and that was the way I wanted things. I had enough of sound and fury during my days; at night and at weekends, I wished to unwind as best I could.

There was another reason, too, for the move, one I barely admitted to myself at the time. I was sick of spending so much time on the streets of London, which seemed to grow more aggressively sexual by the day. On every corner, they were there. Boys in dark eyeliner and leather jackets, with shaggy mops of hair and skin-tight jeans, smoking cigarettes and staring at me through half-closed eyes. They gave off a powerful call that was difficult to ignore, and I did not like my response to it, the way my eyes were drawn to them. They seemed to be calling me back to a former life, one that filled me with self-loathing and shame. I wanted nothing to do with them. The thoughts that plagued me internally were one thing; those I could not always control in the way I would have liked, but I did not want them made concrete. I wanted myself out of temptation's way.

★   ★   ★

Laura settled into Brenchley and soon became a regular parishioner at the church, going without fail every Sunday to morning and evening service. Her faith was unswerving, unquestioning; I envied it. Once or twice, I went with her to church, but it was useless. I recall standing there in the candlelit interior at dusk, letting the hymns flow sweetly over me, staring up towards the altar and registering its beauty. But that was all there was for me — a beautiful hollow shell, devoid of significance. I could not find in it what Laura found. Perhaps I did not try. Deep down I believed that if every man was in some way sinful, then I was irredeemably so; the seeds of my damnation had been sown years before, and it was too late to uproot them.

I watched Laura pray sometimes before bed, her head bent and her hands clasped, lips moving with words I could not catch. Sometimes, I would ask her what she said, but she would never tell me — like a child not wanting to share a wish made with the blowing out of birthday candles, in case the telling prevented it from coming true. I often wondered what they consisted of, these bargains she made with a God I did not believe in. Even leaving religion aside, I was sceptical of the concept — the mere notion that sacrifice and denial could reap any kind of reward other than a sterile and ultimately unfulfilling sense of self-satisfaction. I changed my mind only when it happened to me.

It was the May of 1974, some three years after our marriage. I had stayed late at the office, and I walked fast towards the train station, my legs aching with tiredness. When I reached it, a scene of chaos met my eyes: hundreds of disgruntled passengers thronging around the concourse, staring up at the bleak array of departure boards, their irritated chatter swelling like a wave. I fought my way through the crowd, found a station attendant. The trains towards Kent were cancelled, he told me; a serious signal failure had disabled a large part of the line, and he was unsure when service would resume. For a few moments I simply stood there, sagging in defeat. A sharp pain was spreading across my temples, and the harsh glare of the strip-lights overhead felt like a constant hammer-blow to my head. I could not bear the thought of waiting in the concourse for God knew how long, in hope of a miracle. I pushed through the discontented crowd and queued for a payphone, fumbling for change in my pocket.

'The trains are down,' I said without preamble when Laura picked up. 'I'm very tired, and I need to get some sleep. I think I may find a hotel and stay tonight, if you have no objection.'

On the other end of the line Laura began to flap; would the trains not resume, how would I find a suitable hotel, would it not make more sense to find a cab and take it back to Kent? She occasionally showed these unwelcome flashes of neuroticism, and they served only to harden my position. I dismissed her objections, interrupted and told her I had made my decision just as my money ran out. I placed the phone back on its holder, feeling obscurely guilty. When I looked around again, though, I was resolute once more. The station was full to capacity and there was barely enough space to stand, let alone to sit and unwind. I struggled back outside, feeling the welcome breeze of cool night air on my face. I knew there was a hotel close by on the Strand; I would head there and take their best available room. Lord knew I had relatively few indulgences for a man in my position. I set off down the road.

At the hotel I managed to book a junior suite, and went up there directly. It was on the fifth floor, and tastefully done, in pastel shades of cream and green, as I recall. One long floor-length window showed a view across the city, the evening skyline brilliantly glittering with lights. I stood in front of it for some minutes, watching orange taxi lights crawling below, winking out like beacons among the harsh yellow morass of headlamps swarming along the Strand. Unaccountably, once I was in the room my tiredness had left me. I felt restless and alert, and I determined to go down to the bar for a short while and drink to dull my nerves.

It was scarcely ten o'clock, but the bar was half empty, and I found a window seat without difficulty. I ordered a whisky and soda, and waited for it to be brought to me. The room I sat in was panelled in dark red leather, with small warm spotlights glimmering from the ceiling, giving it the air of a Lothario's lair. There was piano music playing softly in the background, something in an old fifties style. As I accepted my whisky and took the first sip, glancing around the room, I felt suddenly imbued with confidence and sophistication. I was used to places like this, but I seldom visited them alone, and I found that I liked it; sitting there with my drink, coolly surveying all that was before me. And then I saw it. The back of a man's head, sitting across from me, gleaming blond in the half-light. He wore a dark suit jacket, cut close around his shoulders. Everything about what I saw, the set of his back, the angle of his head, was so powerfully familiar, so reminiscent of Roman, that I felt my breath catch in my throat. My head spun. I felt as if I were seeing a ghost.

As if he felt my eyes upon him, the man turned in his seat, and I saw him look straight towards me. He was perhaps twenty-five years old; a taut, sensitive face, high arched eyebrows and cut-glass cheekbones. The resemblance was strong enough to keep me staring. The man looked back, and in the steadiness of his gaze I caught a breath of sexuality, powerful and unmistakable. It was I who broke it first, looking back down into the amber liquid swirling in my glass. My heart was beating very fast in my chest, making my vision blur. I knew it was irrational, but I felt an unstoppable rush of tenderness, so fierce that it threatened to bring me to tears. I finished my drink, swallowing down the last drops even though I no longer wanted them. I knew I should leave, but my legs felt paralysed, no longer part of me.

Just as I was about to force myself to get up, the stranger rose easily to his feet. He was tall and slim, his dark velvet suit skimming the lines of his body. As if in a dream, I watched him come towards me. He stopped only for an instant at my table before continuing on his way out of the bar, but in that instant he dropped a folded piece of paper into my lap. I saw his eyes flash with meaning as he did so — commanding, promising. I unfolded the scrap of paper. On it he had printed only a number: 403.

As I walked towards the elevator I found that my legs were shaking, threatening to give way beneath me. My heart was still beating hard and fast. As the elevator rose, I caught sight of myself in the mirror, and I barely recognised the man staring back at me. I got out on the fourth floor and walked softly along the corridor. Outside Room 403 I leant back against the wall, staring at the door. I did not really need to see what lay behind; I could picture the stranger vividly, my mind flooding with images that made me close my eyes and draw breath. For a moment, I moved towards the door. Then I swung away violently, walked back down the corridor, climbed the extra flight of stairs. I locked and bolted the door behind me with fingers that did not want to do my own bidding. I was breathing deep and quickly, as if I had pushed my body to the limit of its endurance.

Swiftly, I crossed to the window and eased it open, pushing the safety catch as far as it would go. I took the paper from my pocket and threw it out into the night, watching it caught by the wind, spiralling out and away from me. When I rested my head on the glass, it felt ice cold against the heat of my forehead, sending shock waves all the way through me.

In that moment I knew I had made a choice that could not be undone. I would never be unfaithful to Laura, no matter what opportunity was presented to me. Perhaps it was only right, I reasoned then, that with Roman's death part of me had died too. I would not let it resurrect itself. I would keep it underground where it belonged. I spoke calmly, logically to myself, but as I stood there before the window, swaying faintly with emotion, I felt a sudden surge of bitterness and entitlement. I had done all I could to commit myself to the life I had. I deserved something back.

Two weeks later, Laura told me that she

was pregnant, and with her words everything made sense and clicked into place. I knew at once that it would be a son. It was what I had always wanted — someone to be everything that I was not, someone whom I could form in the image of the man that everyone believed I was. My sacrifice had finally borne fruit. My reward was you.

Saturday, 3 July

Up early again this morning. Last night was karaoke night at the resort, and the soulless shrieks and caterwauls of the guests below eventually drove me out into the town. I found a little Spanish bar — a rare thing in this place of Irish pubs and full English breakfasts — and stayed there until after midnight, barely drinking at all, simply sitting in the relative calm, where no one seemed to care who I was or why I was there. By the time I returned here, the karaoke had wound down, but I could not sleep; I seldom can these days for more than a couple of hours at a time. I seem to be forgetting how to lose my grip on the world. Strange that such a basic knack can be so easily lost.

I remember that when, in my office, the telephone rang on the morning of February the fifth, I snatched it up before the first ring was out, instinctively knowing that no client or associate would be on the other end of the line. I was right. Laura had gone into labour, two weeks before time, and I was wanted at the hospital. I caught the first train down to Tunbridge Wells in a state of contained excitement. Outside the hospital an opportunist flower-seller lurked, showcasing his wares. I can see his face — cheeky, rat-like — and his breath steaming out into the winter air, as clearly as if it were yesterday. I bought some flowers, a huge bunch of white roses, tied up with silver ribbon. In the maternity ward I clutched them to me, scarcely noticing the thorns until I looked down and saw the palm of my right hand bright with blood, a scratch running from the base of my index finger all the way to where my lifeline curled around the palm. There was no pain; only surprise.

Laura had wanted to be alone. I sat and waited, my eyes on the cool green metallic door in front of me. I could hear nothing behind it, and the silence chilled me more than any screaming could have done. From time to time, a jovial nurse appeared to update me; everything was progressing just as it should. I smiled and nodded, but inside I did not trust her. Now that I was here, waiting for my son to be born, I feared the worst. I imagined you handicapped, mangled and deformed, stillborn. Ugly images crowded my head, sending shivers of nausea through my body. By the time, six hours later, I was finally called to the room, I had convinced myself that they were premonitory. And so when at last I saw you, perfect and sleeping in the crib next to where Laura lay gazing at you, your small golden eyelashes curled perfectly skywards and your face chubbily serene, it seemed to me that you were nothing less than an angel.

We had chosen the name Jonathan months before your birth. It was a name, for me, entirely without associations, untainted by the memory of anyone I had known or of any family forerunner. From the moment of your birth I saw you as a clean slate — innocent, imprinted with no other's sin, come into the world with nothing but your genes to guide you. I knew that you would make your name your own.

I had planned to write at length of your early years, but I find now that I cannot. The small, grinning boy with the blond mop of hair, whose enthusiasm took life by the throat and rattled it, feels now like someone entirely separate from my story. He belongs to another world. It was one in which, for a time, I believe I was truly happy, and to recall happiness is more difficult sometimes than recalling pain.

★ ★ ★

I suppose that every father sees something special in his son, but in many cases this uniqueness is invisible to the world at large. With you, the opposite was true; even as a teenager, your qualities shone out too brightly to be ignored, and it scarcely needed me to remark upon them. Your beauty was undeniable — the best of Laura and myself had come together in you, marking you out from the pack. You were intelligent and determined, but without the insularity with which such qualities often go hand in hand. Above all, you charmed all who knew you, seemingly without effort or design, simply gathering strangers to you as friends.

It is possible that many of these were so dazzled by your surface that they never saw beneath. For you had your demons just as everyone does — a tendency towards selfishness, a single-mindedness that sometimes veered into the more dangerous territory of heartlessness. You often found it hard to care what others thought and felt, if it went against your will. So greatly were these failings outshone by your other attributes that many disregarded them altogether. I loved you, not with the sick reluctance with which I had loved before, but with joyous, unswerving constancy. This much I hope you knew.

At eighteen you left for Cambridge, to study law. I was content — more than this, I was delighted — for you to pursue my own career: it gave me some validation that the example I had set was worthwhile. All the same, I was glad that you had not chosen Oxford. I had no wish for you to follow so exactly in my footsteps. The thought of you there, walking unknowing along the corridors where I had been, perhaps lying in the same rooms where I had lain all those years before, would have been too close for comfort, too much for me to stand.

We took you up to Cambridge at the start of your first term. I remember the pulse of shock, agonised and fleeting, that passed across your face as you took in the empty bleakness of your new room — the wooden blind half drawn, the walls bare and whitewashed, the single bed pushed up into the corner. We left you standing desolate and forlorn, your case half unpacked in the centre of the floor. I drove back home in silence as Laura cried quietly in the seat next to me. I did not try to console her; it was best to let her purge the sorrow of parting, and besides, I had my own sorrow to wrestle with. That night I lay in bed and every bone in my body felt your absence. I tried to trick my mind into imagining you in the next room and found that I could not. I could only think of your face, smiling bravely as we went, but full of uncertainty and dread at what might lie ahead. Of course, our fears were entirely unfounded, as was made abundantly clear when we made a surprise visit at Laura's insistence some two weeks later and found you reclining in a neighbour's window-seat, surrounded by fellow students and lying in the proprietary arms of a recently acquired girlfriend. When you saw us, there was a look of polite enquiry, chased briefly by mortification, before you found your manners and sprang up to greet us. You were affable and good tempered that day, showing us the sights, but there was a new distance there. You had cut the apron strings, and although this was just as it should be, I felt distress, as any loving parent surely must, at the knowledge that I was not needed as I had been before. You were becoming a man. I could only sit back and watch, and hope that you would manage the task more successfully than I had done.

By the time you left Cambridge, a

succession of girls had had their hearts broken at your hands. I met a few from this jumble sale of abortive girlfriends; blondes and brunettes, exotic-looking waifs and English roses. Laura feared that you were promiscuous, and too careless with love, having had so much freely bestowed upon you. For my part, I did not care; indeed, a secret, furtive part of me welcomed every one. I had no doubt that when you were ready for some deeper connection, you would find it with ease.

Soon after graduating you expressed your desire to follow me into the firm; I passed on your wishes, and naturally an opening was found. I believe I worried, briefly, at the time that things were coming too easily to you. Your academic ability was natural and effortless, as was others' attraction towards you, and you had moved into a London flat on my money; perhaps when it came to finding a job, it would have been better for you to have had to work for your position. You had never had to justify your existence to anyone. And yet such fears were far outweighed by the rush of pleasure I felt when you announced your intentions. It was the beginning of a renewed closeness between us; of journeys taken together in companionable reading of the morning papers, frequent lunches snatched together in office hours, new and mutual understanding of each other's ambitions. I saw something of myself in you — enough, but not too much. When, in your twenty-sixth year, I was invited to become a partner at the firm, no one was happier for me than you. Your delight in my achievement allowed me to feel something of the same.

At home things were less idyllic; things were changing between Laura and me, had been doing so ever since you had moved away. Without you we were left to our marriage, and all the energy that had been focused upon your head was left to turn itself inward, to poke through the embers of what remained between us. The discovery was not a comfortable one. My regard for Laura had not diminished, but regard was not what she wanted. Our physical encounters, always a little less frequent than I sensed she felt comfortable with, dwindled to once-monthly affairs, then fewer. It was not that I felt revulsion at making love to her. It was simply that as the years went on I began to find the process more difficult than before; found that to lie with her and kiss her left me with a strange, numb feeling of nullity. I began to wonder what the point of it all was — it felt like a charade, two ageing homemakers playing at being lusty teenage lovers. With each time we played out this farce I grew less able to stomach it.

The truth was that it was around this time, years after I had ceased to expect it, that Roman began recurring in my dreams. His face and body came to me with heart-stopping familiarity, more clearly than I could by then recall them when awake; the shine of his pale green eyes at once brittle and soft, the voluptuous curve of his lower lip, the exact width and breadth of his chest. In these dreams he was alluring, compulsively enchanting, just as he had been in life. I found myself sitting coldly in my office by day, staring out of the window unseeing. I longed to sleep in the hope that he might come to me again, despite the loathing that was stirred in me each time I woke with the tail-end of such fantasies still lingering around me. In sleep I rediscovered the eroticism that there could be in touch — from the briefest brush of a hand against mine to darker, deeper contact, things which shocked me when I woke with the graphic force of their passion. It shamed me that these dreams were the only place where I could find this, but not enough to wish them entirely gone.

I know that to you, if you had known all, this would have seemed a waste of a life. To make you understand my position would have been impossible. I can barely explain it myself, save to say that all my life I had grown within restricted boundaries, led by my father's sense of decency and of what was expected of me, and that these boundaries have always been just as much a part of me as anything else. I fulfilled the destiny that was marked out for me, not the one my heart would have chosen. I could not see — can still not see — another option. As I grew older I saw, with resentment, that society had changed. What had once been universally shunned and despised was now cautiously tolerated in some circles, openly embraced in others. This fawning permissiveness had come too late for me, and I grew to hate it.

One evening in the winter of 2000, as rain lashed the windows outside and the night drew in, I moved my things into the second bedroom. As I placed my nightclothes at the foot of the bed, I could see my wife's shadow, reflected in the window glass where she stood motionless in the doorway behind me. When at last I turned, she was leaning against the door frame as if she needed the support, a reed blown in the breeze. Mutely, her eyes sent an appeal. As I looked at her, I saw the all too familiar stripping back of pretence, the dissolution of the quiet confidence she radiated in public. When it was just the two of us together, Laura seemed a wholly different woman, her dependence clawing at me, always asking things, wanting too much.

'Have I . . . ' she began, so low that I could barely hear, and she cleared her throat to force the sound out. 'Have I done something to displease you?'

I shook my head; she had done nothing, nothing that I could make an example out of. I knew that the fault was mine, but I could not bring myself to say so. I stood up straight by the bed, the distance between us three feet or less, but enough to feel like a chasm that would never be bridged again. 'I think we will both be happier this way,' I said, hating myself as I heard the hypocrisy in the words. She knew, as well as I did, that her happiness had little to do with the matter; it was for my own peace of mind and no one else's that I wanted to sleep alone. As if to highlight my insincerity, she left a moment's silence before she spoke again.

'Perhaps we have left too much unsaid,' she said, and I thought I caught an unfamiliar hint of scorn in her voice, but when I looked at her sharply I saw her face strained and miserable, without subtext. 'I won't try to change your mind, but I will say one thing. If you intend this as the first step of many away from me, I would prefer that you take the rest at once. I couldn't bear for this,' and here she raised one thin hand and encircled the air, as if to encompass the depth and breadth of our life together, 'to fall away slowly.'

I moved awkwardly towards her and placed my hand on hers, feeling it twitch under my touch. 'I have no wish to break up our marriage,' I said. 'That choice is for you to make, if anyone does.' My words were intended to comfort, but as she looked up into my face, her eyes searching mine, she began to cry.

I knew that what I was doing was unfair; that what I said was tantamount to telling her to fly, when I knew full well that love for me had caged her. I hoped, entirely without foundation, that when she was able to see the matter clearly, she would find that she was content with what I had to give. What I had told her was the truth. I could not contemplate divorce, or the destruction of the life I had fought so hard to maintain. It was simply that I was not suited to the intimacy that is the foundation of marriage, much as I rose to its other tenets. I was a provider, a protector; I kept a roof over her head and food on her plate; I would have defended her to anyone who dared to malign her. There are many others who do not give as much. I hoped that she would come to find it enough. From that day onwards, I have done my best with Laura, but it is only now, as I set these thoughts down in ink, that I am truly able to see that no amount of chivalry and civility will truly be able to compensate for what was lost. As to what my way forward is from here, I am at a loss to know.

In those first nights, as I lay in my new solitude, the bedsheets arranged over my body with clinical coldness, I reflected that I had failed in her eyes as a husband. The realisation was inescapable, and it could lead to only one conclusion: I determined that I would not fail as a father. Our relationship was the one thing left that I genuinely prized. My attention had always been upon you, willing you to succeed, to make out of life what I knew you could, but with the sea-change between myself and Laura, it became doubly focused, like a torchlight that intensifies the nearer it draws to its subject. I was determined that you should make good on your potential. I saw your future mapped out before you — a future as a successful professional and the head of a family. You would have all the gifts I had myself, but with one salient difference: you would be happy.

Perhaps this pressure was too great for you. Now that the possibility of any change or redemption has vanished for ever, I can see the tiny signs that I glossed over, the flashes of insecurity in you that should have given me pause. You would exaggerate your successes in the office, presumably unaware that I had eyes and ears effectively over the entire building. If I passed sarcastic comment on anyone or anything, you would laugh too quickly, too loudly, as if to show me your solidarity. You were swift to agree with me in almost everything, to such an extent that one of our associates once joked that we must share a brain. It was a conceit that I seized upon greedily. In my eyes, we were two halves of the same whole — you my better self, the bright side of the coin, your attributes outshining my deficiencies. I did not stop to wonder whether this was a role you wanted, or one that, albeit without your conscious knowledge, it was fair to impose upon you.

Looking back now, I can reinterpret the nervous twitch of your fingers upon the telephone as you sat at your desk from day to day, my eyes upon you; the sharp, tense turn of your head whenever I spoke your name. They build a picture of a man who itched to strike out against a life, and a father, that seemed to be trapping him without his consent. It comes as a bleak shock to me now to realise that what you really thought of me,

I do not know. At times you looked on me with what I thought was love, inept as I was at recognising such things. At other times, it seemed that you sensed something dark in me that even I could not . . . almost that you feared me.

Sunday, 4 July

I wrote for too long yesterday; it has exhausted me. Last night I dined at a small restaurant on the coastal tip, a dilapidated place with flaking yellow paint and bright woven sombreros hanging from hooks around the walls. Despite the crudeness of my surroundings, my seat afforded me a view of the one unspoilt thing in this place: the sea, beautiful and vast, stretching out in glittering turquoise like a skein of liquid silk. I watched the boats glide across its surface, their movement sending up lace-like sprays of white foam. When the waiter slid to my side and asked me whether anyone would be joining me, I shook my head. I was reminded of another time, back home at the Sherbourne Club, when Laura and I had been asked the same question by much the same obsequious breed of waiter, and when the answer had been yes. We had been waiting for you, and for the girl who had been your secretary for the past few weeks; a girl whose name and face I did not yet know.

It had taken me some time to notice your absence from work that week — you had moved into a new enclosed office, away from my scrutiny, and it was a period when the demands on my time were especially great. It was not unusual, by that time, for us to pass a day or two without encountering each other. When it struck me, however, that I had not seen you since the Wednesday morning, two days before, I went directly to your office, and I found it empty, the curtains drawn. Your green desk lamp was burning unattended; I went and switched it off. Standing there, looking around the empty walls, I was dragged back to another memory: standing with the porter in Roman's deserted lodgings, the dark room scattered with papers, leaving no clue as to where he had gone. The recollection gave me a sick pang of unease. I stood there quietly for some time, taking in your absence. And then my eyes alighted on the desk across from yours. I remembered that you had taken on a secretary for the summer, a gap-year student. I had seen her only from behind, making her way from reception to your office. I conjured up her image; a slim but curvaceous figure, clad in tightly fitted suits, dark hair tumbling down her back. Her disappearance gave yours meaning. I sat down at your desk and dialled the number for your mobile. It rang three, four times, and then I heard you pick up.

'You're not at work,' I said before you had a chance to speak. To state the obvious was to give you a way in to the conversation, not to antagonise or intimidate you, but to my surprise I heard your voice come back nervous and stammering. You told me that you had everything under control, that you would be back in the office on Monday. I wondered at your tone, but I did not press you for an explanation. Instead I simply asked what I already knew. 'The girl — is she with you?' A pause. *Yes — yes, she is.* You knew that this was something I would understand. You knew how accepting I was of your affairs, numerous and meaningless though they were. I could have left it there, but something compelled me to speak again. 'Well, perhaps the two of you would care to join us for lunch tomorrow,' I said. 'We'll be at the club at one.'

I scarcely knew myself why I made the offer, and I fully expected you to refuse. It was not your style to share your conquests with me; you preferred to keep your private life just that. Instead, you gave a swift, relieved bark of laughter and accepted with alacrity, then hung up almost as if to forestall me from changing my mind. I sat there in the darkened office, listening to the dialling tone ringing in my ears. A glimpse of knowledge came to me then — a sense that this affair could be something other than the rest had been — and it made my heart lift with excitement. You were thirty years old, and unmarried.

The next day at lunchtime, Laura and I sat in the warm, indulgent atmosphere of the club, waiting for you. We had taken our usual table, a raised banquette that allowed us to keep watch over the restaurant's comings and goings, and I saw you before you saw me. You were holding her hand, and even this was new. She was slighter than I remembered, her head barely reaching your shoulder, dressed in a short dark dress dotted with flowers, and I saw at once that she was very young. As you led her towards us, I saw something else: your face, alert and searching, already seeking my approval in a way I had never seen before.

Violet was nervous over lunch, her fingers shaking as she picked up her wineglass, her voice cracking as she talked. I liked her at once, but I was deliberately cold with her, wanting to test her mettle. I asked her about herself, about what she did in her spare time, about her parents. I saw her chin lift in defiance when she told me that her father was a mechanic and that her mother no longer worked. I did not reply; there was nothing to say. In truth, I cared little for the girl's background. The need for an aristocratic lineage in all those I encountered was one of the few of my father's shackles that I had managed to shake off. I shot a glance across at Laura to note her reaction, and as I did so, Violet rose abruptly to her feet and excused herself, wheeling sharply away from the table.

'I hope I didn't go too far,' I said to you, hearing my voice light and cold. I half expected you to rebuke me, but you merely smiled, as if you had barely noticed our conversation. I saw at once that you were in love, and that it had made you benevolent and self-absorbed, unaware of any tension around you. The realisation tightened my throat and for a moment I fought with the urge to sob. Happiness made me reserved, turning in on itself, settling with a warm glow in my chest. I nodded.

'I hope that you approve,' you said, and again I saw a flash of something, almost pleading, willing me to acquiesce. Your eyes darted across to Laura, and your hand crept up to your collar, unconsciously loosening it. 'I know this is all rather sudden, but I think it's serious. I apologise for staying away from work. Not very professional.' You grinned, displaying your easy charm. Across the room, I saw two young women staring at you, whispering, their eyes full of admiration. Ordinarily, some instinct would have made you notice them. That day you were oblivious, all your attention focused elsewhere.

'Of course,' I said, and was rewarded by your smile widening as you exhaled with what must have been relief. 'She seems charming.'

'She's very pretty,' Laura said. She glanced at me as she said it. It came to me that there was a hint of jealousy in her words, as if she feared some primitive response from me to the girl's physical charms. The thought was so incongruous that I almost laughed.

'And she has spirit,' I said, turning my attention back to you. 'She's very young, of course, but that's all right. If anything, it's a good thing. I see no problem with an age gap, if you are both dedicated to making it work.' I was talking as much to myself as to you. I meant what I said: something told me that you would tire of a woman your own age long before she tired of you.

You nodded violently, your hand reaching out to grasp the stem of your wineglass, as if to still the excitement rushing through you. 'She's very special,' you said, and in that instant we saw her returning, picking her way through the tables around us, humming with vitality, her face lit up by some unknowable delight, eyes shining.

★ ★ ★

It was barely two months after that first meeting when you came to us and told me that you had asked Violet to marry you, and that she had accepted. You were bubbling with pride and exhilaration, intensity crackling off you, as if gripped by religious fervour. Laura cried, as was to be expected. I congratulated you, embraced you. I said that perhaps we could look into some venue options for the following winter. You turned on me, shaking your head hard and fast. 'No, no,' you said. 'We must get married at once. I was thinking of December the twenty-third.'

It was then late November. 'It's very soon,' I said slowly. 'I doubt you would even find a venue at such short notice, let alone be able to arrange everything to your satisfaction.'

Your wide blue eyes rolled back in your head for an impatient instant. 'My satisfaction?' you cried, raising your hands as if to implore the heavens. 'My satisfaction is to marry Violet. That's it. I don't care if we have to get married in a poxy little register office, or out the back of a village hall, or in a bloody barn somewhere. I just want to do it.'

'I doubt that will be necessary,' I said after a pause. For almost the first time in my life I was at a loss. I had not expected this from you. You had always, as far as I had seen, fought shy of romantic commitment, preferring to enjoy the pleasures of women and then cast them aside for a newer distraction. This volte-face smacked of a decision too hastily made. I knew that it was within my power as your father for me to, if not forbid you, then at least to plant a significant seed of doubt in your mind as to the wisdom of so speedy a union. I opened my mouth to set out my position, but as I did so, I found myself nodding instead. 'Well, you know best what you and Violet want,' I said. 'I won't attempt to change your mind.' I saw Laura glance my way; saw shocked reproof in her gaze. She would never openly defy me, but the defiance was there all the same, a tangible presence in the room between us. She believed that you were rushing things, but with the two of us united against her, she knew that it was not worth her while to say so. You ignored her disapproval, not maliciously, but with that incredible force you had — the ability to block out anything you disliked or which stood in your way.

A suitable hotel was found to have a late cancellation, and you married four weeks later in a whirlwind of Christmas lights, tall white candles, hastily assembled guests. Violet was radiant in pure white, her dark hair dotted with starry hairpins. You barely left her side. It was a happy day; the kind of tremulous, agitated happiness that is perhaps doomed not to last. When I look back on it now, I am convinced more than ever that my first instinct was right. Had you waited, taken more time to discover each other's strengths and weaknesses, reached a deeper understanding, then all might have been well. As it was, you stole that time from yourself. Even now, I blame myself for not preventing you, for the small furtive voice that made me override what I knew was right. *You want him married*, this voice whispered to me. *Now is the time to settle it*. I thought perhaps that to seal you up in wedded bliss would be to remove the last of my fear that you would never fulfil the destiny I wanted for you. I acted stupidly, selfishly. I paid for this selfishness, and am still paying for it now.

★ ★ ★

When you moved to Brenchley, soon after your marriage, I was gratified and pleased to have you near us. You gave me no reason for the move, but I suspected that the London penthouse flat, bought with my money, had begun to feel like a youthful embarrassment to you — a thread of dependence you no longer needed. Once you were settled in Brenchley, we saw more of you than we had done in years. It was a happy time for all of us, or so I believed. I grew fond of Violet — she was intelligent and not without personality, but she clearly worshipped you, and deferred to you in most things. Sometimes I would catch her staring at you across the table, thinking herself unobserved, and the hunger in her gaze told me that she wanted you to herself, that she would not share you with anyone. I believed you needed this kind of adoration, and for some time you did indeed seem to thrive on it. You had eyes for no one but her, your earlier promiscuity forgotten. I sensed a new gentleness in you, the calming of a storm. And so when things began to change, at first I could hardly give my suspicions credence.

A little over a year after your marriage, something seemed to steal over you, insidious and relentless, like an unseen disease. You appeared restless, dissatisfied. You came to us just as often, but there was a new reticence in your manner. Sometimes, I could speak with

Violet and Laura for minutes on end and be left with the impression that you had heard nothing of the conversation. You seemed weary of us, your thoughts elsewhere. What began as the merest hint in your behaviour soon intensified into an all-pervading oppressiveness that was difficult to ignore. Your temper grew shorter, and you would snap at any one of us as easily as blinking. I knew that you were working longer hours, returning to Violet at ten or later every night. Often, she would appear at our door in the early evening, seemingly without purpose or motivation. I suspected that it was simple loneliness and nothing else that drew her there; the chance to sit with others for a few hours to dull the pain of waiting for you to come home.

On one particular occasion, the two of you had come over for afternoon tea; it was a Saturday in late August, but summer had ended early, and it was too cold to sit out on the lawn. We drank tea and ate scones in the drawing room, making undemanding small talk. I remember that you wore a dark linen suit, as if dressed for work, and that you did not eat, but kept your hands clenched on the table as if tensed for battle. In a lull of conversation, your mobile rang. Within seconds, you had snatched it up and left the room. Through the window, I saw you walk out on to the lawn, the phone pressed to your ear, and stride away down towards the apple tree. I looked across at Violet, but she kept her back to the window, chatting quietly with Laura, pretending to ignore your disappearance. Only a certain tension in her shoulders told me that she had registered it, and that she wondered, as I did, what or who had made you leave with such thoughtless urgency.

I rose to my feet and excused myself. Quietly, I pushed open the back door and looked out across the lawn. I could see you there, pacing back and forth, your head bent down, still talking into the mobile. I strode down towards you, and when I drew near your head jerked up and you saw me. A look of fear and anger passed across your face, and without preamble, you hung up, clicking the phone shut. Standing there beneath the apple tree, you looked cornered, like an animal that knows it will have to fight its way free. I took in that look, and with a tremble of nausea, I knew that there was something badly wrong.

'Jonathan,' I said, 'what's the matter with you?' The words came out cold and irritated, a master reproving an errant schoolboy. I saw that you did not like my tone, and your silence underlined it. I tried again, lowering my voice. 'If there is something wrong,' I said, 'it should be talked about. You've seemed troubled for weeks now.' I did not say what was really on my mind, unavoidable though the thought had been to me at the sight of your hunted face moments before. *You are sleeping with another woman*, I thought. It was something that, with dispassionate realism, I had always known to be a possibility. I saw no reason why it could not be nipped in the bud and smoothed over, cut off before it had the chance to damage your marriage beyond repair. I hoped, perhaps, that you would break down and confess to me in the manner of a sinner at the altar, but of course you did no such thing. All the same, my softened tone took away some of your antagonism. You leaned back against the trunk of the apple tree, watching me warily.

'I'm having a difficult time,' you said, and something in the way you said it made me wonder whether it was an affair at all. Your words hinted at something deeper, more fundamental. I thought of your erratic moods, and considered the possibility that you had somehow got yourself entangled with drugs, or that there was some financial problem of which I was unaware.

'Whatever it is, you can talk to me about it,' I said, wishing I could rid my voice of the instinctive stiffness I could not but use when talking of such matters. You looked back at me, almost speculatively, before shaking your head. 'In that case, you should talk to your wife,' I said, and you laughed. It was a sudden, violent burst of laughter that brought tears glistening to your eyes, and it frightened me.

'I'm sorry,' you said when you had recovered. 'I don't mean to be rude. Everything is fine. Really. I know I've been distracted lately, and I apologise. I'll make more of an effort — with all of you, with Violet especially. There's nothing for you to worry about.'

The words sounded hollow, untrue as I already knew them to be, and I had nothing to say. You were watching me through narrowed slits, gauging my response. Silently, you lit a cigarette, then offered me one, and I took it. I lit mine from your own, and in that brief moment, our heads bent together, I felt the closeness between us, a closeness that had always been there, from the moment of your birth. I had never thought that you would lie to me. We smoked in silence for a minute, looking back towards the house. 'She loves you, you know,' I said, and you nodded, and I saw your face, averted from mine, briefly twist with pain.

Monday, 5 July

I slept last night, and wished I had not. In the back of my mind, as I laid down my pen soon after eleven, I knew that the moment was approaching when I would have to write of Max Croft, and accordingly he crept up on me in my dreams. I dreamt that I was walking through an unfamiliar forest, following some unknown path, with his footsteps behind me, sounding out stark and menacing in the silence. When I turned I could see only his shadow. In the ripple of a second, another scene: myself lying in a sanitised hospital bed, prone and helpless, and his eyes above the doctor's mask bending over me, dark and burning like coal. I have had such dreams before, and it is always the same. I see him in pieces, never fully revealed, never wholly knowable.

I saw him first in the January of your last year. You and I were taking a stroll, across the orchards and into the village. The frost had settled overnight, and a thin covering of ice skimmed the bare branches of the trees and tipped the grass at our feet. As we came down from the footpath to the high street, you suggested that we stop off at the Rose and Crown for a swift drink before turning back. I agreed, and we turned our steps towards the pub. As we neared it, I saw a man walking up the high street towards us. What struck me first was his size; his height, the muscular set of his shoulders and the powerful length of his stride. Next I registered his clothing — dark jeans, a black shirt with sleeves cut off above the elbow, and no jacket. The temperature was a little below zero, but I saw no sign that he felt the cold; he seemed fuelled by some internal furnace, indifferent to his surroundings. As he came closer still, I saw him stop and look closely at us both. His face was hard and striking, good looking in an aggressively masculine fashion. I averted my eyes, wishing to pass by unremarked, but I felt an irrational chill of unease at the intensity of his stare.

'Don't remember me, do you?' he said at the moment we passed him. His voice was harsh and guttural. Common. I stopped and looked back. He was standing motionless in the street, arms folded now, a faint mocking smile making the corners of his mouth twitch. His face sparked off no association in me. I shook my head. Next to me, you shifted, stamping your feet on the ground to fight off the cold. 'Max Croft,' he said. 'Pat and James's son. Suppose it must have been ten years, so I'll let you off.' He spoke as if he were doing me a favour.

Looking at him again, I felt a start of surprise. I knew James and Patricia Croft, although not well; they lived a mile or so away from us, and we occasionally met at village events and the soirées of mutual friends. I remembered their daughter, Catherine, but I had forgotten that they had a son. Even now, with him there in front of me, I could not recall ever having seen this man before. 'I'm not sure we ever met,' I said.

'Well, *I* met *you*, Harvey,' Max said. There was a note of ridicule and triumph in his voice when he spoke my name that I did not like. I was not accustomed to others making me feel foolish. 'Back when I was fourteen or so. Saw you several times. I've only just moved back into the area. Was living up in London, but thought I'd settle here for a bit.'

I mustered my habitual cordiality and nodded. 'I hope you find it congenial,' I said, although to what, I could not imagine. Max was no longer looking at me. His eyes were trained on you, sweeping, appraising. I thought I saw him glance at the heavy gold watch you wore, the expensive cut of your coat.

'Hello,' he said.

You smiled. For you, there were no strangers; only friends you had not yet charmed. 'Jonathan,' you said, and as I stood there beside you, you shook his hand.

* * *

In the months that followed I saw Max perhaps three or four times. At the time I believe I felt little beyond a contemptuous stirring of dislike, but it is easy, looking back, to imbue these sightings with a sinister significance. On two of these occasions, you were with him. Once in the pub, where I had come to meet an old friend. Upon entering I found you already there, carrying two pint glasses to the table where Max sat, smoking viciously and frowning down at the tabletop, stubbing his cigarette hard down into the ashtray.

I was not surprised; it was in your nature to form bonds with others of a similar age, and Lord knew the village provided few entertainments and plenty of opportunity for casual, chance meetings. All the same, I cannot pretend that I thought Max to be a suitable friend. It was not a question of class; more one of attitude. There was something unpleasantly ruthless about him; an indefinable threat he wore about him like a force field. I sat with my friend on the other side of the pub, keeping a discreet distance, but I could not stop my eyes drifting over towards the two of you, as you talked intently, laughing from time to time. Later that evening you went to the pool table to play a couple of frames. Max held the cue with practised surety, taking fast, accurate shots that sent the balls rolling smartly into the pockets. When he bent low over the table, eyes burning in concentration, the waistband of his trousers crept an inch or two lower, exposing a strip of taut brown flesh. He beat you easily both times, grinning like the devil as he did so.

The second time was some months later, when, crossing the road on my way home, I glanced through a restaurant window and saw you sat there with him, eating and chatting. There was something about the way you sat together which seemed easy, companionable, as if your acquaintance had shifted to a higher level. As I watched, I saw you shake your head, put your hand to the back of your collar and rub it along your neck in a way that seemed troubled, and I wondered, idly enough, what you were talking of. I stayed at the window for some moments, but you did not turn towards me.

'Do you see much of Max Croft?' I asked you a few days later, and you shook your head and looked at me with suspicion, as if you wondered why I should concern myself with your friendships. We were entering into your last summer now, the period when your affections had begun to shift and change, and you were not as forthcoming with me as you had once been. 'It's simply that I think he's a rather unsavoury character,' I said. 'He'll be asking for money if you're not careful, mark my words.' I scarcely knew why I said it — I had no reason to believe that Max was especially under financial strain — but your reaction was outraged and scornful. I dropped the topic, not thinking it worth my while to argue the point.

Setting these facts down in print, it seems incredible to me now that when I confronted you that afternoon in the garden underneath the apple tree, it did not occur to me that Max Croft might somehow be connected to your distress. In my defence, unsettling though these incidents were, they were little but minor ripples in the grander scheme of things, and my attention was elsewhere — on you, on Violet and Laura, and on our own relationships. I thought, perhaps, that no outsider could have a significant impact upon your life. It was a streak of complacency in me that was only broken some three weeks after our conversation that day. The date was 3 September. I have tried to forget it, but it is a useless exercise. That date is branded upon my brain, a scar that will not fade with time.

You had come over for dinner, without Violet — a rare evening with an old school-friend had taken her out of town. After eating we sat in the lounge with Laura and talked; it was the kind of conversation that is forgettable hours later, but which at the time serves to foster a sense of comfort and ease. I believe we talked of plans for Christmas, of possible presents for Violet. I had been gratified to see a change in your manner towards her since our conversation, oblique and inconclusive though it had been. I had begun to relax, feeling the tension of worrying about the two of you draining from me like poison from a wound.

As we sat there in our familiar luxury, the cream-shaded lamps glowing warmly and the lights turned low, I was filled with expansive bonhomie, almost exhilaration. I have heard of such things before — an inexplicable happiness, moments before disaster — but at the time I trusted my contentment. When the doorbell rang, it was only mild irritation and curiosity that I felt, nothing more.

I rose and went slowly through the hallway; whoever it was, there could be no harm in them waiting. When I opened the door, I saw Max there, leaning against the porch, his shirt dishevelled and open at the collar, his eyes unfocused and staring through me. I was hit at once by the smell of alcohol that rose off him; sharp and sweet, making me draw back. He was too drunk to speak clearly, and at first I could not catch what he mumbled at me. I glanced back into the hallway, checking that it was clear.

'What on earth are you doing here?' I asked. I was careful to keep my voice low, but imbued with the right quality of coldness and disgust.

Max jerked his head back, and it connected with the wooden frame of the porch, a sharp, decisive crack that should have hurt. He seemed oblivious, still struggling to focus on me. After a moment he seemed to gather his resources and spoke, the words slurred and indistinct. 'I came to ask,' he said, 'if Jonathan could *come out to play.*' His tone was bitter, dripping with sarcasm. 'I know he's here,' he added. 'The lights are off at his house, and I saw the little wife leaving.'

The words gave me a powerful sense of unease. *The man is stalking my son,* I thought, and with the thought I felt my hackles rise, the instinctive desire to protect. 'I think it's best you leave,' I said. 'I don't know what you want with Jonathan, but in any case, he isn't here.'

Max frowned, then smiled, an ugly smile that looked strange and out of place on his face. 'You're a liar,' he said, and came nearer, swaying on his feet. He drew so close that I could smell the alcohol again on his breath, so close that I could have reached out my hand and touched the dense black rash of stubble that grew around his mouth. For a moment I thought he would push his way past me, but he simply fixed me with a look I could not understand, as if he were searching through my soul. 'Tell him,' he said, spitting out the words with care, one by one, 'that I came for him.'

I shut the door on him, and bolted it. On the other side of the frosted glass, I could see his shadow lingering like a malevolent ghost. I stayed there until I saw it pull back and fade into the dark, and then I went back into the living room.

'Laura,' I said, 'I'd like a word with Jonathan in private.' Laura's head went up sharply; she glanced from me to you, and her lips parted as if she would speak. After a few moments, she collected up her cup and saucer and left the room in silence. I turned to you. You were looking at me attentively, a shadow of fear between your brows.

'What's this about?' you asked. You were

already defensive. I could see it in the rigidity with which you held yourself, the hard set of your mouth.

I crossed to where you stood and placed my hand lightly upon your shoulder for an instant, but I did not smile. 'We have just had a visitation from Max Croft,' I said. 'The man was drunk out of his skull. He asked for you, and I can only describe his manner as threatening. I should like to know why.'

Your face twitched as I spoke, and it seemed that you were fighting with a host of conflicting emotions, not knowing which to pick. When you had sorted your thoughts into clarity, the anger that shone from your eyes made my breath catch in my throat. 'You shouldn't have sent him away,' you said, so quietly that I strained to catch the words, but with an undercurrent of fury that chilled me.

'The man was drunk,' I repeated, raising my voice and finding some comfort in it. 'He was abusive, and I wished to avoid an ugly scene in my own house. I think I am entitled to that much? I'm more concerned about what business he has with you. What on earth have you got yourself into, Jonathan? I thought you knew better than to mix yourself up with his sort.' I was aware that my tone had become hectoring and scornful, and checked myself, but it was too late. You had

269

wheeled round and left the room, pulling your mobile from your pocket as you did so, and I heard your footsteps, swiftly mounting the stairs. An instant later, a floorboard creaked through the ceiling above me; you had gone to your old bedroom, up in the eaves. I hesitated for a moment. The room was taut with silence, as if at any second it might crack into chaos. Quietly, I followed you up the stairs, and when I reached your closed door, I leant my body against it, pressing my ear against the wood. As I did so I felt a surge of revulsion. It was not in my nature to spy, and I knew that it would not cross your mind to suspect that I would invade your privacy so crudely. The act made me feel contemptible, and yet some instinct, too strong to be ignored, told me it was necessary.

For a moment I heard nothing; then your voice, low and urgent. *I know*, you said, *I know. But you shouldn't have come here.* Another pause, then a muffled sound, a sigh of what could have been frustration, or despair. *I'll meet you in the churchyard*, you said. *Ten minutes.* And then, barely audibly, I heard the snap of your phone closing. Breaking quickly away, I hurried softly back down the stairs, pulled the living room door to behind me. I heard your footsteps, strong and sure. As I had anticipated, you did not return to the living room. A moment later I heard the front door slam. I stood motionless, counting seconds in my head. When I had reached one hundred, I walked into the hallway and took my keys from the rack. Reflected in the hall mirror, I could see Laura, worriedly hovering, not knowing whether to speak or remain silent. As she saw me head for the door, she started forward, but I ignored her, slamming it behind me, and made for the car.

I drove slowly, with the headlights off. The roads were dark and empty, with no sign of your car ahead. I parked at the top of the high street, and when I got out of the car, I registered the stillness; the low, expectant hum of the air. I walked swiftly down towards the church, where light shone from one high window, leading me on. Still in the back of my mind, I felt the nagging tug of shame. I spoke sternly to myself. This unpleasant strategy was the only option open to me, if you would not trust me enough to confide your troubles. As I crossed the long narrow path leading to the church and swung back into the churchyard behind, an image of your face as you had stood in the living room came clearly to me — shock, anger, and something close to fear — and it made my throat tighten. It was my duty to protect you, with or without your consent.

It was pitch black in the churchyard, and it took my eyes some minutes to adjust to the darkness. Slowly, I began to make out the outlines of shapes; sloping stone tombstones, the dark drooping branches of trees. I stood motionless, listening. At first I heard nothing. Then, so faint that it could have been imagined, the sound of someone speaking. I could not make out the words, but I knew as surely as if I had seen you, with the instinctive recognition of love, that the sound had come from you. Barely breathing, I glided forward. At the base of the churchyard, where hedges ran along the boundary, a thin shaft of light illuminated the pathway. I saw you there in the distance, facing him. You were close together, close enough to touch. Straining to see, I thought that his attitude was threatening, but as I drew nearer, I found that I could not at once make sense of what I saw.

The space between the two of you was even less than I had thought. You were smiling, and the strangeness of seeing that smile froze me to the spot. You touched the side of his face, and even then, as my brain fought to process the gesture, I registered the tenderness with which you did it, the affectionate simplicity which comes only with having done a thing many, many times before. And as I watched, he took your hand, pulled you towards him, and kissed you hard on the mouth. With that same audacious, unthinking ease. As if it meant everything, and yet nothing at all.

★　★　★

What followed is blurred in my memory even now. I must have made some sound, enough to break your embrace. You swung round, a hissed expletive escaping from your lips. I remember running, stumbling back through the churchyard, my feet catching on uneven stone, blood pounding in my head, barely seeing. Instinct drove me back through the dark and out on to the street. My fingers fumbling with the car keys; then only your figure in the road as I drove past, your face a mask of horror as you recognised the car. At any other time, you would have looked comical. Of the drive home I remember nothing. Afterwards, I lay in my bed awake for hours, but if you were to ask me what I felt, I could not tell you. Some thoughts are too deep and too dangerous for words.

Tuesday, 6 July

When I woke this morning I could not remember where I was. My eyes traced the pale yellow walls, the crude stencil of olive leaves around the window. This place is fast receding from me. I can think of nothing but what is dead and gone. Outside I could hear the splashes and squawks of children in the pool, drifting up on the wind. I rose, pulled on my dressing gown, hung the Do Not Disturb sign outside the door, and as if drawn by magnetic force, came to the desk to open this book again.

The day after I had discovered you, I travelled to work as usual, dressed in my grey starched suit. I sat on the train, and marvelled at the way my fellow passengers' lives continued uninterrupted and unknowing. I found myself staring at them, and the unwelcome interest made a man look up and scowl, his ugly forehead splitting into an uneven map of grooves. I looked away, and stared out of the window as the train rattled crazily along the track; London rearing in panicky chaos around me, the buildings piling up in relentless, industrial layers, making it hard to breathe. I walked to the office, keeping my eyes on the ground. Inside, I shut my door and pulled down the blind, switched

274

my computer on. The emails that popped up — missives from clients, bringing work that it was my duty to handle — seemed to hail from a foreign land, making no sense at all.

It was almost eleven before I heard you outside my door, arguing with my secretary. She was telling you that I did not want to be disturbed, that I had expressly told her that no one was to be admitted all day. Your voice was raised, imperious. You pulled rank on her, telling her that you were my son and could therefore choose to see me whenever you wished. A moment's taut silence; and then you pushed open the door and came in, closing it tightly behind you. Your suit was crumpled, and your unwashed hair fell over your forehead. You appeared haggard and ill, as if you had not slept, and as I looked at you I remembered the professional mask of my own face in the mirror that morning, and felt briefly scornful that you could not hide your feelings from the world as I did.

Now that you had found me, you did not seem to know what to say. You stood indecisively in the centre of the room, looking everywhere but at me, one hand pulling convulsively at the knot of your tie. I was silent; I would not make this easy for you. At last you sat opposite me, and the look you gave me was full of a pain I had not wanted to see. You leant forward, clasping your hands together so tightly that I saw the knuckles whiten. You were shaking.

'Father,' you said, and I registered the strange formality, a term of address I did not think I had ever heard you use before, 'of all the ways I would have chosen for you to become aware of this situation, this would have been the last. I hardly know what to say.'

You stopped, as if you expected me to guide you gently towards the right words. I felt the familiar coldness descend on me. 'Do you think,' I said, 'that this is an appropriate time and place to say anything at all?'

You gave me a sharp look, and your mouth twisted as if you might laugh. 'I don't know what would be the right time and place,' you said. 'You always have such a sense of what is right and proper.' The comment landed like a rebuke, and I stiffened; instantly, you saw your mistake, and hastily stumbled on. 'I can't imagine what you must be feeling,' you said, 'and I'm not sure I can explain. Max and I — '

I interrupted you then; the wave of fury that came over me when I heard his name frightened me. I feared that I would not be able to keep it in check. 'I'd thank you not to speak that man's name to me,' I said.

You winced, as if I had slapped you. 'OK,'

you muttered. 'That's understandable, I suppose. I know you've never liked him, in any case. I know he doesn't behave well towards you. It's only because he's frustrated by the situation. He knows you'd never accept it.'

I gritted my teeth. I had no desire for you to be Max's apologist, and as I listened to you, all I could feel was incredulity, pure and simple. I could not stop myself from asking the question that had rolled around in my mind ever since I had seen the two of you together. 'Leaving all else aside for a moment,' I said, 'why him? It seems to me that the man is nothing but a charmless thug.' I felt some satisfaction in the condemnation, but when I saw your face tighten with hurt, I wished I had not watched your response. 'Whatever insane diversion this is,' I snapped, 'why choose him?'

You did laugh then, mirthlessly, a sound like breaking glass that you swallowed up an instant later. 'If it was a question of choice,' you said, 'don't you think I would have chosen to be content with Violet?' I was silent, sorting through your words in my head. 'I'm sorry,' you said then, your voice lower, and your head dropped down to your chest, as if you were exhausted. 'I know that this isn't what you want.'

'It is not what *you* want,' I said. The words came without thought, with sudden cast-iron conviction. In that instant, as never before or since, I felt the truth of them immovably within me, and I could see that my certainty shook you. You blinked, ran your tongue uneasily over your bottom lip.

'I don't know,' you said.

'You love Violet,' I said. Again, I knew that I spoke the truth. In the early stages I had watched you together, closely, almost obsessively. There had been none of the telltale reserve that characterised my relationship with Laura, no sign that you were settling for anything less than passion. You were not skilled enough in deception to fake such a performance.

You nodded, jerkily, your eyes full of confusion and regret. 'It's not that,' you said. 'Violet is everything I could want in a woman. It's only that I want something else, too.' You paused, considering how much to say. 'You should know that at college I had several affairs,' you said. 'With women, and with men. Perhaps you knew that already.'

I shook my head. Already I felt myself closing off from these words. The world was not as it had been forty years before. If you had had affairs, I told myself, they had been driven by idle curiosity, hedonistic youth, the

278

permissiveness of your peers. Nothing more.

'Lately,' you said, and your voice was tentative, as if you knew that to speak these words could be to alight upon a landmine, 'I've been wondering if Violet and I married too quickly. If part of the reason I married her was that I knew it was the only acceptable thing to do. In *your* eyes,' you said, and for the first time I caught a hint of anger blazing behind your despondence, a flame extinguished almost as swiftly as it had lit. You collected yourself, took a breath. 'I don't expect you to understand,' you said. 'How could you understand something like this?'

You were unaware, of course, of the irony in your words, but I was not, and they brought a swell of nausea to my throat that I had to swallow down. I tasted bitterness, sharp and sudden on my tongue. I thought of Roman, and I felt a sea-change, a sudden wave of compassion for you that left me feeling tense and suspended, unsure of what to say. I looked at you, slumped before me across the desk. I saw the bruised mauve shadows beneath your reddened eyes, the sad droop of your head. In that moment, my resolve faltered, and I thought, unavoidably, of the acceptance that could never have been shown to me — the utter inability that my own father would have displayed to understand who or what I was. I could give you something of this acceptance. I could show that I understood you more than you knew.

As I tried to imagine it, I felt myself close up. I thought of divorce, of social gossip. I thought of all the things that seem so hollow now, but which on that day, sitting with you in that room, seemed to pile up like mountains, far too high to climb. 'It has to end,' I said, and the relief that flooded me as I heard my own words told me that I had made the right decision. I met your gaze head on, and I felt the steel force of my will pass from me to you. 'If the man becomes difficult, he must be kept silent. Given money, if necessary.' The thought was distasteful to me, but it seemed a small price to pay for the recapturing of your happiness. 'I will say nothing to Violet,' I said, 'if you end this thing now.'

There was a long silence. I saw your eyes flick back and forth, assessing, weighing up the options open to you. At last, you nodded. You did not speak.

'You will get over this,' I said, and again you nodded. You rose to your feet, swaying slightly, as if you were drunk. You clasped my hand for an instant before you drew back and went out of the room. I was left sitting alone, staring unseeing at the computer screen. I did not understand the source of the sudden sadness within me — a deep pang of regret that made my head ache and my eyes sting. I believed I had acted correctly, and yet something told me that pushing this business underground would not be as easy as I hoped it would be; not for you, and not for me.

★ ★ ★

I told myself that you would be true to your word. Two days later, you came to me, white and drawn, and said that it was done. I had no reason to doubt you. I cut you off from telling me more; I had no wish to discuss the matter with you ever again. What must have come across as dispassionate lack of interest was in fact closer to fear. I found myself thinking of the black doctor's briefcase that had belonged to my father, and how I had thought as a child that if I opened it all the ills of the world would flood out and fill our house. This was a case, I told myself, which must stay locked, even if it meant unhappiness on your part. Better a temporary sadness than a terminal disruption to your life and the lives of those around you.

In the weeks that followed I heard of Max more than I saw him. He had come to be a figure of whom many in the town were wary.

Shopkeepers would comment confidingly on the brusqueness of his manner; the landlord of the Rose and Crown volunteered the information that he had twice had to remove Max, drunk and disorderly, from the premises. This information was not unexpected, but precious to me. It served to reinforce the conviction in my mind that he was crude, socially inept — an unsuitable and corrupting influence. I saw him, in those weeks, only once. He was sitting in the memorial garden, set back from the high street, slouched on a bench and staring straight ahead as if he could see nothing of the beauty around him. His legs were slung carelessly apart, tightening the fabric of his jeans around his crotch. In his coarse way, he radiated a powerful sexuality, and it repulsed me. I slowed my steps as I walked past the entrance, even though I had no intention of talking to him. The look he gave me was more eloquent than words; a look of embittered contempt, as a child might look upon another who has snatched a favourite toy. His eyes told me that you had acted as you had professed, and that I had won. After a few moments, he looked away, staring up at the shining blue canopy of sky.

I had thought that he might confront me — even attack me. I wonder now whether the reason he did not was that he somehow knew that your absence was only temporary.

It was only as October began that I started to notice a change in you again, and that only because of the closeness with which I was watching you whenever we met. To the outside eye, the change may well have been imperceptible, but to me it was as blatant and as shocking as if you had advertised it in neon lights. I can describe it only as a heightening of fever in you — a shifty light behind your eyes, a new nervousness in your movements, a willingness to laugh, loud and quick, at any given provocation. I saw the signs, and I felt my heart tighten with dread, but I did my best to block them out, to persuade myself that I was wrong. I succeeded too well. As I have said once before, I have always been good at blinding myself to obvious truths. And so when your phone call came, on the evening of Friday, 15 October, it shocked me more than it should have done.

You called my mobile phone; I was out in the garden alone, shivering in the last of the cold bright sunshine, raking the first of the autumn leaves from the flower bed. When I saw your name on the screen, I thought that you were calling to finalise plans for your next visit, of which we had vaguely talked a few days before. I dusted the earth from my hands, laid down the rake and answered the phone.

There was no preamble. You sounded calm, serene. 'I've tried, but it's no good,' you said. 'I'm calling to let you know that I intend to tell Violet tomorrow that I'm leaving her. It's not her fault, but I need to be with Max, and I'm tired of this subterfuge.'

Your words had knocked the breath from my body, and I felt dizzy. I reached out and leant my hand against the branch of the old apple tree for support. 'I don't think you realise what you are saying,' I said.

'I realise it absolutely,' you said; again that baffling tranquillity in your voice, as if you had been drugged. For a crazy instant, I wondered whether this was, indeed, a possibility. 'I know it will be hideous, and difficult for everyone concerned, but this is the way it has to be. I'll speak to you tomorrow.' You drew breath, as if to say goodbye, and I felt the sharpness of recklessness, an urgent need to reach you.

'Wait!' I shouted, and on the other end of the line, I felt you pause, struck by the uncharacteristic desperation in my voice. 'Do one thing for me,' I said unsteadily. 'Meet me tomorrow, before you speak to Violet.'

You sighed. 'It won't do any good, Dad,' you said. 'My mind is made up.'

'All the same,' I said. 'You owe me this much.' It was a cheap shot, a strategy that from anyone else I would have despised, but I knew that it would resonate with you. I had indeed given you much over the years: an education, a house, effectively a job. You were sensible of your advantages, and you knew that they had not come for free.

You hesitated for a moment, and then sighed again, but this time I heard the softness of acquiescence in your tone. 'If it will help you, then yes, I will meet you,' you said. 'But — '

I cut you off. 'Two o'clock,' I said, and then stopped. I had not thought so quickly as to have planned where to meet you. My house was out of the question; I already knew Laura to have arranged a lunch with several of the village wives. I ran through options in my head, dismissing each as too public, too close for comfort. 'Meet me down by Hunter's Lake,' I said at last. 'You know it?'

I heard the baffled note in your voice, but you agreed. I have asked myself countless times since what drove me to select the lake as a meeting point, but there is never an answer. There was no sinister motivation to my choice. It was simply a matter of alighting upon a thought, snatching at a hastily conceived solution. That much I am certain of, and yet sometimes when I wake in the middle of the night, in the oppressive silence of my room, I feel the ugly doubts stirring; the suspicion that somewhere, in some dark unacknowledged part of myself, I acted with meaning. These thoughts are the stuff of children's nightmares. By day they are ridiculous, puppet monsters without significance. And yet by night their power is so great, so all-consuming, that I could swear that they were real.

Wednesday, 7 July

I could not continue yesterday. When the moment came for me to write of the day you died, I found myself wanting to lay down my pen, put this diary aside and retreat into the denial in which I have lived for so long now. This morning my thoughts are different. It is useless to stop now, when I have said so much, and when there is so little left to say.

I drove to the lake at two. I wanted to be there early, before you, to compose my thoughts and decide on the best course of action. Sitting on the old wooden bench in the sharp autumn sunshine, looking out across that sparkling stretch of water, I thought of how I could make you see sense.

Possibilities came to me which seem ludicrous now. I thought of appealing to your better nature, of explaining the distress that you would cause to Laura if you pursued this course. I thought perhaps a child would cement your bond with Violet, give your life some deeper meaning. I thought even, in my desperation, of suggesting that you accorded yourself the luxury I had never given myself; an occasional indiscretion with some faceless man, enough to stem some physical need, with no threat posed to your marriage. These thoughts blinded me, and I did not see you approach until you were almost upon me. You had not shaved that day. You wore an old shirt and jeans, more casual than your usual style of dress, and it seemed that your appearance sent a signal, as if you were casting off the shackles of another life.

I saw at once that you had been drinking. Alcohol did not sit well with you, and it gave a hectic flush to your cheeks. Looking back, I can see that it was courage you wanted, but there and then, your drinking smacked of dissolution — just another sign that you were destroying the life you had built for yourself. It infuriated me, but I kept myself in check. To lecture you would be to lose any advantage that I had gained by bringing you here. I motioned for you to sit, but you shook your head, and instead I rose to join you. We stood facing each other, and I saw then that you were smiling. When you spoke, your voice was filled with the same serenity you had displayed on the phone the day before. You spoke with the smug surety of a religious leader, one who is unshakeably convinced of the righteousness of the course he follows, and who merely wishes others to be the same.

'I can't say much to you that I haven't already said,' you told me. 'I've made my decision. I'm sorry to have disappointed you, but I love Max, and he loves me, and that's an end to it.'

You did not sound sorry. You sounded calm, almost pitying, as if you could not hope to make me understand the purity of your feelings. I thought of Max — his saturnine, grinning face, the wicked flash of his dark eyes, the muscular roughness of his body. There were limits to my empathy. I could no more understand how you could be in love with this man than I could fly to the moon.

'I believe you are making a mistake,' I said, but my words sounded hollow even to my ears. Now that you were there in front of me, I sensed truly for the first time what I was up against; the relentless tidal wave of the conviction that had been awakened in you, that single-mindedness I had once admired, and which had always been impossible to overcome.

You shook your head slowly. 'I've tried for long enough now,' you said, 'to be the person you want me to be.' I could hear nothing of the anger that the words should have carried with them. Your voice was quiet and resigned, a little slurred. I looked into your eyes, and I saw no resentment there. They were as blue and clear and innocent as the day you were born.

'This is ridiculous,' I said, or something like it. I felt you slipping through my fingers, and that I could do nothing about it. I felt an ache somewhere deep within me, spreading through my body.

'I hope that one day, you will be happy for me,' you said then, and again you smiled, a smile of such shining certainty that for a second I felt my heart twitch unwillingly in response. An instant later, it enraged me. It was as if the thing were settled, that there was nothing left for me to do but to sit back and watch you throw away all the gifts that had fallen into your lap. I saw what you wanted from me, and I would not give it. There would be no easy absolution. I could feel my body shaking with the outrage of it, the self-centred assumption you made that I could forgive you.

'I will never be happy for you,' I said, spacing the words out with brutal clarity, and for the first time I saw your face twitch with anger. You made as if to leave, shuffling backwards, glancing back at the path down which you had come. If you had walked away from me then, I would have let you go. You moved a little away, and then you stopped. It was as if an idea had struck you at random, and seemed to you suddenly so meaningful that it must be shared.

'You know,' you said, and your tone was thoughtful and almost casual, 'it's not my fault that happiness has not come as conventionally to me as it did to you.'

I cannot explain the effect of those words, except to say that when I heard them, I was filled with a sudden fury that blotted out all rational thought and action. I felt myself transported, my whole body burning with rage. I made no decision to step forward — what drove me was deeper, instinctual. I gripped you by the shoulders and pushed you hard. Caught off guard, you stumbled back, and I saw the sudden fear in your eyes in the instant before you launched yourself forward again to meet me. We grappled together, and I felt the unexpected strength of you, the width and breadth of your body. You were young, but I was taller, and drink and disbelief had slowed you. I felt the blood humming in my head, the powerful, quick thud of my heartbeat. My hands reached out and pushed you again, and this time you fell back. I saw your foot skid against the uneven earth, saw you fight for balance and lose, and when you hit the ground, the angle at which you fell, the savage force of it, and the sickening crack of bone against rock, froze me to the spot. I stood there in the silence, watching you, for I do not know how long.

I did not touch you. I did not need to. You were entirely motionless, and your eyes were wide open.

★   ★   ★

I have sat here a long while. My mind strayed to petty matters. My plane leaves tomorrow morning. I must start to pack my things. I thought of the smoothing and folding of clothes, the wrapping of presents, the cool grey light of the airport, the sickening pull of the plane straining against gravity and rising, rising.

Useless to write of what I felt at that moment by the lake; impossible to conceive of a day when it will end. I still find it incredible, the effect of that one instant's anger. I spoke earlier of the randomness of disaster, but in reality, there was nothing random about your death. I caused it as surely as if I had planned it, and sometimes I wonder whether there is really so much difference, after all, between a planned crime and one that comes from nowhere. It strikes with just as much devastating finality. I do not believe in an afterlife. And yet somehow I still find myself obsessed with the worry that, somewhere, you are watching, and that you have not forgiven me.

The evil I have done is one I must keep with me, always. I have never known how much Laura knows. It is possible that shock has jumbled time in her memory — that she has never wondered why I returned that day white-faced and shaking, hours before your body was discovered, or that she has somehow cast my behaviour in the light of a premonition, foreshadowing tragedy. The way in which she looks at me from time to time, thinking herself unobserved, tells a different story, and I am not sure how this story ends.

The night after your death, I lay and watched the doorknob turn, saw her creep forward and pull back the covers, slide into bed without a word. I said nothing. And so it is that, with you gone, we have returned to the first years of our marriage, sleeping side by side, or at least pretending to do so. Perhaps she simply seeks comfort, even from such an unsatisfactory source. Perhaps it is more than this.

As I write I feel the familiar numbness descend. I have found this year that there are limits to what a man can feel. The pain, at times, is indescribable. But it cannot be sustained. This lack of feeling is my respite — the belief, however temporary, that to feel at all is futile, that there is after all nothing that can be done, and that the past is best forgotten. I do not look to the future. If I try to imagine it at all, I can see only blankness. Vast rolling swathes of time, holding nothing but what is already here.

I once read that the cruellest lies are often told in silence. It seems sometimes that my whole life gives truth to the words. I have kept silent, too much, when I should have spoken, and this quiet has tainted all whom it has touched — my father, Roman, Laura, Violet, you. It seems surreal and strange that the absence of a thing can do so much hurt. Far more than any words I could have said, far more even than the violence with which I struck you that day.

This silence is what holds me together. It will not break.

PART THREE

Violet

July

2008

I have been living my life nine months ago. The words come to me as if spoken by somebody else, hard and clear in my head. It is only now, standing out by the lake in this quiet, dense morning heat, that I realise the extent to which I have put myself on hold. Here Max is, waiting for me to speak, and I can see in the unblinking steadiness of his gaze that my words, as yet unknown to either of us, are crucial. The sensation is strange. I have grown used to being out of kilter; for months I have felt that I can have no influence on the world, nor it on me, but now something is changing. Whatever this moment is, I know that it is more real than the memories off which I have been existing. It is important. I have never felt such power, and yet I have no idea what to say.

'Harvey has been good to me,' I say at last, and as I speak his name an image of his face flashes vividly before me — attentive, unsmiling, heavy with secrets.

Max frowns, and he tilts his head to one side as if examining me. In the sunlight, his features have clarified into slashed, bright lines; sharp dark brows, cut-glass bones. I can see the strength humming beneath his skin. 'Good to you?' he repeats. His voice is gentle and puzzled. 'You mean, he lets you live with him? Gives you money? Treats you nicely?'

I nod, for after all, yes, this is what I have meant; these are the things that matter. Without Harvey, I cannot imagine where I would be.

Max comes closer and takes my hand in his; I feel the heat of him passing into me. 'You think it's goodness that makes him do those things,' he says, 'but it's not. It's *guilt*.' On the last word his soft tones snap. He spits it out like poison, and I flinch. I can hear the bitterness spilling out of him, and I can tell that whether or not he is right, he believes passionately in his words, and he cares about what he is saying. He cares, surely, for me.

All at once I feel my legs give way, and I sink to the ground. I sit by the bank of the lake, trailing my hand in the water, trying to think. It's no good; my mind feels slow and stupid, cushioned in cotton wool. I am so out of practice at exercising my judgement that I have no idea how to galvanise it into action. I watch the clear blue water swirl and envelop my skin as I sweep my fingers lightly beneath its surface.

'I don't want you to do anything,' I hear Max say. His voice is somewhere above me, seeming far away. 'I just need your house keys. I just need to get to him without causing a disturbance, catch him unawares. That's all. You don't have to be involved.'

I turn the request over in my head. It seems so small; it could be over in a moment. I imagine pulling the keys from my pocket and passing them to him, and try as I might I cannot imbue the act with any kind of tragic significance. I sit still, wondering what this means.

Max seems to take my silence for something else. He sits down beside me, slipping his arm around my waist, and at his touch I feel an inappropriate leap of desire. 'Look, I know this is a shock to you,' he says. 'Maybe this wasn't the right way to do it, but I had to tell you. I know it must be a shock,' he repeats, almost as if he expects me to nod and agree. I do not tell him that the strangest thing is that his words have come as no shock at all. The capability to kill is not something I have ever had reason to match to Harvey in my mind before, but now that the two things have been put together, there is no sense of incredulity. From our first meeting, I saw that hardness running through him — a capacity to crush emotion, or to channel it into violence. It is not the concept of Harvey killing which troubles me; it is the question of why.

'Harvey loved Jonathan,' I say, and this I do believe, without doubt. I spent years watching the two men together; the quick, unspoken bond that could flash between them in a simple look, a grimace, a roll of the eyes. I saw Harvey's face in the church when his son and I married, and I have not forgotten the pride I read in it, a pride so fierce and joyous that it seemed as if he found it almost unbearable.

Max shrugs. My eyes are on his profile, but he looks straight ahead, frowning intently out at the shimmering line on the horizon where water blurs into sky. His lips tighten, as if to press back words.

'So why would he have done such a thing?' I continue. It's a simple enough question, but as I speak, the calmness of my voice, belying the melodrama of what is behind the words, suddenly sounds ludicrous. I have to bite my lip to stop myself from giggling. The sense of unreality strengthens — the strange silence of the air, the shiny unmoving landscape around us. For a moment, I wonder whether I am still asleep.

Max looks at me now with something close to fear. 'Do you really want to know?' he asks. I nod, and he runs his tongue quickly along his lower lip. I see his throat bob as he swallows. 'This will hurt you,' he says, 'but Jonathan was having an affair.' He watches me warily, waiting for me to scream or sob in protest. I do neither. I think of all the times that I shouted the same accusation in my husband's face, burning up with rage and grief, until I grew so tired of his constant denials that we settled, in those last weeks, into an uneasy truce. The suspicion had never left me, but after his death, it had receded in the face of a deeper grief. I had told myself that I would never know for sure, and that torturing myself over the unknown was less than pointless. Now, as I watch Max, his eyes darting across my face, searching for some hint of emotion there, I realise that Jonathan does not have to be alive for me to discover the truth, and I am not sure that I want to.

'Who was it?' I ask nonetheless.

'You don't need to know that,' says Max. He speaks in a monotone. I cannot tell whether his words are intended to protect me, or to put me in my place.

'That's not for you to say,' I reply.

'I'll never tell you.' Those four words carry such conviction that I do not bother to ask again. I would have expected the question to matter more, but in this moment it seems unimportant. I need to hear what he will say next.

Max turns his face away, as if it is easier to talk without me watching him. 'Jonathan and I were closer than you knew,' he says. 'He confided in me. He told me that he wanted to leave you. He was planning to do it on the day he died.' Dimly, I register the lack of gentleness with which he says these things. It seems that he is no longer so concerned for my feelings. Each sentence echoes in my head, and I wait for the pain, but there is nothing, only numbness.

'I don't see,' I say, 'what this has to do with Harvey.'

Max looks at me curiously. I can tell that he is surprised by the coolness of my reaction, that he is wondering whether, after all, his initial estimate of me as *a cold fish* was near the mark. Perhaps he is thinking that I never loved Jonathan at all. At the idea, I feel the corners of my mouth dully twitch.

'Harvey found out,' he says, 'and he was furious. He couldn't bear the thought of Jonathan divorcing you. The man's a control freak,' he adds, with sudden bitter levity. 'You know that. I . . . I'm not sure what happened. I think they met up. I think Harvey wanted to talk him out of it, but Jonathan wasn't budging. I don't know if he planned it. He might not have meant to do it. I . . . I don't know.' Somewhere along the line, Max has lost his earlier conviction. He's floundering, and once again he looks suddenly insane and desperate, as if he is making this up as he goes along.

'So really,' I say slowly, 'you have no idea what happened. You don't know that Harvey killed him.'

'Oh, I *know*,' Max says. His voice cracks with defiant certainty. 'I know. I just can't prove it.'

I am not stupid. I know that he has not told me the full story, that there are things he is hiding from me. I can see it in the way he holds my gaze without a blink, the way he did not miss a beat before answering me, as if my scepticism was anticipated and reasonable. I barely know him, and yet my instinct tells me to believe him. Try as I might, I can think of no reason he would have to lie. I look at him: the sloping dark eyes, bruised by shadows, the hard yet sensuous line of his mouth. I think of his muscular arms pinning me back against the wall in the dark bedroom the night before, and the rough touch of his hands against my skin. A tremor runs through me, and I realise how closely lust and terror are linked, so closely that I am not sure which it is that I am feeling.

'Why do you care?' I ask. It strikes me that this is the crux of the matter. A fortnight ago, I had never seen Max before. As far as I had known, he had been no part of the fabric of our lives, and the realisation that somehow he has been woven into my past for all these months without my knowledge unsettles me in some queasy, nebulous way I can barely define.

'I care about justice,' Max says. His voice is level now, and he does not seem afraid to meet my eyes. 'Answering to your crimes. Like I said, I can't prove it. Can't see myself trotting along to the police station and saying to them, *He killed him. I know, I just know.*' For an instant he slips into a scornful parody of himself, uncannily capturing the mad waver and crack of his voice minutes before. 'But it's not just that. Jonathan was a good man,' he says. There is something in his tone that, bizarrely, reminds me of Laura, and I realise that it is because there is something faintly evangelical in the way he speaks. I realise, too, with an obscure pang of guilt, that it is the first time that Laura has come to mind, as if she is irrelevant in all of this. Max is still speaking, and with an effort I drag myself back to focus on his words. ' . . . didn't deserve this,' he is saying. 'I owe it to him to set this straight.' Not for the first time, I register the way he talks in euphemisms, almost coy, sidestepping the real brutality of what he means.

I get up from the bank, feeling the world dip around me. I realise I am very tired. 'I need some time to think,' I say. 'Call me tomorrow.'

Max scrambles to his feet, placing his hand on my arm. 'You mustn't tell anyone what I've told you,' he says. I feel his grip on my arm tighten. 'You have to promise.' I nod. 'Promise me,' he says again, and I say the words. He releases me, and a shadow passes across his face. 'I don't have your number,' he says. And there, under the willow trees by the lake in the strengthening sun, we take out our phones and exchange numbers, for all the world as if we were just two ordinary people getting to know one another, making a date.

'I'll speak to you tomorrow,' I say.

Max frowns. 'It's miles to town,' he says. 'Let me drive you somewhere.'

I shake my head. 'I'm going to stay here for a while,' I say. 'You go.'

He hesitates, then nods. Awkwardly, he leans forward and touches his lips to my cheek. They feel cold and ungiving. On impulse, I twist my head round and quickly cover his mouth with my own, pressing my lips hard against his. The violence of the kiss takes me by surprise. When I pull away I am panting, as if he has knocked me to the ground. He stares at me, and I hear the sharpness of his breath too, hoarse and ragged. It doesn't sound like desire. It sounds like fear.

★　★　★

I stay out by the lake for hours, until my limbs feel heavy and limp in the heat, drifting in and out of sleep. When I finally sit up, I see that the sunlight has shifted across the water, casting a sparkling shadow on to the bank. It is only this, and the fuzzy pounding in my head, like sunstroke, that tells me how long I have lain here. I look around. A few metres away, a family are picnicking — the parents in slacks and cotton shirts, two little girls in pink dresses wriggling and kicking on the picnic blanket, and a fat golden dog sprawled on the grass, panting foolishly and happily, its tongue lolling from its mouth. The parents are talking in low voices, occasionally glancing across in my direction. I am used to this. For a while, I became a kind of tragic celebrity in the village; people would come up to me and press my hand in corner shops, or keep a respectful distance, shaking their heads in pantomime sorrow. These days, and this far out of town, these occurrences are fewer. People are forgetting Jonathan — forgetting not only his life, which few of them knew anything about, but his death too. Some people's memories, though, are longer than others', and as I watch the couple, their heads bent conspiratorially together, it seems as if I can hear their whispering, louder and louder, like wind rushing through the trees.

Abruptly, I stand up, and as I do so the dog starts from its position and ambles towards me, slowly at first, then breaking into an uneven, shambling run. I turn my back and begin to walk up towards the road, but it follows, lolloping crazily around my feet, its panting loud and rasping, its fur warm and soft on my legs. Behind me, I hear a call, then the sound of footsteps rushing to catch up with me. The woman has come to fetch her dog. As she tugs on its collar, coaxing it away, her eyes are gleaming with recognition.

'So sorry,' she says. 'He gets a bit overexcited.' I make some noise of acceptance and move away, but her voice pulls me back. 'I'm sorry . . . ' she says, and this apology is not like the last one; diffident and yet demanding, forcing me to listen to her. 'You're Violet Blackwood, aren't you? I remember . . . I'm so sorry about your husband.'

I stare at her. I have never known how to respond to this kind of thing, and in the light of what has passed between myself and Max, it feels even more false, even more surreal. The woman cocks her head to one side. She bites her lip, and her eyes flood with pity. 'I suppose you must come here a lot,' she says. It's an innocent enough statement, but the sentiment behind it enrages me. This woman has no business to think that I am stuck in the past, too pathetic to move on, even if it has been largely true up until now. My silence seems to unnerve her. Like most people, she wants it filled with words, feels uncomfortable with any other kind of communication. 'If you ever need a friendly face to talk to . . . ' she says, even though the wild look that flickers in her eyes for an instant tells me that she knows that she is talking nonsense now, grasping at straws, ' . . . well, I'm here. We're all here.'

Yes, I think. *All here, watching me, never off duty.* Suddenly it strikes me that the time I have spent with Max will not have gone unnoticed either. Even now, someone will be talking, starting the trickle of gossip through the village. My throat tightens with panic, and all at once I know that I cannot be here today. The thought of wandering around the village alone, fending off other people's stares and overtures, is too much to bear, and I don't want to go back home either. I don't want to face Harvey yet, to have to look at him in the light of Max's words and discover how they have changed him in my eyes. I must get away. I walk fast, up towards the road, leaving the woman with her dog behind me, ignoring her call. Blood thumps in my head as I walk faster and faster, my feet stumbling on the uneven ground. I have turned in the direction of the station, but I still do not know where I am going. Possibilities scramble through my head, popping like bubbles instants after they are formed. When the solution comes to me, I feel calm spread through me for an instant. Of course. I will go to London, to the Sherbourne Club, where Jonathan and I used to go together. I will take a room and stay overnight in the hotel above.

I am walking with new purpose now, my steps quick and strong. I can see the club as vividly as if I stood there; the green-panelled walls, the heavy oak beams, the polished tables and the sumptuous carpet that led to the restaurant. And Jonathan, groomed and striking, moving easily through the crowd, nodding his greetings to everyone he passed.

It is only when I try to put myself into the scene that my imagination fails me. It was never truly my world. Whenever I was there with him, I felt peculiarly unreal, transparent like a ghost, and from the way the eyes of the other members looked blankly through me, I might as well have been. What once seemed like an irritant is now an advantage. It will not be how it is in Brenchley — the oppressive knowledge, the unwanted attention. No one will recognise me, even if they have seen me a dozen times before.

Lost in my own head, I become aware of the vibration in my pocket some seconds before I connect it with the sharp, tinny sound that suddenly fills the air. I pull my phone from my pocket, not slowing my steps, and look at the caller display. *Catherine* flashes on the screen. I hesitate for a moment, then push the button to accept the call.

'Hello? Hello?' I hear her say, before I have a chance to speak. Her voice sounds strained and agitated.

'It's me,' I say. This conversation is already muddled, the wrong way round.

'Are you OK, Violet?' she asks.

'I'm fine.' The words are automatic. I have long since realised that they are what people want to hear, and the truth is too complicated to discuss. 'Why wouldn't I be?'

There is a pause at the other end of the line, and I hear her sigh. 'Well, no reason, really,' she says. 'It's just — I know you were meeting up with Max this weekend, he told me. I just thought . . . well, I just wanted to check that you weren't getting in too deep with him. I know I encouraged you, but maybe it was stupid. I got a bit carried away. I don't think you're right for each other. He's not — '

I feel confusion wash over me. I am still walking, and her voice drifts in and out of earshot as cars zoom past on the road. 'Wait,' I interrupt her. 'What's the problem? Has Max said something to you?'

'No, no.' Catherine sounds worried and wary. 'I know he likes you, but . . . I'm not sure it's more than that. Like I said, I don't think it would work out.'

'I think that's for us to find out,' I say eventually. I am baffled by this whole conversation. I frown as I walk along, turning up towards the station's entrance. I feel a spark of anger at Catherine, who has always seemed so sweet and unthreatening, and wonder what she would say if I told her the truth. *Your precious brother fucked me up against a wall last night. Why don't you ask him if he does that to everyone he 'likes'?* For one heady instant, my lips part and the words threaten to spill out. I force them back. 'I'll see you at the shop on Friday,' I say instead.

'I don't want you to get hurt,' she says, as if I have not spoken. It seems that everyone is desperate to prevent me from getting hurt. They want me wrapped up in cotton wool, locked in an ivory tower with my hands tied behind my back, so that I can come to no harm. All except Max. I cannot voice these thoughts to her — that to have someone treat me with such roughness, bordering on violence, is a perversely sweet relief after all these months of protection. It is better to say nothing at all.

I snap the phone shut and switch it off. Up ahead, I can see a train pulling in, its brakes grinding and screeching as it judders to a halt on the track. I gather my strength and run fast towards the platform.

★ ★ ★

The building that houses the club is larger than I remembered; a tall stone façade, an unmarked gilt-edged door. I once asked Jonathan why there was no name plaque outside, and I still recall the amused twist of his mouth as he told me that anyone who did not know what this building was had no business being there at all. At the time, the words gave me a thrill. The pleasure of knowing that I had been accepted into this inner circle, albeit by proxy rather than achievement, felt almost sensual. Now, these words come back to me imbued with a coldness that makes my stomach lurch. Across the street, I watch as two well-dressed men approach the door, pushing their way inside with easy confidence. I rarely think about my age — it seems irrelevant, and I sometimes feel that a whole lifetime's experience has been confusingly compressed into my twenty-one years — but as I stand there, breathing deeply to calm my nerves, I suddenly feel very young.

I smooth my hands down my dress, and as I do so I realise that I have worn the same clothes since yesterday morning. The material of my mauve sundress feels stiff and rough against my skin, and when I bring my hands to my face I smell smoke and burnt ash. I feel dirty, in need of a hot shower. The thought of walking into that pristine building in these clothes is frightening, but when I glance at the shop window behind me I am reassured. I look neat and clean, my appearance betraying nothing of the story behind it. As I gaze at my shadowy reflection, I think of Max's hands on my dress, wrenching the straps off my shoulders and the zip down my back, his fingers snaking roughly up the inside of my thighs. A shiver passes through me, and I turn away and step out into the street, blinking in the bright sun.

The gilt door is heavy and cool on my skin. I push it open and see the reception ahead, a warm green cocoon tucked into the back wall. I walk towards it. I think I have seen the woman behind the desk once or twice before. She is dark-haired and exotic, a perfectly tended hothouse flower under the pale green spotlights. Her skin is olive-tinted, and her eyes are narrow and sloped, hinting at Chinese blood. She smiles when she sees me. There is no suspicion in her face, and emboldened, I step forward.

'I'd like to take a room for this evening,' I say.

The woman nods, turning to the computer. 'Are you a member?' she asks.

'No,' I say, watching her closely for signs of sarcasm. I would be surprised if this club had any members as young as I am; it is reserved for the great and the good, for those — largely men — who have achieved some level of success in the legal profession. The woman's face is pleasantly impassive as her eyes scan the screen. She asks me for my name, and I tell her. When she hears the surname, she pauses for a fraction of a second, her fingers hovering over the keys.

'Blackwood,' she repeats as she taps it in.

'My father-in-law is a member,' I say. 'Harvey.' She nods, but I can tell that this has not extinguished the spark of memory that the name has fired up. As she takes down my details, her eyes look vacant, as if she is searching the recesses of her mind.

I hand over my credit card and watch her ring it through. 'You're welcome to use the main restaurant and the Long Bar, but I'm afraid the Circle Bar is reserved for members only,' she says. This much I know already. Jonathan used to joke about the magic circle, the place where none but he and his kind could come. I remember its secretive dim lighting, the way its curved chairs used to gleam in the semi-dark. 'Your room is number nineteen. Will you be wanting the key now?' she asks.

'Yes, please,' I say. After a tiny hesitation, I take the key she holds out to me. She gives me a painted smile, and turns back to the computer screen. I am dismissed.

The lift carries me up to the first floor with a soft, sinister hum. Its shimmering golden doors slide slowly apart to reveal a long low-lit corridor, tiny spotlights glimmering down on to a plush royal blue carpet. I walk along the corridor, my footsteps cushioned in the soft carpet. The numbers are carved into the doors in dark wood, etched in curled strokes. Number 19 is right at the end, on the left-hand side. I slot the heavy metal key into its lock and turn, pushing the door open. Inside, the same low lighting, this time tinted red; a bulb glowing from a crimson lampshade, the wall behind the bed painted burgundy. The bed is huge and luxurious, draped in dark silk sheets with fat plumped pillows piled up against the headboard.

I stand in the centre of the silent room, not wanting to sit down. Unbidden, a thought creeps over me. *He was here.* I have grown used to sensing Jonathan in the places I know he has been — the Blackwoods' house, the village church, the lake — but never before have I felt this strange, ghostly sense of his presence in an unknown place. Out of the corner of my eye, I think I see something moving, a strip of light sliding under the door of the en suite bathroom, and I shiver. It takes no imagination at all to feel that at any moment he could push open the door, wet from the shower and naked, and step out into the room to face me. I cross to the bathroom door and swiftly push it open, letting it swing back to reveal the empty room inside. Marbled walls, gleaming fixtures, a long low mirror with the strip-light above it flickering.

As I watch, the light fizzes, burns out and goes dead.

I swallow down the rise of panic and turn back into the bedroom. I switch on the large plasma-screen television, but the blare of noise that fills the room jolts my nerves even more, and I quickly hit the mute button. I watch the bright pixellated pictures, light bouncing off the screen and swimming across the walls. Carefully, I sit down on the bed. It is almost eight o'clock. As I stare at the television, I cannot stop the images in my mind, fighting with those on the screen, blocking them out. I think of Jonathan's bright blue eyes travelling over someone else's body, his hands tracing the path his gaze has taken. I feel my eyes sting. I concentrate on the rhythm of my breathing, coaxing myself into a kind of trance. It feels as if I could have been in this room for a matter of seconds, or for several hours. Time has lost its meaning here. It is simply something that must be endured, that has to be got past.

After a while I swing my legs off the bed and go to the door. If I stay here all evening, I know I will be unable to sleep. I will go out, find a place to sit and drink, and then return late and get into bed without switching on the light.

Out on the street the air has cooled, and

the breeze against my bare arms and legs chills me. Dusk is falling, and all the way down the street, lights twinkle out warmly from the windows of shops and pubs. I walk silently, taking in the scene around me. I am struck by the strangeness of this situation, and I think of Jonathan — of what he would say if he could see me here now. I imagine his face, washed in confusion and surprise, and have a sudden bizarre impulse to laugh out loud. I press my lips together and turn into a bar at random. It is all smooth metal surfaces, with twisted, sculptural light fittings exploding like electric-blue fireworks from the ceiling. In the half-darkness, I see groups of men huddled around tables, heads briefly swinging to me and ranking me, sizing me up, before turning away again. I approach the bar, but all at once the thought of asking for a drink seems exhausting and daunting. I do not want to speak to anyone. I swing away and find a table in the corner of the bar, slump down into the chair. There is a little tea-light in a bright blue holder in the middle of the table, its flame dancing and sparking in front of my eyes like a camera flash. I stare at it, and my mind empties.

The voice filters through to me slowly. Someone is saying my name. 'Violet,' the voice says. 'Violet Blackwood.' Hesitant at first, then insistent. I look up and see a woman there, swaying faintly above me. She is staring at me, and I can see the blood draining from her face, her perfect porcelain skin lightening and lightening until she looks almost ghostly under the pale blue lights. Her painted red lips fall open. At first I do not recognise her. And then, as my eyes travel over her gleaming fair hair, not a strand out of place, and her tightly fitted black suit, I realise that it is Alice, the receptionist. Somewhere in the back of my mind, I had assumed that she had left the club. Looking at her now, I know that she is in uniform, and that her appearance here signals a shift just ending, or one just about to begin.

I know that my silence is unnatural, but I cannot force my words out. In Jonathan's last months alive, I carried an image of this woman with me everywhere I went: sat behind the reception desk, her hair bright and blonde against the smooth slippery green wall, looking up through her eyelashes and smiling, smiling. It is an image that has faded over time without my realising it, and as I bring it back to the forefront of my mind it feels remote and strange. I think of the accusations I hurled at my husband — the ugly fantasies of him and her together that whirled through my mind as I did so. I believed them, but now, seeing her here as flesh and blood in front of me, I cannot fit the theory with the reality. I can see the fine lines at the corners of her eyes, the hints of imperfection behind the veil of foundation she wears. She is shorter than I thought; shorter than I am.

'Violet?' Alice says again. 'It is you, isn't it?' I cannot see myself through her eyes, cannot imagine my own expression, and the muscles of my face feel so stiff that I am powerless to change it. As she looks at me, she seems almost frightened. 'Wait here,' she says, and backs away. The thought flits across my mind that I could get up and walk out of the bar, but I cannot seem to send the message to my body. I sit there, feeling my heart start to thump, as if I am being dragged out of a deep sleep.

A minute later Alice returns, holding two glasses and a bottle of white wine. I don't want her to pay for my drink, but I can't summon up the energy to tell her so. 'Drink,' she says. 'You look like you need it.' She pours the wine, and I watch it falling into my glass, a sparkling translucent stream. I have no idea what to say.

In the end it is she who speaks again. 'I haven't seen you around for months,' she says. 'I expected you to come back to the club long ago, after Jonathan died.'

I remain silent. There is something brutal about the simplicity of her words. People generally use euphemisms, or talk around death, not wanting to make it real. I sip my drink, and its coolness eases my throat, fluid and supple. Alice drinks too, her eyes on me.

'I think I know why you're here now,' she says; whether to challenge or reassure me I cannot tell. She is strangely elusive, the subtle signs that dart across her face impossible to pin down or interpret.

I realise that I must speak now, and with difficulty I unlock the words in my head and draw them out into the open. 'I'm not here for any reason,' I say, 'except to be alone. I'm staying at the club tonight, and then I'm going back home.'

Alice peers down swiftly at the key I am still clutching in my hands. 'Nineteen,' she says, and her face twists with something; shock, maybe, but spiked with something else, some dark amusement or irony. I sense a realisation dawning, the recollection of some secret I do not yet know.

I feel a tiny stab of anger. The knowingness in this woman's eyes taunts me, but her hand is outstretched in concern. I don't want her to gloat over me, and nor do I want her sympathy. I will make her change her tune.

'You know,' I say, hearing my voice come out louder and sharper than I intended, 'Jonathan was having an affair.' Her face is a beautiful mask. She does not look surprised, but neither does she look particularly guilty. 'And I think it was with you,' I say, acutely aware that I sound absurd, like some foolish woman playing detective in a parlour game. I no longer know whether or not I believe what I am saying.

Alice does not seem to care about my turn of phrase. As I speak, her face suddenly springs to life — she looks incredulous, then amused. The change is too quick to be faked, and in that instant I am certain that she has never been near my husband. The realisation is dull and anticlimactic. I stare down at my glass, watching the bobbing spotlights above dance and swim in its depths until my vision goes fuzzy.

Alice is speaking, her voice cool, but tinged with compassion. 'Jonathan and I were friendly, to a point,' she says. 'He was a regular customer. He flirted, in the way that such customers usually do. But to have an affair with someone he essentially regarded as staff would have been impossible for him. Ridiculous. He wouldn't have stooped so low. I'm surprised that, having been married to him, you don't realise that for yourself.' The last words sound more bitter, and I glance sharply up at her. It is possible, I think, that she loved him; perhaps even that she made an approach, and was rejected. She has no loyalty to me, after all. I turn her words over in my head. My instant reaction is rebellion. After all, they do not fit with how Jonathan and I first became lovers . . . the summer secretary, seduced by her dashing employer. But perhaps it was different for us, or perhaps he saw me in a different way: a temporary fixture in his firm, but destined all the while for greater things. I know that Jonathan was bound by his class; that my own humble background was a source of subtle agitation for him throughout our marriage.

Alice takes my silence for acceptance, and laughs a short brittle laugh. 'Besides,' she says, 'I don't think I was his type.' Her voice is loaded with a meaning I cannot understand. Her face changes again, grows serious. For the first time, I feel her really look at me — as a woman, an equal. 'You look ill,' she says, 'and so much older. To be honest, I think you should do your best to forget about Jonathan and move on. You weren't right for him. You weren't right for each other.'

Her words bring an acute sense of déjà vu. I realise that they almost exactly echo those spoken to me by Catherine on the phone earlier, warning me against my involvement with Max. *I don't think you're right for each other. I don't think it would work out.* Who, I wonder, would be right for me in other people's eyes? I feel a sharp twinge of exasperation. I do not know what right these outsiders think they have to comment on my relationships. It is as if they do not want me to be happy — and yet even as the thought flashes through my mind it is replaced by another; the consciousness that I am not happy, have not been for some time, and that even when I was it was tinged by the desperation of fearing that it would not last.

I raise my eyes to Alice's again, and I know that there is a subtext to what she has said to me. 'How do you know?' I say slowly. 'Is it because you know who he was sleeping with, if not you?'

Her silence hangs between us like a wire, taut and buzzing, ready to spark into life. Her fingers begin to tap against the side of her wineglass, betraying her agitation; the high faint sound of her long, red-painted finger-nails hitting the glass buzzes in my head. She purses her lips, as if remembering some private scene, and glances back at me, deciding how to shape her words. 'In my position,' she says at last, 'you have to learn discretion. Sometimes, customers appear with guests who are not their partners, and ask for a room for a few hours. Sometimes erratically, sometimes regularly. They usually always take the same room. They tend to make the booking in the other person's name. As the receptionist, who has seen them come and go for years and knows their families, their histories, naturally I am aware of the situation — but to comment on it, or to draw the attention of their partners to what is going on, would be entirely inappropriate. I'm sure you see why.'

She is speaking in generalities, but my blood is fizzing through my veins, my heart beating with unexpected adrenalin. I know that she is talking about my husband. I must tread carefully, not antagonise her. I make my voice soft and pleading. 'What name?' I ask. 'What name would the booking be made in?' I wait for Alice's answer, suddenly tasting bitterness at the back of my throat. Behind her, shadows glide across the smooth metal wall, reflected darkly in its brushed surface. She hesitates, and I feel the pendulum swinging. This woman owes me nothing, and yet mixed with that unpleasant glee we all feel when dropping a bombshell and watching the shards scatter all around us, I see what looks like genuine pity in her gaze.

She leans forward, and her voice is a soft

whisper, her eyes tense and watchful, as if I am a snake that might strike at any moment. 'Does the name Croft mean anything to you?' she says.

* ★ *

I push my chair back with a screech, stand up and walk quickly away from her, across the bar. I have drunk hardly anything, but my head is swimming, and all around me the tables of chatting customers rise and fall, shrink in and out of focus, shade from light to dark. She does not try to follow me. For an instant I simply stand there. Across the room, I see the barman looking at me, his face ruffled by bored concern. He looks like a figure in a dream, a cardboard cut-out who I could peel out of the scene as easily as stretching my hand out. I blink and turn away, pushing my way through the milling groups of people out to the street. The cool summer night breeze lashes my body, and I feel a shiver pass through me, all my hairs prickling.

Catherine. I see her face before me, stamped across the vista of the street ahead. Feathered, platinum hair, clear green eyes, pixie features whose natural setting is innocent and sweet. I see what is behind them now. She has lied to me all along. Pretending that she did not even know that I had been married, when all the time she had been screwing my husband behind my back, seducing him, perhaps even loving him. I do not want the images that come to me, but I can't shut them out, can't close my eyes against them. Her head tipped back in ecstasy, her mouth half open. His hands around her neck, threatening yet loving, his body moving over hers.

I can see it as clearly as if I were there — and after all, I have been there, myself, there beneath him hundreds and hundreds of times — and I hear myself make a sound, a harsh sob of pain that I cannot silence. Out on the street, a man swings round when he hears me and looks at me quizzically, wondering whether I am all right. I shake my head and begin to walk back to the club. I block my thoughts out as best I can, force my way through the heavy doors, let the lift carry me up to my floor. When I unlock the door of Room 19 once again, I wince as I enter. I approach the bed, but the instant I lie down I feel as if it is branding me. I cannot lie where they might have lain. I pull the pillows off the bed and drag the cover with them. Curling up on the hard floor, pressed against the wall, I close my eyes. I tell myself that I will not open them again until morning. Willpower is one thing that I have. I can control myself, if nothing and no one else.

When I sense the light stream in, pulsing across my closed lids, I do open my eyes. I have no idea whether I have slept at all. In the warm light of the morning, the room looks innocent and drained of all sinister meaning. Slowly, I pull myself to my feet, feeling my limbs ache and strain. I go to the bathroom and draw back the shower curtain, turn the water on. Naked, I step in under the stream. The water is hot and steaming, stinging my body. I feel that it can never be hot enough for what I need — to be stripped and reborn, my skin peeling back to reveal another me, bright and new, untouched by tragedy. As I stand there I can feel the tears rolling down my cheeks, mingling with the water, but I make no sound. I am crying out my weakness, because when I see her I will need to be strong.

I dress in the same dress for the third day running, feeling dirty and tarnished. I cannot face her like this. I will go back home, change my clothes and then set out for the shop. The decision gives me purpose. I set my teeth as I walk down to the reception. Alice is there, calm and serene, her shining blonde hair plaited neatly against her neck. She looks at me as if I am a stranger.

'Checking out?' she says sweetly. 'I hope you had a pleasant stay.'

So this is how it is to be. I nod and sign the paper she pushes towards me. In a way I am grateful. I do not want to acknowledge the favour she has done me, a favour that is no blessing at all. As I thank her and sling my handbag on to my shoulder, I see a brief, almost imperceptible spark of meaning in her eyes. *I have given you this knowledge*, it says. *Do with it what you will.*

I take the train back to my nearest station without buying a ticket, not caring whether I am discovered. To negotiate the ticket office seems like too much effort, an unnecessary distraction. All the way back, I stare out of the window at the scenery that moves past; the hectic jumble of city buildings giving way to vast calm green fields, the blossoming trees that line the track. While I see these things I do not need to think. They are simple, uncomplicated by emotion. I must put my feelings on ice until I need them again.

At the station I hail a taxi back into Brenchley, and I let the driver chat to me, his words rolling over me like a wave, occasion- ally making some sound of assent or surprise. When we pull up outside the Blackwoods' house I pay him and offer a tip, and he beams in good-natured thanks. It seems that this is all it takes to make people happy: to smile and nod and pander to their conversation. Perhaps I have not been passive enough in the past. It would be easier to move through life without complaining, without even noticing what is wrong, if I could only manage it. I have never stopped fighting, and much good it has done me.

I unlock the front door and go quietly inside. The house is silent and dark. After two days away, I feel as if I am seeing it for the first time. The elegant carved banisters, the dark woven rug across the hallway, the long narrow painting at the foot of the stairs. These things are no part of me, but as I see them I feel an odd pang of homesickness and regret, strange and unsettling to feel now, when I have come back home. The smell that hangs in the hallway is familiar, a subtle mix of musk and spice. I climb the stairs quietly, and go into my bedroom, to the window-seat. I look out into the back garden, and there is Harvey. He is working at the flower beds, his shirtsleeves rolled up, pushing a spade into the earth. From time to time he reaches forward and grasps a stem with his bare hands, ripping the weed out by the root, then tossing it on to the pile of debris at his side. As I watch him, my eye is caught by something flickering in my peripheral vision. I turn my head and see Laura where the left wing of the house juts out, standing at the upstairs window, just across from me. She has drawn the lace curtain back behind her. I can tell that she has not seen me. She is staring down at Harvey, intently, never taking her eyes off him.

As I look between the two of them, as they think themselves unobserved, a sudden sway of vertigo hits me. I feel like a ghost; that even if they were to look in my direction, they would look through me as if I were not there. The words I have blocked out, Max's words, drift back into my mind. *His own father. His own father* . . . I look at Harvey as he thrusts the spade into the earth. I can sense the unswerving purpose with which he works, can imagine the soft hum escaping through his teeth. I know him so well, and yet barely at all. As I glance back at Laura, there is something in her face which unsettles me. Her lips are compressed tightly together, her expression rigid, and suddenly, with sickening clarity, I realise that she is frightened of him.

I cannot think about this now. I must handle one thing at a time. Breaking away from the window, I strip off my clothes. I pull on crisp new underwear, a vibrant red top, a dark denim miniskirt, a pair of heeled sandals. It is the kind of outfit I have not worn for some time. It clings to the curves of my body, and as I look at myself in the mirror I feel sexy and powerful. I glare at my reflection, feeling the anger coming back, flooding me from top to toe. There is a violence inside me, simmering beneath the surface, waiting to explode. I know it — I acknowledge it. Now I will use it. I turn on my heel and leave the room, and I feel the anger rising inside me. With every step I take, it grows stronger. Outside, I follow the familiar route towards the shop, my head held high. When I see the curvy letters dancing ahead, *Belle's Boutique*, the sign swinging in the light breeze, I do not falter. I walk straight up to the door and push it open. I can feel the static crackling off myself, creating a force field, buzzing all around me.

She is alone. I do not stop to think of how I would have acted had the shop been full of customers — whether it would have stopped me. She is sitting perched on the stool by the side of the till, drinking her mid-morning mug of tea. Her fingers are curled prettily round the cup, her fingernails painted in that ludicrous shade of emerald green.

She is playing at being a little girl, but I know better. I know what she is capable of. When she hears the bell she looks up and smiles in surprise to see me there. I'm not expected today, and she puts down her tea and slips off the stool to come forward and welcome me. She has barely taken two steps before she freezes. She has seen my face. I stride towards her, feeling hot and sore behind my eyes with the effort not to blink. I snatch a bag from the display cabinet, and I hurl it across the room. It hits the wall with a satisfying thwack, but it's over too soon. I cross to the till and snatch up the mug.

Catherine is crying out now, asking me to stop, to tell her what the matter is, but I ignore her. I throw the mug with all my force, watching the remaining contents spilling out dark and brown, scattering against the white wall; then the shattering crack of ceramic against brick, the shards spilling out in all directions. Catherine cowers behind the till, her eyes huge and wide.

'For God's sake, calm down!' she cries. 'What the hell is going on?' She is looking round, her gaze fastening on the telephone. I don't want her calling the police. I must get straight to the point. I summon all my fury and turn the force of it on her, and she shrinks back, her hands forming defenceless fists on the tabletop.

'Bitch,' I spit out. 'Scheming bitch. I know what you've done — Alice told me. You probably don't even know who she is. She works at the Sherbourne Club — you know that, don't you? You've been there often enough.'

Catherine shakes her head, and her long glass earrings jingle crazily from side to side, clashing and jumping against her platinum hair. 'I don't know what you're talking about,' she breathes, her words spilling out over each other as she stutters with fear. 'I've never heard of it, or of her.'

'Oh, come on,' I shout. 'Have you forgotten already? All those nights you spent there screwing my husband can't have been so unmemorable, or you wouldn't have kept coming back for more. How long was it going on? All through last year? Or even earlier? Come on, you can tell me! It's not like it matters now — he's dead, after all — he's dead.' With horror, I realise that I am crying. Tears spill from my eyes and pour down my cheeks, over my chin, collecting in the hollow of my neck, trickling and staining the fabric of my top. Stopping them is unthinkable. With every tear I cry, a tiny bit more of my strength fades away, until I'm left standing there shaking, barely able to support myself, left with the anger trapped inside me, unable to get out. Dimly, I register Catherine's hand on mine, pulling me towards the sofa at the back of the shop. I sit down, blinking the tears away, trying to bring my surroundings into focus. When I manage to look at her, her outline still trembling through my blurred vision, she is looking intently serious, biting down on her lower lip.

'Violet,' she says. 'I never even met Jonathan.' Her voice is low, but it shakes with the force of the sincerity that she is trying to express. 'Not once. I've been away, away at college, remember? While you and Jonathan were married, I wasn't even living here. And even if I had been, I would never go after someone else's man, much less . . . ' She cuts the words off, shaking her head. 'I never even met him,' she repeats.

My mind feels stiff and slow, fumbling for comprehension. There is sense in what she says, and yet I know that it cannot be true. I draw in breath heavily and carefully, hearing it crack. I blink again, and this time the room snaps fully into focus. We are here, sitting on the sofa, so close that we are almost touching. Her hand stretched out palm upwards, lying on the turquoise fabric, as if waiting for me to take it and comfort her. The heels of my sandals digging into the furry cream rug at our feet, pressing the fibres down into sharp flattened holes. I cannot stop shaking.

'Alice told me,' I say. 'She told me that

Jonathan would come to stay at the club, and that he would book a room in your name. Croft. Are you saying this is just a coincidence? Are you saying she's lying?'

Catherine shakes her head. I see that her eyes are wide and bright, brimming over with unshed tears. 'No,' she whispers. 'I don't think she's lying.' And then, not with the devastating and instant certainty of previous revelations, but slowly, insidiously, drip by drip, I begin to understand.

★ ★ ★

'I had no idea it was Jonathan,' Catherine is saying. We have been sitting here for what feels like hours. She has turned the shop sign to CLOSED, switched off the lights and pulled the shutters down, so that it feels as if we are somehow here illegally, hiding in the darkness after hours. 'Max never tells me much about his affairs,' she says. 'I knew there had been a relationship last year, and that it had ended badly. I didn't know anything else. Do you believe me?' She has made a fresh pot of tea, and every so often she takes a sip. It has cooled in the mug, a thin clear film running across the top of the liquid. Behind us, the stain is still trickling slowly down the wall, indelible and dark.

Catherine runs her fingers through her cropped hair, ruffling it softly. 'You were the first woman Max has ever really shown an interest in,' she is saying. 'I suppose I got carried away with it. Max is gay. He doesn't broadcast it, but he always has been, and it's never been a problem for him. I don't know why I thought it would be different with you. But by the time I realised that I was being stupid, it seemed like it was too late, that you were already involved — and then when you told me what Alice said, it just all fell into place. Why he was interested in you at all.'

This is not the first time she has said these things. She has been saying them, or subtle variations on each phrase, for an hour or more. We are stuck in a groove, remorselessly grinding back and forth, unable to spin off the track. She presses her fists into her eyes and breathes in shakily; she is crying again. 'I feel I'm to blame,' she says. 'For getting you involved with him. I should have known.' She hiccups the words through sobs, but my own eyes are dry. It's strange, but I feel as if I will never cry again. 'I wish you hadn't had to find out,' she says. 'You don't deserve this.'

She is a little older than I am, but she seems younger. She does not understand that I would rather have reality, however unpalatable. Even now, I would rather have truth than ignorance. I feel oddly released, my body light with relief. The worst has happened now, and I will not have to hear it again. I want to smile, but I bite it back. I don't want Catherine thinking that I am mad. Even as things are, I can see her looking at me anxiously, wondering why I have not spoken for God knows how long. I search for words, but there is really nothing to say.

All of a sudden I think of Max and myself, in the attic room two nights ago; his eyes glittering in the darkness as he came towards me, the force of his strength as he pushed me back against the wall with something that I now see was close to disgust, carrying out a task that had to be performed. There is no pain attached to the memory. I see clearly that I am not in love with Max. I realise now that something in me knew, deep below conscious thought, that things are not always as they appear, that sex is not the same as passion. My body knew the difference. He has not tricked me as much as he thought. I see his face again in my mind's eye, and I feel nothing. Even so I do not dare, yet, to conjure Jonathan beside him.

Catherine's hand is on my arm, stroking the bare skin rhythmically, as if she is trying to bring me back to life. 'What can I do for you?' she says. 'Tell me how I can help you.'

All at once a sentence jumps to my lips. 'Is that a trick question?' I ask. Catherine is silent, frowning, worried. I have misjudged the mood; my words have sounded too flippant, unworthy of the gravity of the situation. I can barely rouse myself to care. I seem to have lost the knack of behaving as others expect. And after all, what would be expected, here and now? This must surely be a unique occurrence, with no decorous social norms attached. This time I cannot stop myself from smiling, and Catherine reacts as if I have slapped her.

'Violet, I'm worried about you,' she cries. 'This isn't normal, the way you're taking this. I mean, this is . . . it's awful, it changes everything you thought you knew.' I wonder why she thinks I need the niceties of the situation spelled out for me; it seems tactless in the extreme. As I look at her, her fragile body curled tightly on the sofa, her green eyes sad and pleading, I can't help but feel sorry for her. She is not strong enough to handle this, but I am. I must extricate her from it.

'It's not your fault, and there's nothing you can do,' I say. This will have to be enough, because I have no more words that I can pull out from inside me. I stand, and for a fraction of a second my head reels and bright balls of colour explode across my vision. I steady myself and move towards the door. I hear her draw in breath hard, but she does not try to stop me.

I walk home in the bright sunshine, feeling it pour over my skin. Everything looks shiny and reborn — trees bursting with emerald leaves and bursts of pink blossom, houses gleaming and clean, the sky above perfect and painted like a photograph. I pass the village church, and music soars from its doors, a symphony of voices raised in song. For the first time in months, I feel completely connected with everything around me. I feel alive and vital, buzzing with excitement; I smile at passers-by and am gratified to see the warmth in their eyes. This is what happiness is: taking pleasure in simple things, never stopping to think why. It is only somewhere darkly in the back of my mind that I know that this is not really happiness, but survival. I must get home, because I have no choice. I must carry on to the next thing, because forward is the only way that time can go.

★　★　★

Locked in my bedroom, I close the curtains. Without the sunlight to warm the room, it feels cold and sterile. I stand looking around me, realising for the first time how few of these possessions belong to my life with Jonathan. Much of the clutter that filled our cottage is above me in the attic, piled up in cardboard boxes. I remember Harvey the week after the funeral, his face taut and emotionless, ferrying the boxes up the ladder and stacking them in rows. In the months since then, none of us has felt inclined to climb the steps to sort through the mounds of kitchen paraphernalia, lamps and vases, bed-sheets and cushions. Out of sight, they have become out of mind too. I do not think that any of us wants to drag them into the daylight again. Only one box remains, and that is buried at the bottom of my wardrobe, unbeknown to anyone but me.

I go to the wardrobe and drop to my knees, burrowing beneath the scarves and shoeboxes that line its base. My hands close on the small wooden trunk and pull it out. Holding it, I move away and sit down in the middle of the floor. Slowly, carefully, I begin to lay the contents of the box around me. The first item is a single cufflink, a translucent opal set in gold. Jonathan wore this, and its pair, on that day in his office, the first day we kissed. Later that night, in his penthouse flat, he tore at his shirt in such eagerness to be rid of it that he sent one cufflink tumbling to the ground, ripped from its buttonhole. I did not remark upon it at the time, but I followed it with my eyes, watching where it lay, a glistening jewel nestled in the luxuriant blue carpet. Later, when he was asleep, I went softly to pick it up, and slipped it into my handbag. I had not known how things would go between us. Some secret impulse told me that if it was to be a one-night stand and nothing more, I would want a souvenir.

I lay the cufflink to one side and turn back to the box. A ticket stub, kept from our first time at the cinema together, and an empty popcorn box. A hastily scribbled note, left for me on the bed some two months in. *Gone to the shop. Back soon. J xx.* Jonathan had not been in the habit of writing notes, and I suppose that this is why I had kept this one, no matter how meaningless the contents. I toss it aside. Next, a small silver spoon, stolen from a restaurant where we had dined with Harvey and Laura. I run my finger over its burnished surface. I remember the guilty thump of my heart as I slipped it into my pocket. It had been a good day, with Jonathan at his most attentive, and as we had prepared to leave I had felt a pang of distress that at the end of it I would be left with nothing but a memory, which was certain to blur with time. I was right. I can no longer remember what we ate, what was said, or even why I had cared so much about preserving it.

The next item makes my chest tighten. A thin metal sparkler, burnt down and charred at one end. We had been at a party, on a boat drifting across the Thames. I can see the cool blue lights strung across the water, their reflection fuzzy and luminous in the depths beneath. The sparklers were handed round as it drew towards midnight, and Jonathan lit one from his lighter, making as if to hand it to me, then drawing back. I made a grab for it and he shook his head, holding his hand teasingly out of my reach as it sparked and shone against the night sky. His eyes fixed on mine, he began to draw letters in the air, leaving a shimmering trail of light. *Marry me.* The letters were crazy and unformed, but I knew. There was nothing else that they could say.

A few wedding trinkets. A handful of red and white confetti, a silk rose, a piece of frosted cake wrapped up in clingfilm; I run my fingernail across it, watching the shards of icing crumble beneath. The honeymoon airline tickets to Russia. A plastic dome cradling a gaudy model of the Palace; memory makes me shake it, and I watch the snowy glitter drift and swirl. A pair of Jonathan's gloves. I remember them, but I do not know why I have chosen to keep them. I hold them in my hands for several minutes, willing it to come to me, but my mind is blank. It doesn't matter. I smooth the woollen material and place them carefully to one side.

Last, flattened in the bottom of the box, his card from our first anniversary. Looking at it now, it seems in bad taste — all fake gold foil and lurid painted roses — but at the time I thought it nothing less than perfect. I open the card and read the message inside, although I do not need to. *Darling Violet, Happy Anniversary. This is only the first of many, but already you have made me happier than I have any right to be. All my love, Jonathan.* Reading it again, it sounds furtive and miserable. I wonder that I ever thought it romantic. Of course, now I have the advantage of hindsight. Knowing what I know now, the words resound hollowly, less than meaningless. They ring in my head as if announced via a distant, crackling speaker, a message from another life.

I do not know why I have kept these things for so long. After our first anniversary I stopped collecting. I knew, even then, that the fairy tale had passed, and that what I was left with was something that would not need commemorating. It must be nostalgia, nothing more, which has forced me to leave this box where it has lain for the past nine months

— that, and perhaps the fear that to touch it and to see its contents again would bring more pain than I could bear. As I sit with the remnants of our life around me, I register that the pain is there. It hurts, somewhere deep in my chest, making it hard to breathe. But it is survivable. I am still here. Looking at the trinkets I have laid out, I realise that they belong to the memory of someone I never really knew. It makes it easier for me to let them go. I collect them together, push them back into the box, and carry it to the window.

Once there, I hesitate. I want to drop it, but the thought of Laura coming across these scattered souvenirs where they have fallen gives me pause. I take the cufflink and throw it as far as I can, watching it soar and land in the earth. The sparkler I toss to the lawn; it would mean nothing to anyone but me, and will be raked up the next time Harvey gardens. I cross quickly to my bedside table and pick up a matchbox, strike a match alight. In front of the window, I burn the objects I can, watching their smoke rise into the air. The matches are hot on my fingers, the flames licking down to my skin, but I persist. Ash falls upon the windowsill, and when I have finished it has collected in a little pile of soft dark soot. I blow it away.

There is nothing I can do now with the

spoon, the plastic dome, the gloves, the wedding cake. I toss them back into the box and shove it back in the wardrobe. One does not get rid of a whole life overnight, and now that I have done it once, I know that I will be able to do it again. I sit down on the bed. Something is nagging at me, refusing to be silenced, a little voice whose words I cannot quite make out. All at once a picture pops into my mind. Max, prowling through the corridors of his home, his head jerked back over his shoulder as he spoke. *It was my birthday yesterday. Always nice to celebrate, eh?* For a moment I frown, unable to work out what my instinct is telling me. I count back through the days. Today is the fourteenth of July. Max's birthday would have been the eleventh. The date means nothing to me. And then suddenly, the little voice in the back of my head comes into focus, its words sharp and clear.

I start from my seat and go to the chest of drawers, knowing exactly where I will find what I want. In the second drawer down, pushed up against the back, is Jonathan's mobile phone. Soon after he died, I was asked whether I knew where it might be. I feigned ignorance. It was all of my husband I had left, and I did not want to give it up; nor did I want other hands touching it, trying to prise open its secrets. Bundled at the back of the drawer beside it is the charger, the wire neatly twisted around it. I plug it into the wall and connect it to the phone. The screen display lights up, coloured bubbles popping across it in waves, and the phone vibrates, a short decisive shiver that makes me start. The familiar message shows on the screen. *Keypad locked. Enter PIN.* Slowly, I pick up the phone. My fingers are trembling as I punch in the numbers one by one. 1107. Jonathan was sentimental about birthdays, like a child. His own birthday, then my own, had been the first combinations I had tried. I hesitate before I press OK. I am not convinced, even now, that I want to know for sure. I grit my teeth and push the key, and although I knew that it would, I feel a soft, sick blow to the heart when the message flashes up. *Keypad unlocked.*

I look through his messages one by one. The inbox is filled with two names: Max's, and my own. My messages are short and banal. They tell him to pick up a loaf of bread from the shop, to let me know what time he will be home. I do not remember writing any of them, except for the last, two days before he died. It says that I am looking forward to seeing him, and that I love him. He could have deleted these messages, but he didn't, and I do not understand why.

Working back, I begin to look through Max's messages. The first is dated September 2007, nine months after our marriage. It is short and perfunctory: *Cheers mate. See you in the Rose and Crown later?* The next few are similarly detached, but it is only a matter of weeks before they start to change. They become cryptic, flirtatious. *You're one to talk. Right back at you . . .* And even, with sickening predictability, *That's not what you said last night.* Moving through the months, the messages grow more confident and passionate. *Can't wait to see you — been thinking about it all day. Can you get here any quicker?* And others, crude and explicit, messages that I can only skim with half-closed eyes for seconds, but which I already know will be branded into my brain for as long as I live. I wish I had not seen these things, but there is no stopping now.

The last two messages are written on the day he died. The first is long: *I know it's difficult, and it's hard on her, but we're doing the right thing. I love you, and I can't wait until I can show them all how much. Call me when it's done, and I'll come and find you.* The second is brief. *Are you OK, Jon? Call me.* Strangely, I find that it is the second missive which hurts more. I can't stop

348

looking at the name, a diminutive I had never used — that no one had, to the best of my knowledge. This Jon is a different person, one I was never allowed to see. Even after death, he belongs to someone else. I look at the message until it dances before my eyes, the screen breaking up into fuzzy pixels of light.

The Sent box is empty. He has left nothing behind but silence. Now, at last, I feel the pain that I had expected hit me, and the brutal shock of it is so great that I have to close my eyes and breathe.

Vaguely through the haze, I hear the door handle rattling, the sound of knocking on wood. Someone is trying to get in. I rise to my feet and go towards the noise, placing my hands on the door frame. The person behind the door does not speak; simply continues knocking, louder and harder. Laura would not try to get in with such force. She would call out to me, implore me to let her in, ask me whether I was all right. Slowly, I turn the key in the lock and push the door open. Harvey is standing there, tall and elegant in the hallway. He is looking at me with taut concern.

'May I come in?' he asks. I step aside, and when he has followed me in he locks the door again behind us. I notice it with faint surprise, but I am not afraid. He stands in the centre of the room for a moment, as if he is not sure where to put himself, then perches on the edge of the bed. 'You look very pale,' he says.

I sit down beside him. I see his eyes go to the mobile phone on the floor, plugged into its charger, and his own face whitens. His lips press together, and that one movement, tiny though it is, tells me everything that I need to know. 'You knew,' I say. 'Didn't you.' It is not a question; not even an accusation, but a statement of fact. I do not have the strength for denials.

Commendably, he does not pretend not to know what I am talking about. He takes a few moments to compose himself, and then almost imperceptibly he nods. He meets my gaze head-on, unfalteringly. He is not the type to hide away in shame. 'If I had thought that it would have served any purpose to tell you,' he says, 'then I would have done it.' I am not sure that I believe this — I cannot imagine Harvey sullying himself to talk of a sordid affair, no matter how close to home — but I nod in return. I am not angry with him, although I am unsure why not. I look at him as he sits on the bed, his elbows bent forward to rest on his knees, his silver head slightly bowed. For an instant, he looks far older than his sixty-four years, and the thought makes my heart seize up protectively. This man has been my father for only a few years, but now that it comes to it, it is harder for me to cut the ties from him than it was with the man who had known me from birth.

I tell him everything. About my time with Max, about our affair, such as it was. I tell him that Max suspects him of being involved in Jonathan's death, but that he has no evidence. That he hates him, and wants him dead. As I speak I am vaguely conscious that my words sound melodramatic and bizarre, but I cannot dress them up in any way that will make them socially acceptable. I force all the knowledge that I have out of me, for him to do with what he will. He listens, and his face is blank. Occasionally he nods, or briefly frowns as if he disagrees, before his brow snaps back to smooth marble. When I have finished he appears deep in thought, but he does not speak.

'Is he wrong?' I ask. Despite knowing what I now know of Max, when I think back to that scene by the lake, the inherent truth of what he has said still reverberates inside me. I believe his words, but part of me still hopes for some kind of miracle.

Harvey is silent for too long, and in his silence I hear the truth. 'That man sees everything in black and white,' he says at last.

'But nothing in life is so simple.'

In my bag, faintly at first, then louder, my phone begins to ring.

★ ★ ★

Max is calling me. Together we watch the screen as it buzzes urgently, then subsides. With difficulty I remember that I had told him I would contact him today. He is not a patient man, and he is expecting an answer to his proposal. He is waiting to hear whether I will give him the keys to Harvey's home, so that he can charge into this fortress and avenge his beloved like a white knight. Vitriol twists inside me as I look at his name.

Harvey watches me. 'You should call him back,' he says.

'I don't want to speak to him.' It is true: I would be happy if I never had to hear his voice again, much less see his face.

'He is expecting something from you,' Harvey says. 'You should tell him that you'll meet him tomorrow morning. At ten, down by the lake.' He sees my face, and shakes his head. 'You won't have to see him,' he says. 'Trust me.'

Trusting him makes no sense, but I find that I do. I dial Max's number, and he picks up almost instantly, cutting off the first ring with his harsh, guttural tones. He sounds strained, as if his tolerance for me is wearing thin. He calls me 'babe'. I think that only a day or two ago, such a term of endearment from him would have set all the hairs on my body on edge with lust, but now I feel nothing. I speak in monosyllables, giving nothing away. I arrange to meet him the next morning, and he sounds relieved. He hangs up before I even have the chance.

I sit motionless, and I feel Harvey's gaze on me, worried and appraising. He is wondering whether I am in love with Max, whether I have been bruised by this new betrayal. 'No,' I say, although he has not asked the question, and I think he understands. We sit in silence for a few moments. I have the eerie sense of normality returning, despite all that has happened and all that is left unfinished; the inability to exist upon a knife-edge for too long at a time. I want to curl up on a sofa, read or watch television, and forget everything. Nonetheless, there is something nagging at the back of my mind, and I know that if I do not get it out now, it will stay there and rot. 'Jonathan,' I say. 'Do you think he ever loved me?'

Harvey looks surprised, as if I have asked something too obvious to need clarification. 'Of course,' he says, in that clipped, crisp tone of his that brooks no denial. 'This business with . . . Max.' He speaks the name with difficulty, and I think it is the first time that I have heard it pass his lips. 'It was a diversion, an inexplicable one, that went too far. Jonathan loved you from the day he met you.'

I think his words over. They sound reassuring, solid. I think, too, of the text messages I have seen — the way they ranged from passion to tenderness, the familiarity contained within them and the little private jokes to which I was not privy. I think of Jonathan's distant behaviour in the months before he died, and of the sadness on Max's face as we had lain together in his attic room and he had asked me what my husband had been like. I must shut these things out. They can bring nothing good. I nod at Harvey, and smile. This, whether it is fact or fiction, is what our lives are built on, and neither one of us wants to rip it away.

Harvey stands up, and his shadow looms across me for an instant before he moves away. 'Laura will be serving lunch soon,' he says. 'I propose that we go downstairs and try our best to have a pleasant day.'

I stand too, but I linger in the doorway. 'This meeting with Max tomorrow . . . ' I say.

Harvey crosses quickly back to my side and puts his hands on my shoulders, pressing down for an instant as if to impress upon me the seriousness of his words. 'I intend to go to meet him myself,' he says. 'There is nothing for you to worry about.'

I shiver, not liking this plan. 'I don't know how he will react to that,' I say. 'He . . . ' I want to say, *He wants to kill you*, but I shrink back from the phrase. It sounds hopelessly melodramatic, not a concept that, away from Max's intense, forbidding presence, I can really convert into reality. 'If you are thinking of talking to him,' I say instead, 'I'm not sure he will want to listen. I'm not sure how you could ever reach any kind of understanding.'

Harvey takes his hands away from my shoulders, and moves towards the hallway again. I think I see a thin smile pass over his lips before he turns away. 'Of all the things that I could want from that man, understanding is the least of them,' he says as he goes downstairs. The finality of his tone tells me that, as far as he is concerned, the conversation is finished.

In the kitchen, Laura is fussing over her pots and pans as usual, flitting from oven to hob to cupboard like an over-anxious fly. She lifts the lid of the largest pot, and I see that she is making some kind of casserole, thick and hearty, an incongruous choice in the middle of July. Tiny beads of sweat have formed on her forehead, glistening at her hairline where her pale hair is drawn back into a bun. She looks tense and distracted, as she almost always does, and with a shock I realise, perhaps for the first time, what a strain it must be living as Harvey's wife — living with a man who keeps so many secrets. Even after what has just passed, I feel that I have barely scratched the surface of what is beneath his coolly polite façade. Even if Laura is aware of more than she would ever divulge, her intuition must have its limitations. As I watch her thin frame strain against the effort of lifting the casserole dish off the hob and on to the sideboard, my heart contracts. I move forward to help her, and she gives a violent start, like an animal surprised by an attacker.

'Sorry,' I say brightly. 'Almost ready?' I smile, so hard that I feel it will crack my face. Laura's eyes flicker for an instant, and then she smiles too. It feels like years since I have seen her smile with any warmth, and the sight floods me with unexpected well-being. There has been enough sadness in this house, and I feel a sudden urgent need to counterbalance it, to have one more happy day here, the way things used to be.

We eat in the dining room with the patio doors thrown open wide, letting the heat of the day stream in. On another day, Harvey might have passed some subtle acerbic comment on the unsuitability of the dish, but today he merely rolls up his shirtsleeves and eats with gusto. He seems buoyant, relaxed. All through the meal he keeps up a stream of conversation, coaxing us in. He talks of gossip he has gleaned from the garden party, the plans of his former colleagues, their trials and tribulations. He mimics Miranda Foster, with cruel and devastating accuracy. Laura does not generally approve of such character assassinations, thinking them unchristian, but even she is reluctantly amused, smiling down into her plate and shaking her head. I had forgotten Harvey's capability for humour, which even before Jonathan's death had been sporadic and unpredictable, lurking somewhere beneath the surface and only occasionally breaking through.

'What's the matter, Laura?' Harvey asks, still in Miranda's sugary cadence. 'Could you pass me the salt, or would that be too much trouble? I wouldn't want to put you out, dear.'

Laura laughs then, pushing the salt cellar across towards him. 'You're very unfair to poor Miranda,' she says. 'She has a good heart.'

'A good heart,' Harvey repeats. 'Perhaps. She certainly has a good pair of lungs. I could hear her halfway across the garden no matter where I went.' He winks at me, including me in the joke, and I smile. I feel suddenly released, as if something has lifted from my chest and left me able to breathe freely for the first time in years. I realise that in our strange little triangle, it is Harvey's mood which influences us all. There are some people, like Laura, whose moods and emotions melt into the atmosphere, leaving little mark. There are others who can cast gloom across a room with the slightest frown, create an oppressive air of tension with a couple of snapped words, or lift an atmosphere with a single smile. It is a gift that Harvey has often misused. Now that it is being put to good use, though, I am grateful for it, and I sense that Laura is too. We soak up his good humour like sponges.

After lunch Harvey offers to help clear the things away, and Laura lets him. When it is done we go out into the garden and set the deckchairs out. All afternoon we sunbathe, occasionally engaging in desultory conversation. Laura reads a book, an uncharacteristically cheerful-looking affair with a bright pink cover. Harvey lays the newspaper out on his knees, but rarely turns a page. He lights a cigarette, blowing the smoke up high into the air and watching it curl and dissolve into the blue sky.

The movement is familiar yet strange, and I realise that I have not seen him smoke for several days. Vaguely, I had assumed that he was trying to give up, but it seems that all that is now forgotten. I put my sunglasses on and lie back, watching the world darken and dazzle before my eyes. I feel comfortably numbed and desensitised. Today, if not tomorrow, I am happy to wrap myself in the insulation of family life, no matter how mundane it may be. At this moment it seems that there is nothing more precious. I do not think of Jonathan. For the first time, I feel him receding into the past. Into where he should be.

As the day grows cooler and the sun begins to set, Laura drags herself to her feet without a word and wanders down the lawn towards the rose garden. From a distance, I watch her move systematically up and down with the watering can, tending the plants. Harvey and I are left alone together. He does not look at me, keeping his eyes on the sky, his profile set and serene.

'It occurs to me,' he says, so quietly that at first I think he may be talking to himself, 'that you should contact your parents. That is to say, your biological parents.' He still does not look at me. His words stun me; in almost two years, Harvey has not mentioned my former life or anything connected with it, and I have not wanted him to. With difficulty, I bring my parents' faces to the front of my mind. They have been buried for so long that the thought of them brings a sharp, unthought-of pain. I can think of no reason why Harvey should be saying this now, and somehow it makes me uneasy and panicky. I stare across at him, willing him to look my way, but he remains motionless.

'Why?' I ask him.

He pauses for a moment, sorting his words into meticulous order. 'Laura and I consider you our daughter,' he says, 'but there is obviously something lacking. It would be different if your parents were dead, or irrevocably estranged. I think that unless you are reconciled, there will always be a void in you, and I wish you to be happy.'

I struggle for comprehension. The emptiness left by Jonathan has been so great that I have barely stopped to consider any other absence. Dimly, in the recesses of my mind, I glimpse the truth of what Harvey is saying, but I have no desire to draw this knowledge out into the open just yet. I parcel these feelings up, push them to one side. When I open this box up again, I will want to be alone. I reply only to the last thing he has said. I say simply, 'I know.'

Harvey blows another plume of smoke up

into the silent air above him, and together we watch it slowly contract and disperse into nothing at all, or at least nothing visible. 'Good,' he says.

Laura serves supper in the kitchen that evening — a slapdash affair of roughly carved baguettes and cheese, crackers and grapes, black coffee brewed and served straight from the pot. Such food is not in her nature; she prefers tidy finger sandwiches, meticulously cut with crusts shorn off, and tea in china cups on delicate saucers. Tonight, though, it seems that the food is secondary. We sit around the kitchen table and talk as we eat, about everything and nothing. The relaxed mood of lunchtime is still there, oiling the wheels of our conversation so that it seems easy to do this, to sit together and talk. In this moment I wonder why it has felt so painful for so long. Laura even talks of Jonathan, lightly and in passing, not leaving him out of her memories. In the past she has often sidestepped him, making him ten times more conspicuous by his absence. As she speaks of him, I grope for the anger I felt earlier in the day, and cannot get a grip on it. The man she speaks of, her son, is someone completely separate from the man who has betrayed me so entirely, and perhaps it is best that they are kept that way.

After supper, when the last of the light is draining away and the kitchen window-glass is wet and blurred with the steam from the coffee pot, I stand up and say goodnight. As I do so I have a strange sense of something being missing, something left unfinished. I realise that for the first day in nine months, Laura has not said grace before our meals. There has been no mention of commending Jonathan's spirit, or of him watching over us all like some black forbidding ghost. I had thought I would feel relieved, if this moment ever came, and yet I feel a sharp pang of sadness somewhere not at first locatable; the point of a knife slipped in beneath my clothes without warning, out on a street in the dark. I linger for a moment, wondering whether she will realise her omission, but her face remains unruffled and calm. In the dim kitchen light, free of its habitual worried lines, her skin looks smooth and almost beautiful.

I am halfway across the landing upstairs when Harvey calls me. I turn and see him there, standing at the top of the stairs with the light behind him, a tall silhouette. Questioningly, I move back towards him. He does not speak at first; then simply bids me goodnight. He leans forward, one hand drifting briefly to the small of my back, and presses his lips to my forehead, then pulls away. The kiss lasts no more than a second, but something about it endures. I feel it burning in the centre of my forehead, a small perfect impression.

'I meant to say,' he says, 'that I brought a present back from Spain for you. I intended to give it to you several days ago, but it slipped my mind. It's in my black case, in the bedroom.' He hesitates, as if he might say more, then breaks away and walks swiftly back down the stairs. I watch his tall back receding until he turns and is out of sight.

I frown, unsure whether I have been promised a gift or given an order. In any event, there is no question of my going to Harvey's bedroom and rifling through his case at this hour. Laura will be there soon, wanting to prepare for bed. I push the information to one side and go into my own bedroom. I can still feel the hard imprint of Harvey's kiss on my forehead, and when I look in the mirror, I am almost surprised to see no jewel-like branded mark there, but the skin white and perfectly clear. I look blankly back at myself for a few moments, my eyes travelling over this skin, this hair, these lips that seem to have so little to do with who I am. An intense weariness comes over me; I do not want to think. I pull off my clothes, climb into bed and pull the covers over my head, lie in the hot dark silence and close my eyes.

★ ★ ★

When I wake with a start the room is full of light. I have been woken, perhaps, by the sound of the church clock in the distance, chiming again and again. I count its peals in my head, and my eyes flit to my bedside clock for confirmation. Ten o'clock. I had meant to rise early, to see Harvey before he left for the lake. In the back of my mind, I had perhaps envisaged that in the untroubled light of a new day, he would decide to let the matter alone and forget the meeting. Quietly, I slip out of bed and draw back the curtain. Laura is already out in the garden, down by the rose garden again, on her knees, digging at weeds. Her face is shaded from the early sun by a large straw hat, so that I cannot see her expression. Beyond her, the row of lime-green elm trees like sculptures against the skyline, perfectly still. It is this stillness which strikes me, as if Laura and I are the only moving points in a suspended world.

Quickly, I wash and pull on some clothes.

The house is quiet as I descend the stairs, but this means nothing. Harvey can exist in a room noiselessly, when he wishes. Systematically I comb the rooms, finding each one empty. On the kitchen table, two plates scattered with toast crumbs, two empty coffee cups. In the dining room, a morning paper abandoned on the table, unopened. In the hall, one pair of shoes missing from the neatly ordered rack.

I go out into the garden and call Laura. She looks up, shading her face with her hand under the wide brim of her hat, and smiles in greeting. I walk swiftly towards her. 'Has Dad gone out?' I ask. Strangely, the word comes easily, with none of that instinctive hesitation I normally encounter. I wait for her answer, my hands twisted behind my back, feeling my fingers hot and damp.

She nods gently. 'Yes, he said he had to go into the village for a few things,' she says. 'He told me he should be back by noon.'

So he has gone. I try, and fail, to picture him and Max alone together, two figures in a silent space. The images do not meld, no matter how hard I try to force them; my mind closes up. I cannot imagine what they will do, what they will say. Laura is looking at me quizzically, waiting for me to speak. Instead I nod, and drop to my knees beside her. The smell of freshly dug earth and mown grass damp with dew rises to meet me. I pick up a trowel, and begin to dig the soil around the base of the yellow rose bush, clearing it of stones and weeds. Dirt creeps in underneath my fingernails, into the pores of my skin, staining my hands. Above me, the scent of the roses, heady and sweet. I concentrate on my task, but out of the corner of my eye I can see Laura watching me, curiously at first, then smiling.

'What is it?' I ask, still working at the weeds around the stem.

She half shrugs, then cocks her head to one side like a bright inquisitive bird, sidling towards an unknown thought. 'It's nothing much,' she says. 'Simply that you are changing. We all are.' Seeing my face, she shakes her head. 'It's not a bad thing,' she says. 'It has to happen, even if it is a little sad. You're a grown woman, after all.'

I am not sure what she means, but instinctively I do not want to push her to say more. I can feel the sadness she speaks of coiling between us, unfurling into something tangible, and I do not want it there. I stand up and brush my hands off, watching the dirt fly in small clouds off my skin. 'I'm going inside for a bit,' I say, and she simply nods.

I walk up the garden, flooded by sudden

restless indecision. I do not know how to fill the hours until Harvey returns. Time has slowed to a trickle, each minute drawn out and separate, drops of water falling one by one upon a blank page. All at once I think of his words to me the previous night, and the veiled invitation in them. They give me a sense of purpose. I climb the stairs and go to Harvey's bedroom. The net curtains stir faintly in the summer breeze, rippling the thin cover arranged over the bed. Next to the wardrobe, the black suitcase is propped up, zipped and buckled. I pull it out on to the floor and unfasten it, pushing up the fabric to see what is inside. He has barely unpacked at all, and I register that this is unusual. Tentatively, I sort my way through folded clothes until my fingers alight upon a small parcel, stiff blue paper wrapped with Sellotape. Already from the shape I can tell what it is — the same thing that Harvey always brings me from his trips away. I run my finger under the tape to tear the parcel open. The bracelet is pretty and gaudy; fake green gemstones set in gold, rising and falling like waves. I slip it on to my wrist. Once more, I check the paper, almost expecting to find some message written there, but there is nothing. Kneeling there in front of the case, I feel a sudden aimless desolation wash over me. Something in Harvey's manner the night before has led me to expect something I have not found — what, I do not know. I remember the tight urgency of his voice, and frown.

Slowly, I turn back to the case. My hands twitch with the knowledge that what I am doing now feels forbidden, unwarranted, but I have the bit between my teeth now, and I cannot stop. I take each item out of the case, shake it out and lay it to one side: clothes, a washbag, a guidebook. When the case is empty I sit staring at it, deflated, no longer able to find the sense in what I have done. I will have to pack the items back. I reach for the first shirt, and in that instant I see it. A ripple in the lining, a change in its smoothness. I put my hand to it and press the material, and I feel something hard beneath the surface, something small and rectangular. Quickly, I lift the folds of the lining, and I see that, right at the edge of the case, it has been sliced free of its stitches, as if slit by a knife. I slip my hand inside and feel for the object, draw it out. It is a leather-bound note-book, dark red in colour. I open it at random, and I see Harvey's writing, sloped and pointed in black ink, filling the pages.

I pack everything back into the case just as I have found it, fasten it and prop it back up against the wall. The note-book in my hand, I sit down upon the bed, and I open the first page. *You must kill the dead, or they will kill you.* I begin to read, and I do not raise my head until I have finished. The last two entries are written in a different colour, in dark green ink.

Sunday, 11 July

I had not thought to continue writing once I had returned home, but in the absence of any other activity I feel compelled to pick up my pen again. I have been back in England three days. I had expected to feel something as the plane touched down on British soil, but in the event it seemed that there was little to feel that had not already been felt before a hundred times. Violet met me at the airport, and at once I detected something different in her — a return of some impetuous rebelliousness that has been buried deep inside her for so long that it came as a shock to see it once again. She was tense and nervous, skittish like a kitten. It would come as no surprise to you to hear that I did not know how to handle her, if indeed I have ever known. The time away has left me even less able to connect with others than usual, and my senses still feel numb and stifled. We drove back home in silence, and all the way I watched her, trying to find some clue as to why this metamorphosis had come about, but I could find none. Laura at least is unchanged. We had an indifferent dinner and retired to bed. There is little more to say.

Yesterday, we hosted the garden party in honour of my birthday. I had dreaded this, but in the event there was little left for me to organise. I dressed in my best grey suit, and as I combed my hair before the mirror I thought that I looked dull and faded, nothing more than a shell of what I had once been. On an impulse, I dug into the back of my wardrobe and found Roman's necktie, the green silk shot through with silver which he gave to me the last time I ever saw him. Holding it in my hands again after so long, I felt myself suffused with a strange defiant contentment; the knowledge that, try as I had, I had not entirely wiped out all trace of the past. I fastened it around my neck, and this time the figure that looked back at me was different, mysterious and filled with a new significance.

Ridiculous that a single item of clothing

can so alter a mood. I felt myself lifted and buoyant, and I made conversation at the garden party with indifferent former colleagues without effort, drawing on all the charm that I can still access. The garden was beautiful, decked out with ribbons and bunting by Laura. I might have come away from the event with a sense of satisfaction, hollow though that is, had it not been for Max's appearance. I do not know why he would choose to come here, knowing as he must that I am fully aware of his history. We did not speak, but once I had noticed him, I felt his eyes on me all day, hard and appraising. It struck me that there was a challenge in his gaze. Later, I saw Violet talking to him, over by the apple tree, alone. I cannot think yet about what this may mean.

I had no wish to engage with him, or to cause a scene, but I could not help being aware of him everywhere I went; the threat in his muscular frame, the way his hair lies close against his skull, the dark burning eyes. I thought of you, and I tried to imagine this man's features reshuffled into tenderness, into someone you could look upon with love. The thought was as impossible as it has always been. It is sad, desperately so, to know that there are some things I will never understand.

The guests, Max included, left by eight, and I was left to sit in the dining room and drink while Laura and Violet sat together in the rose garden. Then, as now, I felt a bleak sense of things falling away; the belief that I will never be able to hold on to anything for long enough to truly enjoy it, ever again. Those brief hours when I felt energised and enthused, spurred on by Roman's old gift around my neck, have in some ways made things worse. It is pathetic to think that it is only through some talisman of the past that I can find a modicum of happiness. This morning I put the necktie away, back in the recesses of my wardrobe. I will not take it out again, but neither, I know, will I throw it away. This is what is left to me: this strange suspension between the past and the present, unable to commit to either. I can see no way forward. I do not know where this leaves me.

Tuesday, 13 July

Violet has gone. Although she refused to say as much, I know that she has gone to Max. I could see it in the hectic flush of her cheek, the sparkle in her eyes that I have not seen there since before you died — not, if I am honest, since long before. I tried to prevent her. I concocted some story, vague and oblique though it was, to make her believe that your history with Max had been an unhappy one, but it was no use. She was already too far gone to listen, and short of forcibly restraining her, there was little I could do. She promised to be back in two days. Without her, the house feels even darker and more quiet than usual.

The source of this man's appeal is a constant source of confusion to me. It seems that he is some kind of magician, casting a spell on all he encounters, and yet to me he still appears nothing more than a violent imbecile. I do not want Violet dirtied by this man as you were. I want him gone, but I can tell already that he will never leave. He will stay here, malevolent and resentful, until he dies. I have thought of moving myself — of upping sticks and abandoning Brenchley, whether with or without Laura by my side — but if my time in Spain has taught me anything, it is that there are some things from which there is no running. Wherever I am, you will be.

Foolish of me to think that in writing there could be some solution, when all it has done is to clarify everything I already knew, everything I have lost. I wish I had the courage to end it, but I know that I do not. There is to be no escape for me there, either. Perhaps I do not deserve one. I will not write in this diary again. I see now that the point of it has gone.

★   ★   ★

I raise my head in the silence, and I can feel the blood pulsing hotly through my veins. I reach for the telephone and dial Harvey's number. It rings for thirty seconds or more before the answerphone clicks on. I repeat this several times, with no variation. I think of Max. Of the strength of his anger, a flood poured into a space too small to contain it. I think, too, of how he would react if faced with an inexplicably willing victim, a victim who did not fight back. My thoughts halt and dry up. I cannot visualise this scene, because, I now realise, I do not know either of the people in it — have never known them at all.

I cross to the window and look out into the garden. Laura is lying back on a sunlounger now, her eyes closed and shaded against the bright sunshine by the wide, low brim of her hat. Her lips are smiling. It might be a smile of innocence. The last flicker of happiness before a tragedy, as yet barely glimpsed out of the corner of her eye, extinguishes it for good. It might be a smile of knowledge. A dark shadow at last vanished into light, a burden of decades lifted. The longer I look, the less I can tell.

Acknowledgements

Many thanks to all my first-draft readers — my agent Hannah Westland, my editor Clare Reihill, Elaine Connell and Charlotte Duckworth. Thanks too to all those from the teams at RCW and Fourth Estate (with special mentions to Mark Richards and Essie Cousins) who have helped to bring this book to print, and to Daniel for his repeated reassurances during the writing process that I would actually finish it.

We do hope that you have enjoyed reading this large print book.

Did you know that all of our titles are available for purchase?

We publish a wide range of high quality large print books including:
**Romances, Mysteries, Classics
General Fiction
Non Fiction and Westerns**

Special interest titles available in large print are:
**The Little Oxford Dictionary
Music Book
Song Book
Hymn Book
Service Book**

Also available from us courtesy of Oxford University Press:
**Young Readers' Dictionary
(large print edition)
Young Readers' Thesaurus
(large print edition)**

For further information or a free brochure, please contact us at:
**Ulverscroft Large Print Books Ltd.,
The Green, Bradgate Road, Anstey,
Leicester, LE7 7FU, England.
Tel:** (00 44) 0116 236 4325
Fax: (00 44) 0116 234 0205

Other titles published by
The House of Ulverscroft:

THE ART OF LOSING

Rebecca Connell

Haunted by childhood loss, twenty-three-year old Louise takes on her late mother's name and sets out to find Nicholas, the man she holds responsible for her death. Now, still haunted by the past, lecturer, husband and father Nicholas can't forget his clandestine, destructive and ultimately tragic affair with Louise's mother. As Louise infiltrates his life, she forms close relationships with both his son and his wife, her true identity unknown to Nicholas himself. Tensions grow and outward appearances begin to crack, as Louise and Nicholas both discover painful truths about their own lives, and the woman they both loved.

A SURREY STATE OF AFFAIRS

Ceri Radford

For Constance Harding — village bell-ringer, devoted mother to perplexingly unmarried Rupert and Lycra-clad gap-year strumpet Sophie — life in the Home Counties is heavenly. But when Constance dips her toe in the murky waters of the blogosphere, she gets out of her depth. Unbeknown to her, Constance's home conceals scandal that would make the vicar blush. As her family comes undone, she embarks on an extraordinary journey: from tripping in Ibiza to riding bareback with an Argentinean gaucho — his only English words 'Britney' and 'Spears' . . . She's about to discover a wider world she thought it was too late to find . . .

ON THE BROKEN SHORE

James MacManus

Leo Kemp lives in Cape Cod with his wife and daughter, working for the Institute of Marine Biology — a seemingly idyllic life that hides heartbreak . . . A few years ago their son drowned in an accident at sea, and the family cannot come to terms with his death. Then Leo loses his job, and his last field trip with the students ends in tragedy when a wave throws Leo overboard. Now, like his son, he's missing — presumed dead — the community is rocked. Yet when a man is sighted, living on an uninhabited island just miles off shore, rumours begin to circulate . . .

I CURSE THE RIVER OF TIME

Per Petterson

It is 1989 and all over Europe Communism is crumbling. Arvid Jansen, thirty-seven, is in the throes of a divorce. At the same time, his mother is diagnosed with cancer. Over a few intense autumn days, we follow Arvid as he struggles to find a new footing in his life, while all the established patterns around him are changing at staggering speed. As he attempts to negotiate the present, he casts his mind back to holidays on the beach with his brothers, to courtship, and to his early working life, when as a young Communist he abandoned his studies to work on a production line.

A FILM BY SPENCER LUDWIG

David Flusfeder

Spencer Ludwig, idealist and filmmaker, is making one of his regular duty visits from London to New York City to tend to his declining but still fearsome father. Driving back from a doctor's appointment, Spencer decides not to take the turn to his father's apartment: instead, they hit the road. Ahead of them will be an emotional ride taking in police and prostitutes, film festivals and gambling in Atlantic City, as father and son try to make sense, not only of each other's lives and hearts, but also their own. And, Spencer hopes, to reach a suitable cinematic conclusion.